Molly Shipton

SECRET ACTRESS

SHERI GRAUBERT

Molly Shipton: Secret Actress

Copyright © 2021 by Sheri Graubert

Summary: England. 1598. Queen Elizabeth rules the waves.
Molly Shipton and her sister lose everything in a plague. To evade the clutches
of Mr. John Barnes, they flee to Stratford-upon-Avon. Disguised as boys, they
earn a living as street performers. After several narrow escapes, they make
their way to London. Here Molly becomes a star of the London stage. She
works with Burbage, Shakespeare and Kempe. However, it is illegal for girls
and women to act professionally. Will Molly get into trouble with the
authorities? Or will Shakespeare find the drama so stimulating he writes a
play with her in mind?
Thank you for buying this book. Please go to: sherigraubert.com/
MollyShiptonThankyou.

Clear Fork Publishing

P.O. Box 870 102 S. Swenson

Stamford, Texas 79553 (915) 209-0003

www.clearforkpublishing.com

Printed in the United States of America

Softcover ISBN: 978-1-950169-82-5

This book is dedicated to those who do not fit
into the mold society has cast for them.

Lila & Sasha, my real life Molly & Juliet; there is no mold big
enough, creative enough, fun enough or
smart enough to ever contain you.
Live life to the fullest.
Follow your dreams, no matter what.

They were loud.

Very loud.

Molly and Juliet cautiously peeked into the dining room. The men wore so much jewelry; Molly thought they must be pirates.

Necklaces, bracelets and gigantic rings sparkled. Earrings dangled or hooped from ears. They appeared larger than their physical size because their personalities were enormous.

They were not pirates.

They were actors.

Prologue

I am famous, so people assume I had it easy.
I am successful, so people assume I am mean.
I speak up for myself, so people assume I am unkind.
I am a strong woman, so people assume, well, there's a lot
they assume, most of it negative and all of it incorrect.
I am dead, so people assume my story died with me.
But it did not.
My story lives on.

MY NAME IS LADY SHAKESPEARE, and I am a ghost.
I'd like to tell you my story so you can know the truth about
me. Then you can make your own assumptions, but your
assumptions will be based on facts.

In my day, I was the finest Shakespearean actress in
London, although most people thought I was a boy; a boy
playing girls' parts. In fact, I was a girl pretending to be a boy,
who was pretending to be a girl on stage. You see, back then,
women could not act. It was against the law.

Darlings, I simply had to break the rules.

But I am getting ahead of myself.

Travel back with me through space and time – to an era

with no electricity, no running water, no computers, no video games, no ballpoint pens; back to a time when there weren't even flushing toilets — yes, there was such a time.

Would you like to know what was absolutely marvelous back then?

The *theater!*

People gathered together in the theater to watch stories acted out upon a stage. The theater is where excitement always takes place, both in and out of the playhouse. The theater, my darlings, is where I grew up.

But let us begin at the beginning, back when I was a simple girl with impossible dreams; back to when I was known as Molly Shipton.

Book One:

UPON AVON

The year: 1598
The place: Bitford-Upon-Avon
A plague has ravaged its way through the village. As much as possible folks stay inside their homes, but they still must go outside for work, for food, for church. That's when the disease catches them.

One

"WE MUST DISGUISE ourselves as boys and escape," said Molly. She clicked open a small silver locket, then closed it.

"I don't like boys," replied Juliet.

She's only eight, thought Molly.

Molly looked around their now empty room. The Plague had devastated London a few years prior. Then, much closer to home, Stratford-upon-Avon had been ravaged by the same pestilence.

Both towns had recovered.

But The Plague wouldn't die.

Country folk thought they were safe. They had dropped their guard. Now The Plague poisoned the countryside. It crept its way through the smaller towns and tiny villages of England.

Molly's dad had ignored the early hints of infection. He thought The Plague couldn't possibly attack a tiny village like Bitford-upon-Avon. He had continued his work as a shoemaker. Molly's twin brother, Ben, continued his work as their father's apprentice. One night, their dad crumpled onto the floor, never to get back up, wracked with guilt for bringing The Plague into the family home.

Ben ran to the doctor's house in the next village, but did not return. They did not know the doctor had already passed away from the disease.

Molly's parents were told Ben collapsed on his way back. He was taken to a local hospital, never to wake up. They were instructed not to collect his body for burial, for fear of further infection.

Molly's mother nursed their dad until the end. She kept her children away from them both. Then she got sick herself. They sold every valuable thing in the house for food, apart from Molly's lute and the silver locket. They burned every wooden thing for heat: the stools, the plates, even the table.

THIS HOME, once their happy place, their safe place, was now a place of danger and loss. Molly tied the locket around her neck, the tiny painting inside seared into her memory: the impossibly alike twins' faces together, with Juliet nestled below them.

"Ben's breeches fit me fine. Can we adapt your skirt to make breeches and a tunic for you?" Molly asked.

"I don't want to be a boy!"

"Julie, listen. I know. I know you don't like boys. Here's the truth. As girls, they'll throw us in the poorhouse," explained Molly. "As boys, we'll be free."

They stared at each other.

"You know I'm right," said Molly. She was in charge now. And this was her plan.

I hope it works, thought Molly.

"Fine," agreed Juliet, reluctantly. "But, just to be clear, I really, really, really don't like boys."

MOLLY SMILED IN ADMIRATION, as Juliet removed her skirt, bit the edge and ripped it right down the middle.

"You've always been a wizard with a needle and thread, like mum," said Molly.

"It's easy," said Juliet with a shrug.

Easy? thought Molly, incredulously, as she watched Juliet fashion a pair of short breeches and a tunic. Then her little sister worked on adjusting Ben's breeches, so they no longer had holes and fitted her perfectly. Molly never had those skills even though, Lord knows, she'd been forced to try, over and over again.

What are my skills? thought Molly. She listed them in her mind.

~

My Skills
by Molly Shipton

1. I can read.

Shocking, I know, for a girl to be able to read, but Aunty Anne taught me. My mother didn't like that. Aunty Anne argued, "If you can read you can change the world. If you can't read, you're vulnerable to ignorance."

My mother fought back.

"Her job is not to change the world," she argued. "Her job is to marry, have children and be happy."

Was that really a job? And was it really *my* job? Surely, I was meant for more than that?

"But these girls have brains! Talent, too!" declared Aunty Anne.

"They're my children, Anne, not yours!" my mother replied. Aunty Anne was left speechless. They both

knew my mother had won that argument. But, as I
learned to read, I was the true victor.

2. I can write.

Even more shocking for a girl to write, but thank you,
again, Aunty Anne. She was always ahead of her time.
Once, a man showed up at our house, riding a horse,
wearing breeches, a tunic and smoking a pipe. The
stranger tied up his horse and demanded he be
allowed into the house. Anxiously, my mum and dad
obliged. Once inside, Aunty Anne pulled off her cap,
let down her hair, threw back her head and laughed! I
wish my mom and Aunty Anne hadn't argued like
they did. I miss her so much.

3. I have an excellent memory.

I have memorized several of Mr. Edmund Spencer's
poems, and some of Mr. Christopher Marlowe's
speeches. Also, *Venus and Adonis* written by a local
poet, called Mr. William Shakespeare, but he lives in
London now. Memorizing poems and speeches is a
skill I've had for as long as I remember. Apparently,
this is what boys have to do in their endlessly long
school days. I can't see how it's useful for anything,
but it's the sort of challenge I like.

4. I can sing and play the lute.

My lute is the last thing Aunty Anne gave me before
she stopped visiting. I sing okay, but Julie? Julie sings
like an angel with wings.

"THAT IS JUST AS WELL," said Molly, out loud, "because we
might have to literally, sing for our supper."

Sometimes, when a village became overwrought with the cruel plague, the villagers shut themselves off to protect the rest of the country. Sometimes, when there were too many bodies, they left the bodies. In Bitford-upon-Avon, they couldn't collect the bodies because there was no one left to collect them.

The few remaining townsmen had to make a decision. Mr. John Barnes had an idea. He lived in the manor house on the outskirts of Bitford. He suggested they set fire to the village. That way, he explained, every remnant of Plague would burn to ashes, rendering the land safe again. What he didn't say was this: once the village was destroyed, he could buy the land for a pittance, expand his estate, and plant an orchard. Any land with a stream would always prove valuable, even after fire.

MOLLY HUGGED JULIET, as they tried to get a last night's sleep in their home. An unexpected and gruff voice cut through the night's silence. The man's voice bellowed in the not-too-far distance, "Halloooo, look to yourselves! Fire's starting!"

"Fire?" whispered Molly to herself, still half asleep. She looked at Juliet, sweetly sleeping on the rushes next to her. Molly thought she must have dreamed it. She rolled over to get a little more sleep.

"Hallooo! Strivers Row! Look to yourselves!"

Strivers Row.

That was their road.

This was not a dream.

Molly started awake. Her abruptness woke Juliet. Molly put her finger to her lips so Juliet would stay quiet. They listened in hushed silence. Molly tried to work out what was happening. She could hear loud bangs on the doors of the houses at the top of their road.

"Halloooo! If you're alive, look lively!" they yelled.

They had stayed inside for so long, Molly did not know The Plague had devastated their entire street, their entire village. That meant:

The Georges.
Jeffrey Smalley.
The Littletons
Little Bethany.
Timmy Brookes.
The Brooktons.

Had all of them…perished?"

"Are they getting closer?" whispered Juliet. She looked up at Molly with her wide, trusting eyes.

"All will be well," assured Molly, not at all sure that it would be. Every muscle in Molly's body was alert. How long 'til the men thumped on their door?

BANG! BANG! BANG!

Five doors away.

"If we reveal ourselves, we're done for," whispered Molly.

"Oh, Molly!" whimpered Juliet, terrified.

Molly, her heart beating fast, reassured her trembling little sister by quietly rubbing her back.

BANG! BANG! BANG!

Two doors away, now. Molly and Juliet clung tightly to each other, arms tight, lips tight, breath tight, trying to make themselves invisible.

BANG! BANG! BANG!

That was their door.

That was their door now.

"Look lively! If anyone's inside, come out now!" They heard the townsman's heaving breath as he listened at their door. Could he sense them? Could he smell them? Would he break down the door? Would he find them huddling inside?

They were stone silent for a minute, which felt like an hour. Then, they heard his footsteps fade away. Without talking, without thinking, the girls gathered their things:

A crust.
A few pennies.
A candle nub.
A ragged blanket.
The lute.
The locket.

"Please don't let them catch us," prayed Molly, as they stole away. She knew if they were caught leaving a condemned house, they were doomed.

Two

FOR TWO DAYS, Molly and Juliet watched the flames gorge on their village. Long after the fire had reduced to embers, long after birds had restarted singing, long after their house had collapsed into ash and burned timber, they sat transfixed.

A blank, thought Molly. *Everything I've ever known is a blank.*

They had settled in the woods behind Strivers Row. A wide stream, which fed into the River Avon, kept them safe from the fire. They had used this stream all their lives: to fish in, to wash in, to play in. Now, it protected them from fiery destruction.

Molly held Juliet while she wept.

She refused to cry. *I'm in charge now. I cannot cry.*

Molly tried to calm her sister. "Julie, listen to me. This... it's the beginning of something. I can feel it."

It shocked Molly to see Juliet's fury break through her grief, like a bear breaking free from its chain.

"How can that be, Molly? Huh?" yelled Juliet. "We have nothing! Where are we going to sleep? Huh? Answer me that! What are we going to eat? Chickweed?"

Molly couldn't help smiling. Her baby sister looked

gawky in her tunic, breeches, and lopsided woolen hat. She was adorable, even when she was raging.

"Chickweed is actually tasty and good for you," said Molly, weirdly light-hearted.

"That's not the point!" Juliet fired back. "Look at us! We're nothing more than beggars!"

"Don't say that, Julie," said Molly, suddenly sober.

"Well, it's true! I'd rather be in the poorhouse!"

"No, you don't! You know what happens to girls there," said Molly. She knew she had made sense to Juliet as her sister slumped back down to the ground.

"Here's how I see it," continued Molly, hoping to sound convincing, "We're alive for a reason."

"You're just saying that," said Juliet, pulling at her unaccustomed clothes.

Molly grabbed Juliet by the shoulders and looked into her eyes. "See, we didn't get sick, did we? Did we?" she asked.

Juliet looked away.

"We were in that house, same as everyone else, same as everyone in the village, but we didn't get sick," continued Molly

"Because Mum and Dad protected us," said Juliet.

The flames from their old house had burned longer and brighter than any other house on the Row. Molly was sure it was their mother loving them from beyond the grave, trying to keep her children warm. And their father, trying to assuage his unnecessary guilt. She was sure it was Ben's love, too.

Ben.

Now Ben was gone, Molly felt no longer whole; as if half of her were missing.

An uneasy emotion bubbled up in the back of Molly's brain; a strong sense of doubt, a consciousness of something unfinished. She pushed the thought back down before it had the chance to wreak havoc in her mind and torture her every waking moment. But the question persisted. It grew in force until it eventually burst forth into the front of her mind, like water busting through a crack in a damn:

Is Ben still alive?

"NO!" Molly said firmly. Juliet looked up at her, questioning.

"It's nothing," Molly said. She put her arm around Juliet. She hoped she was as reassuring as their dad could be. She felt too churned up to be certain.

Ben had run out of the house so fast, he didn't even have a blanket to keep him warm. He had no food, no money, no nothing. Molly pulled the blanket more tightly around her body. She still felt cold.

No.

If the pestilence hadn't got him, the January frost would have finished him off. He had perished, just as they were told. She must stop her mind playing childish tricks and accept cold, hard, grown up facts:

Her father was gone.

Her mother was gone.

Ben was gone.

Their home was gone.

Everything was gone, save Juliet and herself.

Molly was mother, father, brother, sister, everything to Juliet now.

She prayed silently to herself. "Please, God. Please. Let this *mean* something."

She waited for a sign.

She breathed.

Nothing came.

"I suppose," said Juliet, sadly, "you can only go forward, if there's nowhere to go back to."

"Julie, you are right!"

Molly said a silent *Thank You* for the message coming from the mouth of her baby sister. There was no going home, as they had no home.

Forward was their only direction.

Three

MOLLY SUDDENLY REMEMBERED she was hungry.

It was more than physical hunger. It was a hunger that made her want to cry out, to yell, to curse the very Heavens with her hunger.

Molly tried to tear their one remaining crust of bread in half, but it had become so hard she gave Juliet all of it. She watched Juliet chew on the end of the tough piece of hardened dough. Juliet finally tore off a piece with her teeth, then gave the rest back to Molly. The work it took to chew the stale crust made them momentarily forget their hunger and the meager bread's inability to quell it.

Finally, they swallowed, jaws aching, as they felt the solid mass move through their bodies.

"Happy birthday," said Juliet.

"What?" asked Molly.

"Happy birthday, Moll."

"That... It's my birthday?" asked Molly, barely believing what she'd heard.

"It's the 14th," said Juliet. "At least, I think it is. Yes, I'm right, it must be the 14th. That's your birthday. So, happy birthday."

"How can it? How old am I?" Molly asked, half in a daze.

"Eleven," said Juliet, genuinely confused. "How can you not know that?"

After everything they'd been through, Molly hardly knew which way was up, let alone the day of the week, the date, the month, or even the year. Sweet Juliet, remembering her birthday. It was too much....goodness.

Overwhelmed, Molly hugged her gorgeous, beautiful, thoughtful little sister. She desperately wanted to cry.

No, she thought. *I will not cry. I must be strong.*

A battle raged within Molly, as she fought to take charge of her emotions.

I will not cry.

I am in charge.

I will not cry.

I will not cry.

After some time, Molly won her internal battle but she had arrived on a different emotional shore. Something had shifted inside of her. An acceptance?

No.

A determination.

"Molly, I'm sorry. I didn't mean to make you sad," said Juliet, wide-eyed and innocent.

"You didn't make me sad, Julie. You made me happy."

"That was happy?" asked Juliet, confused.

"Yes," giggled Molly shyly.

"But, I don't have a gift for you," insisted Juliet.

"Oh, Juliet. You are the gift. You were always the gift." Molly tenderly, lovingly, tucked a stray lock behind Juliet's ear.

"AYE, AYE!!"

A gruff man's voice cut through their reverie. "Come 'ere, you two. NOW!!"

Marching towards them, on the other side of the stream, came a red-faced and blustering Mr. John Barnes.

"Come with me or it's the orphanage for you two!" he said

Molly tensed, ready to run as soon as she could. She nodded *get ready* to Juliet.

Mr. John Barnes charged to the edge of the stream, which he had to cross to catch them. He used the stone crossing the girls had placed there, years ago. They both knew the fourth stone was loose and must be skipped.

"You won't survive in these woods," he said, wobbling on the first stone. "The wild beasts'll have two scrawny lads like you for dinner," he added, wavering on the second stone.

"We're not going to the orphanage!" said Molly, defiant.

"Stubborn are ye?" said Mr. John Barnes, trying to keep his balance. His woolen cape must have cost a fortune.

"Tell you what. I'm building an orchard. I need strong hands and nimble feet to get the trees planted," he said. He cautiously jumped to the third stone.

Everyone in Bitford knew what happened to young boys at Mr. John Barnes' manor. He drove them hard from dawn to dusk. The lads slept together on the floor in the big hall. Not that that was unusual. What was unusual was how badly he treated them. He would hunt down boys who ran away, and not give up until he found them. Only one had ever escaped; that's how they knew how terrible Mr. John Barnes could be. He would punish runaways by locking them in the cellar with the rats. He would discipline others by locking them in the dog kennels. Molly remembered Charlie Beaumont, the boy who escaped, said he preferred sleeping with the dogs. It was warmer, for a start.

"You'll have three solid meals a day, Sunday mornings off for church, and you'll be safe," said Mr. John Barnes, as he prepared to step onto the fourth stone.

"What do you pay?" asked Molly, already knowing the answer.

"Insolent! You'll be paid with your board and lodging, like

everybody else." Mr. John Barnes was about to jump onto the fourth stone. Molly wrapped her hand around the lute; Juliet tightened her grip on her knapsack.

"Which is more than you have now-owww."

Splash!

Mr John Barnes, of the manor house just outside Bitford-upon-Avon, had fallen into the water. His woolen cape soaked up the frigid water, pulling him down, down, down to his woolen cap. He spluttered about in the shallow depths. He flailed and helplessly spat out fruitless curses.

Once she assessed Mr. John Barnes was going to live, Molly grabbed Juliet and they ran. Molly shouted behind her, "Thanks, but no thanks!"

She'd had a much better idea.

Four

"I CAN'T BELIEVE I let you talk me into this," said Juliet, as they trudged their way to Stratford.

"Stop moaning, keep walking," said Molly.

Please let my idea work! she thought.

Molly's bright idea:
Get to Stratford.
Make money.
Escape Mr. John Barnes.

Her aching limbs complained, but what choice did she have? Besides, how far away could Stratford really be? Both towns were 'upon Avon' weren't they? Bitford-Upon-Avon, Stratford-Upon-Avon. The River Avon wasn't that long.

Was it?

EVERY FEW YARDS, Juliet complained:

"Why Stratford?"

Trudge.

"Why do we have to go to Stratford, anyway?"

Trudge.

"What's so special about Stratford?"

Trudge.

"When do we get to Stratford?"

Trudge.

"Are we there yet?"

Molly, breathing heavily from walking, stopped and turned to Juliet. Her complaints were eating into Molly's brain like a petulant earworm.

"Stratford's a big town, right?" said Molly.

"It is?" replied Juliet, exhausted.

"Yes!" answered Molly, her own exhaustion causing her brain to melt. Why did her sister have to be so, so *exasperating*?

Molly continued,"That means Stratford has more people, right?"

"Right?" said Juliet.

Molly stopped. She reminded herself. *Juliet is three years younger than me.* Molly changed her tone, to make it sound more like an adventure.

"We're going to play music and sing," said Molly.

"We are?" asked Juliet.

"We need to make money and that's how we're going to make it," Molly continued.

"Oh! Right!" said Juliet, oddly over-exuberant.

"We need-.." started Molly.

"No, no, I *fully* understand," interrupted Juliet.

"Good," said Molly, not sure she did.

They paused for a moment. There was no one around. They could perish and no one would ever know. Is that what had happened to Ben?

"When did you decide that?" continued Juliet.

"Just now. I mean before," said Molly.

"And you didn't think to tell me?" asked Juliet.

"We had to get away from Mr. John Barnes!" said Molly,

crossly. Did she really have to consult her baby sister on everything?

"Shall I go on?" asked Molly.

"You will, anyway," said Juliet.

"What?" asked Molly.

"Nothing," answered Juliet.

Juliet was driving Molly senseless. *Why can't she accept I'm in charge now?*

With studied patience, Molly continued, "Stratford means more people-"

"Got that bit," said Juliet.

"And more people means more money," Molly said, with a flourish.

"I said I understand!" snapped Juliet.

"Good."

That was more exhausting than walking, thought Molly, ungenerously. She stopped herself and gave her sister a hug.

"All will be well," she said. "I have a plan."

Molly started to walk again. After a few minutes, she got the feeling no one was behind her. She turned to find Juliet, in the same spot, still thinking. Molly walked back to where her sister was standing.

"How much money?" asked Juliet.

"Lots of money!" Molly smiled. "Plus, there's this poet from Stratford, who went to London and got rich. Maybe we'll do the same."

"Or maybe the poet can help us?" suggested Juliet.

"I doubt it. But, you never know!" said Molly, trying to sound hopeful.

"Does that mean we have to go to London?" asked Juliet.

"...Not necessarily," said Molly, cautiously. Going to London was a plan growing in her mind.

Get to London and make our fortune; just like Dick Whittington. But she wasn't ready to share that with Juliet. Not yet.

"Plus, it'll be easier for Aunty Anne to find us," said Juliet.

That comment stopped Molly short. Aunty Anne had left after one extremely nasty argument with their mother. She had never returned. Did their Aunty even still care about them? Did she even remember them?

No.

If Aunty Anne had cared enough, she would have made up with their mum and visited. She would not mysteriously disappear out of their lives. But she hadn't, so she didn't.

I wasn't good enough, or smart enough, or nice enough for her to come back for, I guess.

No.

They were on their own.

Molly hugged Juliet tightly.

"Get off!" Juliet said, even though Molly knew she liked it.

Revived, they continued to follow the path along the River Avon. They knew they were getting closer to Stratford, when they saw clusters of workmen's houses connected to estates, outside the town.

Nearer still to Stratford, they encountered a wall enclosing an enormous estate. The gatehouse, protecting the entrance, was larger than their old home. A burly, bearded man, dressed in a fancy guards uniform and holding a pike, came out of the gatehouse.

Molly approached the guard and asked, "Whose estate is this?"

"Why? Are you two jackanapes planning to rob it?" sneered the guard.

"C'mon!" said Juliet, pulling at Molly's sleeve.

"Now look," said Molly, offended by the guard's insult. She had never been called anything so rude as a "jackanape," in all of her life!

"If we were planning to rob this estate, would we present ourselves at the front gate?" she asked.

"Who knows, a pair of wastrels, like you," said the guard. His equally massive colleague popped his head out of the gatehouse. To tease the guards, Molly became as gracious as possible.

She said, "Kind Sirs, if you would do me the honor of telling me whose estate this is, we'll be on our way."

"Not that it's any of your business," said the first guard, "It belongs to His Grace, the Duke of Armington. Now, hop it!"

"Thank you, Sirrah," said Molly, smiling her insult.

"Oy! Watch it!" said the guard.

"Come on!" said Juliet, pulling Molly away.

"The little lad's got the right idea, mate!" called the other guard from inside the booth.

When they were safely out of earshot, Juliet tore into Molly. "Why did you talk to him like that? Who cares whose estate that is? Who cares! We'll never go there. We'll never meet him. Plus, those guards might have worked out we were girls and then what? We'd be done for!"

Molly grinned.

"But they didn't," she said.

Five

EXCITED THEIR DISGUISES ACTUALLY WORKED,
Molly and Juliet marched on to Stratford with renewed vigor.
The path followed alongside the wall surrounding the Duke
of Armington's estate.

"Does his land ever end?" gasped Juliet. "This Duke must
be really wealthy."

"And very, very rich," added Molly.

They both laughed.

They chanced upon a part of the wall obscured by a tree
and some overgrown hedgerow. They were a long way from
the guardhouse now, at what seemed to be a forgotten part on
the far side of the estate. Molly noticed a breach in the wall,
covered by gorse bushes. She decided to find out more.

"Wait here," said Molly, as she darted into the bushes.
"Keep a watch."

"What? Why?" complained Juliet. "Why do you have to
be so-" Molly had disappeared into the undergrowth.

"-sudden," finished Juliet, now quite alone.

~

JULIET SLUMPED TO THE GROUND. Her feet hurt. She started to say so, but realized there was no one to tell. It was the first time Juliet had been alone...ever. She didn't like being alone.

She felt a rising tension in her chest.

She *truly* didn't like being alone.

MOLLY PUSHED her way through the unruly bushes. The bushes pushed back. The plants didn't give up without leaving a few scratches and tears. Molly saw the semblance of a small, overgrown path and followed it.

This would be impossible in a dress, Molly thought.

She continued to push her way through. The forgotten path led directly into the wall. Was it going to be a dead-end, after all?

That can't be, thought Molly.

She dug further and was delighted to see a small hole in the bottom of the wall. This breach led directly into the grounds of the estate. Molly took a sharp intake of breath. She was about to do something she had never done before: trespass onto another person's property.

Needs must, she thought and squeezed her skinny frame through to the other side.

Please don't let me get caught, she thought.

AFTER A FEW MINUTES, Molly returned to the main road.

"Where were you?" asked Juliet. "What did you see?"

"Oh, you know. Nothing much," answered Molly, mysteriously.

"Urgh! You're so annoying!" said Juliet.

"I'll tell you later," said Molly. She had found a possible

place to sleep. She wanted to surprise Juliet with it. In the meantime, she had made an important decision.

"You're up to something. I can tell by the look on your face. Molly?"

Molly looked away.

"Molly!" insisted Juliet.

"The name's Walter," said Molly.

"Walter?" asked Juliet.

"You must call me Walter from now on. When we're in public."

"Walter. But that's-"

"Dad's name. I know," interrupted Molly.

"But, if you're Walter, who am I?" asked Juliet.

"You're, well, you can be Julian. Jules for short," said Molly.

"Can't I be Ben?" asked Juliet.

"That's. That would be too hard," said Molly, quietly.

"Like this whole thing isn't hard?" Juliet asked.

"I know, I know-" answered Molly.

"I'm fed up with it already!"

"I mean it, Julie. It would be very hard calling you Ben, knowing you're not...Ben," Molly explained.

"I know!" shouted Juliet, even louder. Molly hadn't seen Juliet lose her temper like this, since she was a toddler.

"Hey, Jules, what's going on?" asked Molly

"I was scared," said Juliet, quietly. "When you left, I was all alone. Everyone was gone. What if you hadn't come back?"

Molly threw her arms around Juliet.

"Listen to me." Molly looked into Juliet's eyes and held her gaze. "I will always come back. Do you hear me? I will never let you go. I will always come back for you."

Juliet threw her arms around Molly and the two clung to each other, knowing they were all they had left in the entire world. Molly wiped Juliet's few remaining tears away with her fingers.

"Walter is still weird, though, don't you think?" said Juliet. "Walter. *Walter*. See?"

"I know. But…It feels like I'm, I don't know, like I'm carrying dad with me," explained Molly.

She returned to trudging towards Stratford.

"And calling yourself after dad isn't weird?" called Juliet, running after her, shrugging her boy's clothes back into place.

Molly stopped. "We never called him Walter, though, did we? We always called him dad."

Molly continued walking.

"This doesn't make you my dad, you know," said Juliet.

"Julie, I promise you, no one is more aware of that than me," said Molly, not slowing down her pace. "Let's get to Stratford, shall we?"

After more silent, grumpy trudging, they turned a corner.

"Julie, look!" Molly declared, breathless.

Before them lay the spires and thatched roofs of Stratford-Upon-Avon.

They stopped for a moment, staring at the site of their uncertain future. They clasped hands and strode toward the town square, hearts on their sleeves, smiles full of hope.

"Please be kind to us, Stratford," said Molly, as they entered the market square.

Six

"A THRUPPENNY BIT!" exclaimed Juliet, excitedly pulling the coin out of their wooly hat. "That woman gave us a whole thruppence!"

"Look at this, though," said Molly. She gingerly held a half crown in her hand. They had never earned anything close to this amount before. Her dad had shown her a half crown once, when he'd come back from working a big job in London. He'd shown her some other coins, too, including half an angel. "One day, I'll bring you an angel, my angel," he had said. Of course, he never did. Coins like sovereigns and angels were out of reach for ordinary people.

"This is a half crown, Julie," said Molly. "This is worth a full two shillings and six pence. That means 30 pennies! We just earned 30 pence!"

Molly ran her thumb over the image of Queen Elizabeth. Their monarch was pictured in low relief, looking to her right across the silver. Her crown cut into the Latin written around the edge of the coin. She seemed to be looking into the future while dominating the present. As Molly held the coin, she realized she was shaking a little.

"Maybe we'll play for Her Majesty one day!" said Juliet, looking at the coin.

"She'd be lucky to get us," answered Molly, knowing full well that such an event was impossible. Not in a million years.

"The woman who threw this into the hat had a funny look on her face," said Molly. "I bet she gave us this as some sort of revenge. Or maybe she just thinks I'm a dazzling lute player."

Juliet pushed her playfully.

"You'd better mean my singing!" laughed Juliet. Molly was always teasing Juliet these days. When she wasn't teaching her, that is. Molly wanted to make sure Aunty Anne's precious lessons were passed on to her little sister. Even though Aunty Anne had abandoned them, her teaching remained.

They'd been playing music on the streets of Stratford for two weeks. Molly and Juliet quickly discovered there was a code of honor amongst street performers. Lucrative spots were divided up between the more established musicians. There were some more aggressive street performers who tried to keep these spots for themselves. Eventually, the remaining performers banded together and stood up to the bullies. That's how they had created their honor system. You had a specific time in the high-traffic areas. If you missed your allotted time slot, too bad, but if you showed up on time, you got to play and make money.

After testing different locations, from the market square to the smaller streets, Molly and Juliet found their perfect spot. It was at the corner of Chapel Road and Chapel Street, in front of an enormous house called New Place. New Place was the second largest house in Stratford. This meant tons of foot traffic to and from that part of town.

The turn in the road was large enough to accommodate a crowd, and the walls provided fantastic sound. Their takings here had been steady and always increasing. They made enough money to buy regular food from a street vendor, but not enough to stay at an inn, or anywhere indoors. However, Molly's surprise for Juliet was a good place where they could sleep safely and under cover. They just had to keep it secret from other street folk.

"That's the most we've earned, so far!" said Juliet.

"That's because we're marvelous," said Molly, strumming a celebratory cord on her lute. "Mar-ve-lous!" she trilled.

"Mar-ve-lous!" sang Juliet, taking it up a register. They modulated higher and higher until Juliet hit a high C.

"Careful, you might shatter my new window glass," said a passer-by, pointing up at New Place.

"Window glass? What's that?" asked Juliet.

"One more thing to worry about," smiled the man.

Molly smiled back, but didn't really comprehend. The gentleman looked like he had money and might give them a tip. On the other hand, she'd learned that the most generous tippers tended to be poorer folk: maids moved to tears by Juliet's angelic voice or scholars tightly dressed in too small suits, enjoying Molly's renditions of famous speeches.

"Could we delight you with a madrigal, Sir?" Juliet asked. "Or my brother here can recite from any play or poem you fancy."

"Oh, he can, can he? Hmmm…" The man thought for a moment. "Well, in that case, young man, do you know Venus and Adonis?"

"Yes, Sir," Molly said, relieved. She knew that one backwards.

"It's one of the greats, Sir," she added.

"So, I'm told," smiled the man.

Molly cleared her throat to begin.

Her mind went blank.

It was as if her brain froze. How could this be happening? She mentally searched for the words, previously so familiar to her. Juliet punched Molly in the arm. The poem came flooding back into Molly's mind.

Juliet gestured *I don't know what happened* to the man.

Molly launched in:

Even as the sun with purple-colored face
Had ta'en his last leave of the weeping morn,
Rose-cheeked Adonis hied him to the chase.
Hunting he loved, but love he laughed to scorn.

Molly noticed the man staring at her. She chose to ignore him. He would certainly let her know if he was displeased. Folks were keener to complain than compliment.

Molly continued:

Sick-thoughtéd Venus makes amain unto him
And like a bold-faced suitor 'gins to woo him.
Thrice fairer than myself, thus she began,
The field's chief flower, sweet above compare,
More white and red than doves or roses are-

A voice, melodic and breathtaking, rose above Molly's words. It sang the line, *more white and red than doves or roses are* and, with the gentleness of a dove, wove intricate, soaring flights of sound through the air. Molly stopped, entranced by her sister, who flashed a cheeky glance at Molly before returning to whatever angelic realm her singing had transported her.

The man stood, transfixed, as Juliet took different lines from the poem and traced melodic patterns through the air with her voice. Molly grabbed the lute, anticipated Juliet's next musical turn, and strummed a quiet but grounding chord.

The effect was transformative.

Soon, a small crowd had gathered. Juliet and Molly

continued to improvise together–Juliet took lines she heard Molly repeat, and Molly added melody with the lute.

Molly felt Juliet's grief move through her, certain Juliet could feel the same. Their shared experience of the past few weeks gathered together and floated from Molly's lute and Juliet's songbird voice. Molly felt herself meld with Juliet, the lute, the words, the grief. They all became one. The melody poured over the audience, entrancing them, the heartache and the beauty, all at once.

After some minutes, Molly felt the final musical wave ripple to the end of the music. They had never played like this before. The words had inspired the singer, who had inspired the musician, who had inspired the audience. They brought the music to a close and stared into each other's eyes. Molly was not sure what had happened, but she knew something had changed.

Clink, clink.

Clink, clink.

Molly and Juliet turned, somewhat bewildered, towards the source of the clinks. They had been in such a trance, they had not noticed how large a crowd had gathered to hear them. The audience members were smiling, crying and pushing their way to the front to drop coins in the hat.

Clink, clink.

The man who had initially requested the verse stood to the side, tears rolling down his cheeks. He grabbed a coin from his cloth pouch and placed it in their hat.

"You remind me of my son," he said, before hurriedly walking away.

Soon, Molly and Juliet were alone again. Juliet pulled out the coin the man had thrown in.

"Is this real money?" asked Juliet.

"Let me see," said Molly. She took the coin and examined it.

"I think it's an angel," she said.

"An angel? He gave us a blinking angel?" asked Juliet.

"Yes," said Molly, quietly looking in the direction of the man's wake.

"How much is an angel worth, then?" asked Juliet.

"Uh. I think it's…it's half a pound," said Molly.

"Half a pound? Are you kidding? And look at all these other coins! We're rich, Molly!" squealed Juliet.

Molly was painfully aware they were now alone. All this cash made them vulnerable. She knew street performers could eagerly spend another's good takings at taverns.

"Quickly, let's hide this," said Molly, knowing streets were never empty for long. Juliet had sewn little money pockets into the cuffs, collars, pocket linings and hat brims of their clothing. Now, they shoved the coins into these secret compartments, as well as into the lute bag. They put a few coins into their cloth pouches that hung from their waists, in order to not draw suspicion to the coins within their clothing.

"We'll count it later," she said.

"Oh my heavens, Molly!" blurted Juliet, crying tears of joy.

"Let's get something decent to eat," said Molly, remembering she was hungry.

Seven

MOLLY AND JULIET had a wonderful place to sleep.

On the forgotten side of the Duke of Armington's estate, a secret structure grew, like a barnacle, out of the side of a hill. As a young man, the Duke of Armington secretly met there with Lady Exeter. He had stained-glass put into the tiny windows, through which light romantically sparkled different colors onto the floor and walls inside. Then the Duke married the person he was told to marry and the secret folly was assigned to dusty memory.

This was all to Molly and Juliet's good fortune. The forgotten folly became their secret home. Plants had grown up around the outside walls and the pathway to the building was wildly overgrown. Molly and Juliet carefully created a trail for themselves without disturbing too much undergrowth.

By contrast, the internal structure of the folly was pristine and undisturbed. Inside the domed room were two cushioned benches, protected from the weather by a heavy canvas laid across them. These served as blankets to keep the girls warm at night.

A small table sat upon a woolen rug. Semi-relief sculptures were inset into shallow alcoves along the curved wall. Delicately carved wooden panels lined the lower half of the surrounding wall. On one side of the rotunda was a fireplace, which they did not use. It was too risky.

Molly and Juliet could not believe their good fortune. It was the grandest palace they had ever seen, let alone slept in.

Something about the incongruence of the size and shape of the architecture nagged at Molly and wouldn't let go. The measurements were off and Molly was determined to find the reason. She tapped on the wood panels. Different panels resonated differently with each knock.

Knock, knock, knock.

Knock, knock, thud.

"Molly, stop knocking on the blasted walls!" Juliet moaned. "I ate too much last night and I want to sleep."

They had had another successful day of takings and had eaten a big meal inside a tavern. It had been heavenly.

Knock, knock, thud.

"Molly! Stop," complained Juliet.

"Listen to this!" Molly enthusiastically knocked on one of the wooden panels near the fireplace. It sounded hollow.

Knock, knock, knock.

"Now listen to this," persisted Molly, as she knocked on an adjacent panel.

Knock, knock, thud.

It sounded dense and landed with a muted boomph.

"I need to sleep!" moaned Juliet.

"Now, here, see?" Molly knocked on another panel.

Knock, knock, knock.

This time the sound was hollow and resonant.

"Maybe it's rotten. Can I sleep?" groaned Juliet.

"That's what I thought at first, but then listen here," Molly knocked in a different place further along, and it sounded dense again.

Knock, knock, thud.

"Urrrrgggh!!!" said Juliet, as she pulled the cloth up and over her head. "Why are you so annoying?" came her muffled voice from under the canvas cover.

"Something's behind here," said Molly, feeling close to solving a mystery.

"Lovely," muttered Juliet.

Molly knocked all over another panel. It sounded entirely hollow. She moved her hands along the side edges of the panel, not knowing what she was looking for but determined to find it. She discovered a tiny indentation, easy to miss. She fiddled her finger into the hollow. To her delighted gasp of surprise, she heard a satisfying 'click.' The panel popped open. It was a tiny door.

"Julie. Julie! Look," said Molly. Juliet uncovered herself and, on seeing the open panel, sat bolt upright.

"What is that?" Juliet asked.

"It's a hiding place," said Molly. "I think it's a priest hole. Wait here-" Molly scrambled through the little door.

"Don't leave me, again!" complained Juliet.

"Ssh. I won't be long. Keep a watch," answered Molly, before disappearing completely through the panel door.

"Keep a watch," Juliet complained. "Why am I *always* the watch? Why can't I be the explorer? Like Sir Walter Raleigh? Or Sir Frances Drake?! Or anyone! But, no, Molly gets to do the fun."

After a moment, a panel at the side of the fireplace popped open. Out came Molly.

"Did you hear a word I said?" asked Juliet.

"It's a priest hide!" declared Molly, in awe.

"No," said Juliet, answering her own question.

"Julie, there's an entire room back there!" Molly jubilantly exclaimed. "Come and see!"

Unable to resist, Juliet crawled through the fireplace panel into the secret room. The small, tight entryway opened up into an enormous space.

"This must have been dug out of the side of the hill," said Molly.

They explored the secret room, wide-eyed with wonder. On one side, there stood a rough-hewn altar and a crucifix. They found tons of secret panels carved directly into the wall. Some were empty. Others hid different articles for a Catholic Mass. They even found a Latin Bible in one. In another, they found a silver chalice decorated with gems. Juliet turned it in her hands. She said, "I wonder how many angels we could get for this?"

Molly snatched it back and returned it to its hiding spot.

"We are not thieves!" she admonished.

"Why is all this back here?" asked Juliet.

"Secret Catholic Mass, looks like," explained Molly.

They continued to explore the dank, dark room. How many Catholics had secretly worshiped here? Why had they stopped coming? Had they been caught? As so much about this odd little building started to make sense, it threw up many more questions.

While they explored in the hushed, solemn silence of this hidden chapel, they heard an unexpected sound from outside.

Someone was coming.

Eight

THEY KNEW THE DRILL.

Molly and Juliet ran around the rotunda as quickly as their legs could carry them. They grabbed their things, darted back into the priest hide and quickly shut the panels.

They were sealed inside.

After they caught their breath, Juliet noticed a stream of light pouring in from the center of a panel door. It was the tiniest of spy holes, but she could see the entire room on the other side. The priest hide was built for non-detection and it served its purpose admirably. They took turns and silently watched as their forgotten little home was transformed by stewards into something splendid.

The floor was swept.

The walls were dusted

A cloth was placed over the table.

The benches were brushed.

Cushions were plumped.

Flowers were decoratively placed.

The path outside was cleared.

With a sharp intake of breath, Molly noticed one of their

small pouches, filled with pennies, lying at the foot of a cushioned bench.

After a flurry of activity, the men left and there was silence
once more. Carefully, stealthily, Molly opened the latch on the
panel door, darted out, grabbed the coin purse and tripped
over the table covering. This sent it sliding to the floor.
Hearing footsteps outside, she quickly put the table back and
re-arranged the cloth as best she could, then dashed back into
the priest hide, clicked the panel shut, just as the door to the
folly opened up again. She threw herself onto the ground,
away from the panel-door, so no one could hear her heavy
gasps for air.

She silently signaled *I'm fine,* to Juliet.

Juliet continued to watch through the spy hole. The stewards now brought in silver plates topped with fancy
delicacies.

One of the stewards appeared somewhat frustrated with
what he perceived as the shortcoming of a colleague's work.
He readjusted the table cover until it lay perfectly flat and
evenly placed. Upon the table, he arranged three plates, all
piled high with deliciously aromatic food.

Plate One:
This was covered in what looked like colorful pebbles.
These were called comfits, which in this case were
sugar-coated almonds.
Plate Two:
This was loaded with sweet, and delicately aromatic,
damson fruit tarts.
Plate Three:
This was piled high with tiny berry pies; their juices
had rebelliously and deliciously bubbled through the
pastry.
Extra Plate:
On this was piled a stack of plate-shaped crackers

waiting to be loaded with treats, before being eaten themselves.

Molly had only ever heard about such delicacies from. Aunty Anne. The sparkle and smell of the sweetmeats made Juliet's eyes widen and her mouth salivate.

For whom was this banquet being prepared? And did this mean the end of their secret home?

Juliet pointed out another spy hole in a perpendicular wall. This gave a view of the pathway outside. Molly watched as the servants rushed away.

Of course! thought Molly. She wondered if there were several more spy holes dotted around the walls of this hidden chapel. *Spy holes kept the congregation safe. Will they keep us safe, too?*

After everything was set up, no one else came.

For a long while.

There was simply silence.

The temptation was too great.

The sweet treats on the table were sirens calling to Juliet's tongue.

"Don't," admonished Molly.

"I want to," said Juliet.

"Julie!" said Molly.

"I need to!" insisted Juliet.

While Molly reluctantly kept a careful ear out for foot-steps, Juliet crept out of the priest hide and grabbed small handfuls of the sweetmeats. She dumped these into her pockets to free up her hands for more. She rearranged what remained so that the plates didn't look bare.

While Molly watched her sister with delight, her own tummy rumbled, and her mouth drooled. She could resist no longer. She rushed to her sister, grabbing crackers and other she-didn't-know-whats, before darting back into the hide.

"Quickly!" urged Molly. "Someone is bound to come soon. Let's not risk it."

Juliet grabbed a few more goodies, then Molly rearranged the plates to cover their misdeeds. They ran back into the priest's hide and Molly clicked the panel shut behind them.

Giggling, they dumped their edible treasures on the former altar inside the secret chapel. They were so beautiful they didn't feel they had the right to eat them. Juliet held up a delicate damson tart. It glimmered like a treasure. She took a breath then sank her teeth into it. Her mouth filled with a sensation she had never felt before.

What was it?

Flowers?

She had no idea. She just knew it was delicious, and she wanted more.

They made a game of trying each one, putting on aristocratic voices as they tried each delight.

"This looks like almonds, Modom," chuckled Molly.

Juliet popped a tiny pie into her mouth. "And what is this, fair maid? Blackberry?"

"Indeed so, Modom!" Molly answered.

Juliet laughed. The sugar was making their heads spin.

"….Might it be boysenberry, kind Sir Walter, Knight of the Realm?" asked Juliet, in a silly voice.

"It may be fair Sir Julian, Knight of the Garter," answered Molly.

They were in fits of giggles by now, as they gobbled down the candied delights.

Slam!

The door to the folly had swung shut.

Was someone in the room?

Wiping their mouths, they crept slowly to the spy holes.

Nine

"WHY DO we have to meet he-re?" moaned a very well-dressed young man inside the folly.

"My Lord. Think of the adventure! I have arranged all of your favorite sweetmeats, see?" said a willowy, elegant woman in a flowing gown.

Could this be the Duke's son? thought Molly, *The Marquis of Armington?*

"How long has this odd little building been here?" asked the Marquis.

"A while," said the Lady. "Surely you explored it as a child?"

"No," answered the young man, in his uncurious manner.

"It was built by your grandfather, and it is filled with secrets," the Lady teased.

"There's hardly any comfits," complained the young Marquis.

"Oh? I gave strict instructions. I asked for all your favorites. Well, there's plenty of everything else," said the lady.

"Berry pies!" said the Marquis, tucking in. Within a few

minutes, he had consumed the entire plate. Then he shoveled the crackers into his mouth. Once full, his petulance returned.

"I'm cold," he complained.

"There's not much I can do about that," said the Lady. "The fireplace is fake."

"Why did he build this odd little place so far away from the house?" moaned the Marquis. "I want to go back!"

"Aren't you curious about the secrets this building holds?" asked the lady, intriguingly. "Curiosity is the key to life!"

Oh no, thought Molly. *Is she going to show him the priest hide?*

She desperately looked for somewhere to conceal themselves. There had been a cloth in one of the secret wall compartments. Would that work if they laid it on the altar and hid beneath?

"Now there should be…" the lady continued. She was feeling along under the rim of the fake fireplace. She found a tiny box.

How did we miss that? thought Molly.

With the flair of an alchemist, the lady clicked the box and the lid rose up by itself. Inside the box was a small key tied with a ribbon.

"Et voila!" she exclaimed. The magic impressed the Marquis.

"Lady Exeter, how did you know that was there?" asked the Marquis.

"This folly holds secrets," said Lady Exeter, mysteriously.

Molly indicated for Juliet to keep watching while she fetched the altar cloth.

"Where is it? Where is it?" muttered Molly, feeling along the rough-hewn walls. She found it! She unfurled the cloth. Dust rose. She tried not to cough as she laid it across the altar.

It had rotted away. It would never hide them.

"Help me with this," Lady Exeter instructed the young man. They moved a cushioned bench about a foot to its right.

"Well, well. What do we have here?" asked Lady Exeter.

There, on the floor below them, was a small trapdoor.

"Molly!" whispered Juliet, vigorously indicating that she should watch this. Molly did so, pinching her nose, trying hard not to cough.

Lady Exeter dramatically pulled up the ribbon, bringing the key out of its box.

"Ha ha!" she said, for no obvious reason.

Lady Exeter pulled back a small piece of wood in the door, revealing a lock. She inserted the key, and opened the trap door. As she did so, she told the youth a story, "Back when your father was very young, it was extremely dangerous to be an English Catholic."

"And?" said the Marquis, disdainfully.

"Your grandfather was Catholic-"

"*What?*" interrupted the Marquis, completely surprised.

"Oh, yes. Your grandfather would host secret Catholic Mass, right here. The congregants would sneak in through this passageway from Stratford. The authorities never found out."

"But we're not Catholics," said the Marquis, a little nervous.

"No," answered Lady Exeter, "not *now*. It was a very confusing time. Your father wanted to keep all of you safe, so he became a protestant."

"Oh," grumped the Marquis. "Any more *tedious history*? I want to play tennis."

"This tunnel comes out inside the vestry of the church, off the market square."

"Oh," said the Marquis, dryly.

"I suppose you're not interested in the priest hide, then" said Lady Exeter,

Please say no, thought Molly.

"There's a priest hole? Really? I've heard about them!" asked the Marquis, suddenly interested.

"Not just a hole - an entire hide. They would hold Mass behind this wall, right here," explained the lady.

"How is there any room back there?" the young man asked.

"Your grandfather had them dig out the inside of the hill behind the folly. It's probably why he had it built in the first place," said Lady Exeter.

"Crafty old devil," said the Marquis.

"Would you like to see it?" asked the lady.

"I would, actually" conceded the Marquis, suddenly intrigued by the revelations.

"All right, then," she replied, finally happy to have piqued the Marquis's interest in *something*. "The latch is somewhere along these panels. Let's see…"

Molly and Juliet had nowhere to hide. Hopelessly, they pressed themselves against the wall around the slight bend, which led to the fireplace entrance.

"Please, please, please, don't let her find the latch," whispered Molly to herself.

She could feel her heart thumping and sweat dampening her brow and hands, as she pressed herself more tightly against the wall. She could feel her younger sister trembling, as her little body pressed against hers.

"It's here, somewhere, listen, can you hear? It's hollow?" the woman's voice muffled through the wall.

"Yes," muttered the Marquis, quickly bored again. He was used to an easy life in which everything came quickly to him. His servants arranged his clothes, got him dressed, and served his meals. He was a man who never had to wait, which had stifled his curiosity.

Molly and Juliet were terrified. All sorts of possible solutions were running through Molly's head, should they be caught. How to explain their situation? Could she say they were Catholics? That they had been trapped here? That they had been kidnapped? Could she pretend they didn't understand English?

Click.

"Aha!" declared the lady.

Molly and Juliet tensed.

"My word!" exclaimed the young man.

"Do you dare go inside?" asked Lady Exeter.

" It smells," whined the Marquis

"It's damp, that's all. It's astonishingly large inside," said Lady Exeter, squeezing herself through the panel into the priest hide.

At the same time, Molly and Juliet quietly clicked open the panel at the fireplace. They crept out of the hide. They were going to make it, after all.

They headed towards the main door of the folly. The Marquis was finding it hard to bend down through the panel door into the priest hide. Molly and Juliet could see his bottom up in the air as he tried to squeeze through the small panel. His pantaloons ripped right along the back. He stood up, twisting in a circle to check his garment. He spun straight into Molly.

They all stopped in shock.

"My, my. What do we have here?" asked Lady Exeter, looking back through the panel.

Molly slammed the panel door shut, locking Lady Exeter within the priest hide.

"Help!" cried Lady Exeter, banging the door.

Molly and Juliet dodged past the hapless Marquis and down into the trap door, pulling it shut behind them.

"Guards!" yelled the young Marquis, after he had taken a moment to recover.

"GUARDS!!!!"

Ten

THERE WERE THREE OF THEM.

They could easily overpower us, thought Molly, running as fast as she could along the dark tunnel. *If they catch us,* she added.

The three stewards *ooffed* and *ouched* their way down the rickety ladder into the underground tunnel. (Molly and Juliet had jumped from an anxiety-fueled need to escape)

The acoustics in the passageway were excellent and, even at a distance, the girls heard the stewards coming after them, coughing and spluttering with the dank, dust, and dirt.

Molly and Juliet bolted along the tunnel. They had traveled through enough woods, rough roads, back alleys and secret pathways, learned from falls, trips and twisted ankles that they were able to whizz along a dark tunnel at speed. The overly dressed stewards stumbled over rocks and each other.

The girls put some distance between themselves and the stewards. After a while, they couldn't hear them anymore. Perhaps, the stewards thought two urchins were not worth ruining their formal attire over. Or, perhaps, they realized the two crafty knaves would have disappeared into Stratford before they got to them.

AT THE END of the tunnel was a wall of rock. Molly blindly felt the stone around her. There was no ladder, no stairs built into the wall, nothing to show a way out. Had the Lady lied about the tunnel?

They sat for a moment, exhausted, bruised, scratched, dirty and plain fed-up.

Juliet nudged Molly and asked, "What's that?"

She pointed to a faint white stone. Molly put her finger on it and her finger brightened. She looked up.

An almost imperceptible stream of light shone from above them. Molly reached up and felt around the ceiling, pushing as she went. She heard a crunch of stone against stone as she felt something give. More light poured into the tunnel.

"It moved!" exclaimed Juliet.

They silently checked if the stewards were coming down the tunnel. They couldn't hear a thing.

Good.

With considerable strain, Molly pushed the covering up still further. This cover was designed to be lifted by a handle on the other side. She continued pushing until there was enough room for a personage, a very *small* personage, to squeeze through. They were bruised; they were battered, but they were not beaten. They had escaped and were free once more.

Molly gave Juliet's foot a heave up as she leveraged herself through the hole. As Molly began to pull herself through, she heard a whimper from Juliet.

Oh no, thought Molly. *Has Julie hurt herself?*

Molly's head and shoulders poked above ground. As her eyes adjusted to the light, she felt herself being pulled up by several pairs of firm hands.

Three pairs, in fact.

Scrabbling to her feet, she saw Juliet in the clutches of the burly guard. He matched in the stature of one man the three stewards who now held Molly. Their smart outfits were dirtied and torn.

Molly and Juliet had been outwitted by Lady Exeter. She had shown the guards the tunnel's exit, and the guards had simply waited for them to arrive.

"Two reasons for the lack of fruit tarts," said Lady Exeter, with a wry smile. "Take them to the Duke."

"We didn't do anything!" cried Juliet

"Please! Let us go!" pleaded Molly. "We didn't mean to... We just...we just-"

"Were hungry?" answered Lady Exeter.

"We just wanted to see the priest hide," said Juliet, scrabbling for an excuse.

"Are you Catholics?" asked Lady Exeter.

"We were curious, that's all," said Molly, backing up her sister.

"It's famous!" added Juliet.

"Well, now I know you're liars as well as thieves. That hide has been one of the best-kept secrets for the last half century. Take them!" instructed Lady Exeter.

"Please! Please, let us go. We won't be any more trouble, I promise," begged Molly.

"It's the trouble you've already caused. Take them straight to the Duke," barked Lady Exeter.

"I hope, for your sake, he's in a good mood."

MOLLY AND JULIET were forced to walk, shame-faced, through Stratford. Scared for their own safety, fellow street musicians secretly watched the peculiar procession of outsized men, two waifs, and a woman who appeared to float along the ground.

Once in the privacy of the Duke's estate, things got worse. Molly and Juliet were pushed, pulled, and cuffed across the grounds. The stewards were unhappy about their ruined clothes, blaming the misfits rather than Lady Exeter and the Marquis.

The girls were thrown through a backdoor into the Duke of Armington's enormous mansion. They could do nothing but await their fate.

Eleven

IT WAS as hot as hell.

They had been thrown into the largest kitchen Molly had ever seen. It looked as if it had built it for giants.

Hot giants.

Sweltering giants.

But it was filled with ordinary people, working hard everywhere. In one area, meat was cooked on sword-like skewers over crackling fires, while other cuts were thrown into bulbous cauldrons. Muscular men carried entire joints of meat from hooks to tables where heavy set women, with wilting caps and sweaty faces, cleaved them into unrecognizable pieces.

In a corner, folks were in different stages of bread and pie making. Some pounded dough as if raging against their fate; others kneaded and stretched it until it was silky and pliable. Others lined different sized pie dishes and poured in sloppy meat or fruit mixtures.

Against a far wall, with doors open to the cold outside, folks hunched in hushed concentration worked on tiny, edible sculptures. Molly marveled at miniature statues, a small chess set and playing cards. The smell was intoxicating.

As Molly and Juliet stewed in their own sweat, they heard the stewards argue: Where to put the captives? Should they go in the basement?

Please, no.

That would not be suitable, as it might interfere with the wines, meads, and ales needed for the guests. Should they go into one of the rooms upstairs?

Yes, please.

This might interfere with the guests who were staying overnight. Molly thought they would be just fine in the kitchens, surrounded by food...

A girl furiously slammed and kneaded dough. She locked eyes with Molly, as if trying to solve a puzzle. When the stewards dragged the girls to a finally decided location, Molly saw the kitchen girl smile.

Then it hit her, like a whack of dough on the side of her head. Molly knew that girl! That was Bess Brookton! She was sure of it. Bess had been a playmate of theirs on Strivers Row. Many a time they had played stickball or *you are it*, together.

A flood of thoughts drowned Molly's brain.

Is Bess an orphan, too?

How did she land a job in the Duke's kitchen?

Can she get me a job here?

Does she recognize me?

Another thought shook Molly cold.

Does she think I'm Ben?

THE GIRLS WERE THRUST into a hallway. The wall opened as a hidden door, behind which loomed a narrow wooden staircase. Molly was pushed up the stairs. She heard Juliet stumble up behind her.

"Hey!" Molly shouted. "Don't be so rough with him. He's only eight."

"Hark at him. *He's only eight*," mocked a steward. "Oh,

what a delicate flower." His voice sharpened. "I was apprenticed here when I was *seven*."

Halfway up the staircase, a door opened on the left. The girls and their scant belongings were tossed inside like so much feed into a chicken coup.

"Hey! That's a lute!" shouted Molly.

"Ooooh, a lute. Must be worth a *fortune!*" sneered a steward.

The door shuddered shut with the distinct click and turn of a lock. Molly immediately looked for ways to escape. She had expected the room to be tiny, but it was enormous. And everything was shut fast.

They were stuck.

They had no choice but to wait and face the wrath of the Duke.

Twelve

"ARE YOU WELL?" Molly whispered.

"Yes," answered Juliet. Molly knew she wasn't.

She gripped her sister tightly. Juliet's eight-year-old body shook and convulsed with sobs as she released the tension from the past few hours. Eventually, Juliet slumped into her big sister's arms, her emotions spent.

"Would they have treated us like that if they'd known we were girls?" asked Juliet.

"Probably not," answered Molly who, in reality, had no idea. She had never experienced such disrespect or physical disregard in her entire life. Not even when she had gotten up to mischief back in Bitford. No one had been that rough with her, *never*, not even when she had done something very disobedient.

Molly took in their surroundings. Apart from the kitchens, they were in the largest room Molly had ever been inside. Over on one side of the room were a series of virginals—keyboard instruments - and various stands for music. In a far corner stood a harp. Other instruments were propped against walls.

One wall of the room hosted two large, ornately carved,

black cabinets with keys sticking out of the locks. Molly's curiosity goaded her into turning the keys to open them, but she was in enough trouble. Whatever they contained was of absolutely no concern of hers.

Sigh.

Molly noticed two of the most beautiful lutes she had ever seen, resting on stands; ornate inlays of delicately shaded wood lay beneath the strings, strips of different colors ran along the bowl, and stunning pegs kept the strings taut and in place.

One of the lutes seemed iridescent to her. Its delicate grace and beauty overpowered her. Her hand was drawn to it of its own accord. She was just about to pick up the lute when Juliet said, "Look!"

Molly turned around. Juliet stared at a small table. On the table sat a plate piled high with sugar-coated almonds, fennel seeds and tiny, red fruit tarts.

Dare they eat them?

Molly and Juliet resisted. Surely, they were meant for other people. Besides, scarfing down delicious treats had caused enough problems. Oh! The aroma! The beauty! Refusing the sweets was like fighting the Wars of the Roses with their rumbling bellies.

Molly had an idea: to distract them from the sweetmeats, why not sing a song? They were in enough trouble, anyway. Why not sing a ballad about their predicament?

Without waiting for her rational mind to stop her, Molly uncoupled the beautiful lute from its stand. It was surprisingly out of tune. Had this exquisite creation not been played for a while? How could anyone leave such a majestic instrument untouched?

Once tuned, Molly struck a melodious chord.

"What are you doing?" whispered Juliet.

Molly strummed.

"There is nothing more for which we can be punished,"

said Molly, strangely defiant. "Therefore, we must enjoy our confinement the best we can."

Juliet giggled, took an almond comfit and popped it into her mouth.

Molly played a series of chords and notes, making up a song:

'Twas a merry time in Warwickshire
With a hey, and a lo, and a lo, nonny-no
When young ones did themselves disguise
With a hey and a nonny, nonny no.

Juliet, laughing, joined in. She made up the second verse.

They'd lost everything they had ever known
With a hey, and a lo, and a lo, nonny-no
And away to Stratford they did go,
With a hey and a nonny, nonny no.

The girls sang with a harmonious connection they had developed performing on the streets. To sing meant an escape from the harsh world to the sublime, if only for a moment.

Their outstretched hands were turned away,
With a hey, and a lo, and a lo, nonny-no
They were quite alone as a cloud in May,
With a hey and a nonny, nonny no.

They improvised a possible chorus

Hey, lo, hey lo and away they go
With a hey and a lo away they're meant to go.

"To London!" sang Molly, in an outburst.
"London?" gasped Juliet.

Avoiding further conversation, Molly quickly returned to the chorus. Juliet sang in her soaring soprano. The two girls delighted in the beauty of the bright harmonies they had created from nothing. Maybe things wouldn't be so bad? If they could stay like this, could they be happy?

Hey, lo, hey, lo, to London they did go
With a hey, and a lo, and away they go,
From Stratford to London Town they go,
From Stratford to London Town they-

"Leaving for London so soon?" a man said. "I can't allow that."

Thirteen

THEY WERE NO LONGER ALONE.

A tall, exquisitely dressed man stood in a doorway, which Molly had previously thought was a wall between the two locked cabinets.

Is this estate completely filled with secret passageways and hidey-holes? she wondered.

Lady Exeter awkwardly squeezed through the doorway. She wore an entirely new outfit. She swished to the table of sweetmeats. Nonchalantly, she took the tiniest sweet from the tray and popped it into her mouth. Juliet's belly rumbled loudly.

"The Duke is very keen to meet you," Lady Exeter said.

"Thank you, Lady Exeter," said the Duke, indicating it was time for her to leave.

"Oh," she replied, obviously upset. "Your Grace."

She curtsied like a wilting flower. Then she glided to the main door and delicately tapped. On the other side of the door had gathered a crowd of well-dressed eavesdroppers, intent on getting a good look at the captives. To Molly, they blurred into an audience of eyes and whispers.

"Make way!" hollered a steward, and the sea of people parted. Somewhat.

As the doors closed, one voice remarked, "They're so dirty!"

"Commoners," explained another.

"What a stink!" scoffed another.

"We were this close to genuine urchins," said another, excitedly, as the doors closed on the gossipy gaggle of gawkers.

The Duke walked toward Molly and Juliet with an ease a lifetime of wealth can give you. His eyes were focused and kind. He was well aware of his privilege and enjoyed it with a generous spirit.

The Duke took a moment and surveyed the room. "It's been a while since I've been in here," he said, with some melancholy.

Molly and Juliet watched him, uneasily. They were keenly aware their fate lay in his hands. His splendor made them feel grubby. Juliet awkwardly pulled at her garments.

"I see you didn't touch the sweetmeats," the Duke observed.

"Were they meant for us?" asked Molly, confused.

"Of course," he said, beguiling them further.

None of this - *none* - made any sense. The Duke wasn't angry about her using his lute? The lute! She was still holding the lute! And *more* of the most delicious food in the world? Weren't they accused of stealing? Something wasn't right.

The Duke laughed.

"Forgive me. It seems I do forget myself. Let me make formal introductions. Good afternoon, gentlemen, may I present..."

Then he stepped to one side, holding up his hands to present where he had just been standing: "the Duke of Armington."

He stepped back to his original position and gave a

gracious, practiced bow. Juliet giggled in spite of herself and started to curtsey. Molly quickly hit her arm. Curtseys were for girls! Molly bowed awkwardly; she had no idea how to bow properly. Juliet tried to bow, but it turned into a half bow, half curtsey, and she promptly fell over.

"I'm...Walter, your Majesty," stumbled Molly.

"I hardly warrant such a grand title, especially when Her Majesty does a fine job herself. *Your Grace* will do. I do not wish to be accused of treason!" chortled the Duke.

"Oh, no, Sir, me neither," gabbled Molly. *Treason? Was he jesting?*

"And you, young man, you are-..?" asked the Duke, directing his attention to Juliet.

"Er, I'm, I'm," stuttered Juliet.

"That's my brother. Julian," said Molly. "He's rather shy, Sir, Your Grace."

"Julian," Juliet said quietly, "yes."

"Master Julian, Master Walter. Enchanté. Do you have a surname? Or should I guess?" asked the Duke.

Molly realized she hadn't thought about surnames. She couldn't use their real last name, in case Mr. John Barnes came hunting for them. Her mind raced. She noticed the name on the lute.

"Harcourt!" Molly blurted out.

"Master Harcourt. I see. Then the lute must be yours," said the Duke.

"I don't think so, Sir, Your Grace," said Molly.

"But it has your name on it, Master Harcourt," insisted the Duke. "Besides, you play it well. I think musical instruments lose their soul if they aren't played often enough."

A look of sadness washed over his face.

"Thank you, Your Grace," answered Molly, now completely baffled. She tried to bow again, but it was awkward and she nearly dropped the lute.

"Careful," smiled the Duke.

"Yes, Your Grace," said Molly. Gently, regretfully, she returned the lute to its stand.

"You were discovered in the priest hide, I hear?" asked the Duke.

"Yes, your honor, Your Grace" said Molly, quickly correcting herself.

"We're very sorry," added Juliet.

"Are you Catholics?" asked the Duke.

"Way back," said Molly. She wasn't *exactly* fibbing but she did remember Lady Exeter's conversation with the Marquis.

"Aha. And you were…curious?" asked the Duke.

"Yes, Sir," replied Molly.

"This is my dilemma. I'm not quite sure why Lady Exeter was in the folly in the first place. Showing it to my useless son, for some reason," the Duke said, disdainfully. "She's very cross with you, you know."

Molly lowered her head in shame.

"It's a curious thing. I've heard tell of a pair of street performers; a lute player and a young boy with the voice of an angel. By chance, might that be you?" the Duke continued.

"I don't know about the voice of an ang-" started Juliet.

"Yes!" Molly jumped in, sneaking a "shush" look at Juliet. This was no time for modesty. "That's us. Lute and angel voice," she added, awkwardly.

"I see. I do understand. Desperate people do desperate things. I really should have you punished. Trespass and all that. But, in some respects, you've done me a favor—you've shown me potential entry spots for trespassers onto my land. That tunnel, for instance. More than that, I appreciate true talent."

The Duke paced the room, fondly touching the instruments. Molly wondered the impossible— would he let them go?

"Everything in this room?" said the Duke. "All of this was for my son." The Duke stopped, lost in his melancholy. "My daughter played too, and quite well, but for *her* that was all about marrying well," the Duke said, dismissively. "My son, though. My son showed genuine talent. The virginals, the organ, the harp, the lute- there's nothing he could not play and excel at," the Duke continued. Then he turned bitter and angry. "All for naught. He'd rather play dice and gamble away his inheritance. I had to ensure he wouldn't lose his entire inheritance in a single throw. My own son!"

He paused for a moment.

"Anyway," the Duke continued. "It had not occurred to me that you might be the musical duo who caught the attention of a certain poet. As I was making my way here, I heard the most breathtaking music. Your voice-"

Juliet blushed.

"Your voice," the Duke continued, "flowed through the door and calmed my mind."

The Duke quietly walked to the main wooden door.

Molly and Juliet snuck a quick smile at each other.

"Move the people away!" he instructed through the door. There was a shuffle outside. The Duke turned to Molly and Juliet, winked, and pointed his thumb at the door.

"My guests are curious and confused. I like it that way," he whispered with a smile.

The Duke walked back into the room and sat down, with great ease, on one of the benches near them. He did not worry about his fine clothes mucking up the upholstery.

"I have a proposal," he said.

Fourteen

"ALL OF THIS IS TO SAY," continued the Duke, who had not stopped speaking, "I am hosting a grand feast this weekend."

Molly and Juliet, whom the Duke had exhausted from his ceaseless talking, snapped alert. The Duke strolled to the wide wooden door again.

"Hence my wonderful array of *inquisitive* guests," he said, loud enough for the inevitable eavesdroppers. It was a jolly game for him. He returned to the chair and spoke in hushed tones to the girls.

"Here's what I propose," the Duke resumed. "You will pay for your trespass by performing for my guests at dinner."

The girls were silent.

Was the Duke *really* asking them to do this? A real, live performance? In a manor house? For breaking the rules?

After a while, Juliet nudged Molly to speak.

"Oh, yessiryourgracesirthankyousir," Molly mumbled, all at once, "Very much. It would be my, I mean, our honor, very much."

"Excellent," answered the Duke, who was used to people saying yes to him. It made life easy.

"Where is your lute?" he asked.

Molly pulled out her lute. The one valuable thing she owned (apart from the locket) had been dragged, beaten, bashed and almost broken. They all looked pitifully at the sickly instrument.

"That will never do," said the Duke.

"It's all I have, Your Grace," said Molly.

"Here!" said the Duke, grabbing the ornate lute Molly had played earlier. "Take it. It's a gift." he said, holding it out to Molly.

"Your Grace is most kind. I couldn't possibly," stammered Molly. The lute shimmered before her. She had never been offered generosity on this scale before, and she didn't trust it. Not one inch.

"Nonsense. Have you seen how rich I am? This lute needs to be played. You are the one to play it. I simply cannot have you appear before my guests with that poor example of an instrument. And besides, this one has your name on it."

He handed Molly the beautiful lute. She felt it vibrating in her hands. Was it the lute shaking or her body?

"Think of it as an investment. Perhaps you could play what you played just now?"

"But, it wasn't-" Juliet started.

"Certainly, Your Grace," interrupted Molly. "It would be our pleasure."

"And you have a few other songs in your repertoire?" asked the Duke.

"We have several," stated Molly. "We can also take requests."

"Excellent, excellent," said the Duke, heading out, his task complete. He stopped, turned back.

"Might you have something else to wear?" the Duke asked.

Their silence answered the Duke's question.

"I see. Well, I'll send someone to sort that out and you'll

play for the banquet - the dessert. Will that suit you?" the Duke asked, already knowing the answer.

"Yes, Your Grace," said Molly.

"Yes!" said Juliet, at the same time.

"I'll have someone bring you a light repast before you perform; can't have you fainting from hunger. After the performance, you'll be given your full meal."

The Duke turned to leave, but stopped again.

"Do you have a name?" he asked. "I mean, apart from Walter and Julian Harcourt?"

Molly and Juliet looked at each other. It had never occurred to them to name themselves.

"Surely you have a name?" asked the Duke.

"We do?" asked Juliet.

"We do," said Molly. "The Secret Minstrels!" She blurted it out, uncertainly.

"The Secret Minstrels. Hmmm. Has a nice ring to it, but, if I may suggest-?" the Duke paused.

"Yes?" asked Molly.

"Everyone, who's anyone, loves everything Italian. This chair? Italian. That desk? Italian. Those pieces?" The Duke waited for them to answer.

"Italian," said Molly.

"These benches?" asked the Duke.

"Italian!" chimed in Juliet.

"Esattamente!" exclaimed the Duke. "How about *I Menestrelli Segreti*?"

"You what?" asked Molly.

"It's *The Secret Minstrels,* but in Italian. I promise you, with an Italian name, the audience will respond to you with great enthusiasm," explained the Duke.

"I Menestrelli Segreti. I Menestrelli Segreti" Molly practiced.

"Excellent. Glad that's settled. Very well," the Duke's task was complete. "Someone will be along shortly. Don't forget the lute. It has a case...somewhere...here it is...and, if I may give you a word of advice?"

The girls nodded, still slightly stunned.

The Duke continued, "Don't let anyone push you around. You two have talent. People are prepared to pay for that. Jusqu'a plus tard. Farewell."

With that, the Duke knocked on the wide wooden door, which the stewards duly opened. An undignified group of the well-to-do clamored in his wake. Lady Exeter curiously peeked at the musicians before the door closed.

Molly and Juliet sat for a moment.

What had just happened?

Molly examined her new lute. Juliet stuffed the sugar-covered almonds and fennel seeds into her pockets and a few into her mouth. She picked up the plate and carefully carried it over to Molly.

"Here," said Juliet. "They were for us, after all."

Molly popped a couple of comfits into her mouth and let the sweetness fill her mind.

She was still in shock.

Fifteen

THE CHAMBER WAS the size of a large cottage.

"Is this all for us?" Molly asked the steward, who had just laid out rubbing cloths next to a bowl filled with aromatic water.

"For now, Sir," answered the steward, in his French-Moroccan accent. "Do you require assistance getting undressed?" he asked.

"No!" answered Molly, somewhat alarmed. "Thank you."

"You must have impressed His Grace," smiled the steward. These two lads were much more fun than the guests.

"We did?" asked Juliet.

"We did," said Molly, throwing a look at her sister.

"If there is nothing else?" he asked.

"No, no. I mean, there isn't. Anything else. Thank you, Sir, I mean, Sir," garbled Molly. She had never given instructions to a servant before.

"*Bon.* I will return when it's time," the steward said. With a bow, he left.

Molly headed straight to the bowl of water. There were all sorts of flowers and tiny twigs floating in it. It smelled like a bouquet of rich spices. Molly recognized cinnamon and cloves, but not much else.

Giggling, the girls plunged their hands into the water. The herbs and spices spun around. Molly took a rubbing cloth and washed herself. Her skin stung where it had endured the cuts and stresses from the last few days. Juliet followed suit.

Suddenly, Molly plunged her entire head into the bowl of water. Juliet gasped, then laughed. Molly burst back up, her eyes flicking open and shut, her mouth wide with the welcome intake of a new breath, her hair slicked flat against her head. Juliet did the same. It was fun to escape the busy world into bubbling nothingness, if only for a moment. Molly delighted in Juliet's joy as she burst back up out of the water bowl. Maybe everything would be okay, after all?

The door opened.

Although they still had their breeches on, the girls darted to cover themselves: Juliet to the curtains around the bed; Molly to the blanket draped over the nearby chair. She flung it around herself, like a cape. Was there no privacy in these fancy homes?

I must remember that, thought Molly.

Bess Brookton entered. She carried a silver tray stacked with tiny pies. She kept her head down as she set up a small table near the door. Molly froze.

"A light fare. To keep you going, sirs. As instructed by His Grace," she explained.

"Begging your pardon, Sir," Bess asked quietly. "Are you Ben, Sir?"

Molly's brain flooded with a million questions. Bess kept her head down, fearing retribution for having overstepped. There was a crackle of tension as both sides wanted to speak, but could not.

"His name is Walter Harcourt," said Juliet, after a moment. "He's Italian."

Molly looked askance at Juliet. *What is she doing?* She thought.

"We are *I Menestrelli Segreti*, the famous Italian duo," said Juliet, unable to stop talking.

"Of course, Sir. I'm sorry, Sir. You just-..You reminded me of someone I used to know. I was hoping-" Bess stopped herself. Molly's heart ached. She had so many questions. She recognized the yearning for her past life in Bess's sad eyes.

"Well, if there's anything else you need, please ring the bell," said Bess.

"One moment? What are these?" asked Molly, in a terrible Italian accent. She wanted to alleviate Bess's obvious pain and also, find out more about the food. Juliet put her hand to her mouth, stifling a giggle.

"Oh, um, they're small meat pies, Sir," said Bess, very slowly and loudly, as if that might help the Italian understand her better. "These little tarts are damson. And fig, Sir. They're delicious. I hope you enjoy them, Sir."

She curtsied awkwardly and rushed out of the room.

"Grazie!" Molly called out after her.

Once the door was closed, Molly lent against it. She was sweating. Juliet burst out laughing.

"You make a great Italian!" laughed Juliet.

Molly said, "At least, she thought I was Ben and not me."

"Molly, look at this."

Laid out on the bed were two splendid outfits.

Molly quickly finished washing and ran to the bed to get dressed before someone else burst the room without knocking. The softness of the cloth caught her off-guard. Were people supposed to wear this? Clean linen underwear? Who wore underwear?

Additionally, there were:

Pantaloons of red velvet, inlaid with white and red silk.

White stockings.

A red waistcoat striped with deep blue.

A red velvet doublet with gold brocade.

Even red velvet shoes with a slight heel, also red, with gold bows on the side.

Juliet looked splendid in her complimentary colors. They both looked perfectly the part: famous Italian musicians!

"Let's eat," said Molly.

The tiny pies tasted like pieces of heaven. Molly pinched herself. Soft clothes? Delicious food? Had she fallen asleep and awoken in a dream?

The door opened again.

People really do enter any room at any time, thought Molly.

"Monsieurs. I wanted to inquire if -"

It was the steward, again.

"Bon! I see you are already dressed."

Their dirty, ragged clothes lay crumpled on the floor like old snake skins. Molly rolled them up and shoved them into the lute case. She didn't want to waste the fabric. Plus, they had once been worn by Ben. She was not ready to let that go. Not yet.

"Gentlemen, are we ready?" invited the steward.

"Ready as we'll ever be!" answered Molly, a bit too brightly.

"Alors! If you might follow me," said the steward.

Molly grabbed the lute, brushed any crumbs from her sumptuous outfit, her mind plagued with questions and doubts: *What happens if we don't please the Duke? Will he punish us for trespass? What if the guests don't like us? What will Lady Exeter say?*

As they followed the steward out into the hall, he rang a little bell, which was echoed by a bell somewhere else, which was, again, echoed by a bell further away.

Truly, thought Molly, *that is a bell which summons us to heaven or to hell.*

Sixteen

STICKING CLOSE TOGETHER, they followed the steward down a series of stairs and hallways, each becoming wider and grander the lower they went. Eventually, a final set of double doors opened into a large room. On one wall arched enormous windows and on the other stretched a grand, ornate tapestry. In between, a massive wooden table was laid for a feast.

"You'll play up there," said the steward. He pointed to a balcony built directly into the sidewall and facing out over the room. It was narrow and looked as if the audience would only see the heads and shoulders of the minstrels.

"How do we get into a wall?" asked Juliet.

"Follow me," smiled the steward.

He led them through a hidden door in the same wall. This led to a tiny narrow staircase up to the minstrels' gallery. There were small wooden stools for the musicians to sit on.

"Bonne chance!" said the steward, turning to leave.

"Wait! Excuse me, do we just sit here?" asked Molly.

"Is there somewhere else you need to be?" asked the steward. Then, he added, "You'll play from up here. At the bottom of the stairs, the door to the left takes you into the dining room. Don't do that. The door to the right brings you to the servant's area. That's where you'll eat after the performance."

The steward turned to leave again, then stopped.

"If Rufus the Minstrel does not show up, do you have enough music to play as the guests enter, and throughout the entire meal?" asked the steward, almost as an afterthought.

"Rufus the Minstrel? Who is Rufus the Minstrel?" asked Molly.

"Probably drunk in a ditch somewhere. That's who he is. If he doesn't arrive soon, be prepared to play for the whole time." With that, the steward creaked back down the rickety staircase and exited through the door on the right, into the servant's quarters.

Juliet stifled a nervous giggle. Molly was concerned. There was so much they didn't know. What were they going to play if "Rufus the Minstrel" didn't show up? On the street, they would repeat the same tunes, with an occasional improvisation for fun. The foot traffic was always changing, so they could get away with it.

"What are we supposed to play?" asked Molly anxiously. "With one audience, for the whole time, what do we do? Just make it up as we go along?"

"You'll make it work, you always do," beamed Juliet, her big, trusting eyes turned up to Molly's. "Look at where we are. You got us here."

Molly gave her sister a warm hug.

Juliet, my sweet Juliet, she thought.

"You're crushing me," squeaked Juliet.

"Sorry," said Molly, releasing her grasp.

From the cramped and stifling minstrels' gallery they watched maids, stewards and footmen bring dishes of food, flowers, and ornaments into the dining hall below. The head steward fiddled and fussed and gave instructions. Eventually, he gave a satisfied nod to himself. Without looking up, he said, "Are you ready, up there?"

"Us?" asked Molly, having forgotten they could be seen and heard.

"Minstrels? Are you ready?" he asked again.

"Yes. Yes! We're ready," squeaked Molly.

"I suppose Rufus hasn't shown up yet?" he asked, making a few more tweaks to the room.

"Rufus? Uh…" Molly didn't know what to say.

The door to the minstrels' gallery burst open, and an enormous, heavyset man staggered up the stairs.

"Rufus has arrived," the steward drolly announced. "Sing and say nothing."

Rufus quietly mocked the steward's stiff manner, for no one's amusement but his own. As the steward turned to leave, he muttered, "Lord save us from drunken fools."

After a moment, the gargantuan Rufus noticed his young companions. "You're *new*," he said, as if being new were comparable to a foul-smelling stench.

"Yes?" said Molly, not sure how to respond. "Are you *Rufus the Minstrel*?" she asked, innocently.

Rufus guffawed.

The door to the dining hall burst open and the steward re-entered.

"Begin!" he instructed.

Seventeen

"DON'T LET them eat your soul," whispered Rufus.

Then he burst into the most beautiful basso-baritone voice Molly had ever heard.

Rufus the Minstrel had a vocal range as wide as his voice was breathtaking. His singing calmed Molly and Juliet, as well as the guests being seated at the splendidly adorned table.

Rufus accompanied himself on a virginal - the same type of keyboard Molly had seen in the music room. He wore an old and torn brown monk's robe. Without skipping a note, he tied a monk's knotted belt around his middle. He winked at Molly, without missing a beat of music. Molly wondered if Rufus was making a silent Catholic protest to the Protestant diners. He wore monks' sandals, even though they were in the midst of February. Surely his feet would freeze once he went back outside.

As Rufus sang, Molly and Juliet sneaked a peek at the diners below them. There sat the Marquis and Lady Exeter amongst other well-dressed diners, but nowhere could Molly see the Duke himself.

Molly and Juliet barely recognized any of the food, having

grown up eating simple pottage. It smelled delicious. The diners ate and drank; Rufus sang and played and Molly's tummy rumbled. Everyone was merry, except for Molly and Juliet. They were nervous.

The second course consisted of game and poultry. Molly noticed the diners never completely emptied the serving dishes; she wondered at their restraint. She could eat the whole lot and then some more.

All the while, Rufus continued to sing and play. While his voice was beautiful, his eyes were rheumy. He looked sad and angry.

As the second course was cleared away, the Duke entered to a resounding round of applause. He smiled with appreciation.

"I trust you are enjoying your meal?" he asked. The diners responded with affirmative croons and purrs.

"Time for the banquet!" declared the Duke. Rufus played a dramatic cord on the virginal.

"You're next," he whispered to the girls.

The servants carried in platters of desserts. Everyone *ooed* and *aahd* as the impressive edible sculptures, shaped into playing cards, dice and a chess set, were placed at the center of the table. Towers of tiny fruit tarts were placed between the diners, along with shallow bowls of comfits.

Pointing to the cards, the Duke said to his son, "These are in your honor." The Marquis snarked an embarrassed smile in return. Then, to the surprise of everyone, the Marquis grabbed one of the playing cards from the splendid display and bit into it.

"Delizioso!" declared the Marquis, grinning.

There was an awkward silence.

Then, to avoid his father's displeasure, the Marquis said, "Thank you, Father. Truly delicious."

The guests applauded and smiled.

"Beloved guests, I have one more surprise for you," declared the Duke.

"Start playing the moment he stops speaking," said Rufus.

"I discovered a talented duo whom I may patronize. I trust they will captivate you as they did me. I give you, *I Menestrelli Segreti*."

"Go!" whispered Rufus.

Molly strummed the chord she had been nervously holding since the Duke started talking. The girls went straight into their first song. Molly's delicate playing immediately shifted the mood of the diners. Her light style was starkly different from the heavier sounds of Rufus, but equally beautiful.

Then Juliet began to sing.

Joy spread over Rufus' face. He started singing base notes, bringing the performance to even greater spellbinding levels. As the guests crunched on the delectable and ornately decorated subtleties, they were transported to an etheric realm by the harmonious blend of sweet marchpane and mellifluous melody.

The Duke smiled.

Molly wondered, "Are we finally safe?"

Eighteen

IT WAS STILL hard to take in.

Their first official concert had been a tremendous success. They now sat with Rufus in the servants' quarters, at a table laden with leftovers. They stuffed themselves with the leftover food until their bellies ached. Rufus drank.

The Duke of Armington had announced he considered being their patron. If that explained the fine clothes and food, then that could only be a good thing.

Right?

"Be careful," warned Rufus. "All of this, the food, the comfort, the warmth, the being *inside*, it can make you forget who you are. It can become a golden prison. It can make you forget your God."

With that, he refilled his glass with ale and gulped it quickly. He stood, somewhat staggeringly, and said, "You two gentlemen, you have talent. Don't waste it on the backwaters, on *Stratford*" (he almost spat the name). "You must get to London! That is where futures like yours are made. London or the Church." He whispered, "The old church. Ssh. The Duke wants to keep you here, working for him. Of course he does! He sees your talent. He's no fool."

Rufus filled up another glass and drank it, as if drinking were easier than feeling sad. He put down his goblet and muttered, "That's what happened to me."

He filled his cup again.

"Before you say yes to the Duke's patronage," he continued, "*Think* about what it really means. Yes, you get food, lodging, a set of clothes, a certain amount of safety, security, even a small stipend. No doubt he'll impress you with all the finery. Do you still want to be here in ten years? In twenty? They love you now, but one wrong move, at any time, and you could lose it all. But, this is my most important question: If you say yes, what dreams will you have to give up?"

He took one more swig of ale, removed his knotted belt and staggered out into the February cold.

The girls were silent for a moment.

"I like it here," whispered Juliet.

"I know," said Molly, doubtfully. Here she would be safe. Her sister would be safe. But, something nagged at her, tugged at her.

London.

It was ridiculous. She knew that.

London.

Molly waved away the thought with her hand, as if batting a fly.

London was impossible.

Nineteen

MOLLY SANK into the most luxurious bed she had ever encountered.

Juliet giggled from her side of the same bed. Molly thought the feather topping on the mattress would swallow her whole. People actually slept on feathers?

"Molly? You awake?" asked Juliet, from her side of the bed.

"Yes." How could she sleep after such a day? The food alone sat heavy in her stomach, like rich gold at the bottom of a clear stream.

Their luck had changed. Only Rufus' comments gave her pause. What dreams was she prepared to give up? What dreams did she want to hold on to so tightly, she could never let them go?

London.

"MOLLY," whispered Juliet, breaking into her thoughts.

"Yes?" answered Molly.

"Aren't you sick of it?" asked Juliet.

"Sick of what?" Molly replied, confused.

"Dressing like boys. All. The. Time. Being treated like boys," said Juliet.

"Do you mean being treated with respect?" asked Molly. "I don't know about you, Julie, but I like it. Having the freedom to go anywhere I choose? Not having to conform to expected behaviors? I like that too," said Molly.

"Ye-s," said Juliet. "But what about the other stuff?"

"Other than being treated with respect and having freedom?" asked Molly.

"Yes!" said Juliet, crossly.

"What other stuff?" asked Molly,

"I don't know. Like men holding doors open for you, stuff like that," said Juliet.

"Uhuh," said Molly, not seeing the appeal.

"And the dresses," said Juliet, finally breaking. "Did you see their dresses tonight? They looked like princesses."

"But they couldn't move much. Or eat much," answered Molly.

"And men holding a chair out for you," continued Juliet, dreamily.

"Do you mean like dad used to?" asked Molly, suddenly understanding. This wasn't just superficial longing. This was something deeper.

"Yes," said Juliet.

"I miss Dad very much," said Molly, trying to express the emotion for Juliet.

"I wish he could have seen us tonight," said Juliet, sadly.

"He would have been very proud of you, my Jewel," said Molly, using the endearment their father had used. "You know, maybe he is with us. Somehow."

"I...hope...so," said Juliet, falling asleep

"We need to stick it out a little longer," said Molly.

"*How* long?" asked Juliet.

"The more success we have, the more money we make. Then one day, I promise, you'll have all the fancy, stiff and unmovable dresses you can wear, and then some," said Molly.

"Mmhmm," mumbled Juliet.

"We have one more concert here, and then we'll see," said Molly. "We will make it, Julie. We'll make it because we have to. Don't you agree?"

Juliet was asleep.

Molly rolled onto her back. She couldn't sleep. Her mind whirled. This concert had proven, beyond doubt, they had talent which people would pay money to see.

It was essential they get to London.

But how?

Twenty

THEY WERE to do it all again.

Rufus had come early to chat with his fellow musicians. They had been told some new folks were coming up from London, but it was the same arrangement for the minstrels. Rufus would open. Molly and Juliet would play during the banquet. Rufus confirmed the Duke did want to become their patron.

"You'll be assessed tonight. By everyone. You'll feel like dancing bears," said Rufus.

"BEGIN!" ordered the steward.

The girls peeped at the diners as Rufus sang. These guests were much more glamorous. Fine jewelry was on display, glistening from ears, necks, wrists and fingers, even stitched into clothing. Several of the Duke's London friends had arrived, fresh from seeing the latest theater sensation.

The play was called, something like, *Bad King Richard*. The story was about a King from York who murdered everyone. The diners quoted "*Now is the winter of our discontent*," and laughed. Molly desperately wanted to know more.

The chatter buzzed with an excited, energized undercurrent. Molly felt it rather than thought it, as she worked out what it was:

London.

Were the streets of London really paved with gold? All Molly wanted was to make enough money to keep Juliet safe.

No.

Molly had to be honest with herself.

She wanted to *perform*. She wanted to change the way people felt through music and stories. *That's* what she wanted.

The door to the dining hall burst open. The room hushed. The Duke entered, very grandly. He wore pantaloons of expensive black velvet, a tilted crown upon his head. He walked slightly sideways, one arm stretched out ahead of him, the other dangling down by his side.

"He's going to *act*," said Rufus, rolling his eyes.

"Now is the winter of our discontent," the Duke began, in an actor voice, *"Made glorious summer by this Son of York."*

The guests cheered. From their comments, Molly worked out the Duke was reciting lines from the *Big Bad Richard* play. Molly didn't think the Duke was a very good actor. His acting felt forced, as if he were trying to impress with his performance rather than simply saying the lines.

"And all the clouds that lour'd upon our house
In the deep bosom of the ocean buried...."

Molly loved the language. The words bewitched her. The Duke continued:

"And therefore, since I cannot prove a lover,
I am determined to prove a villain.."

"He does – he says that!" said one guest, delighted.

"Oh! He's good, isn't he good?" said another.

"Marvelous!" exclaimed another guest.

"Dad!" moaned the Marquis. The Duke looked directly at his son.

"So wise so young, they say do never live long."

"Why does he always *do* this?" whined the Marquis. Lady Exeter chided him with a playful tap on the shoulder. The Duke pointed to Lady Exeter and said, *"Dispute not with her: she is lunatic."*

Molly noticed how much the diners enjoyed the performance, even though it wasn't very good. Was that how theater worked? As she watched them laugh and react, Molly's eyes rested on one of the new guests.

She froze.

A familiar face in an entirely different costume: fancy hair, pearls, white make-up, red lips. Molly dipped back behind the balcony, visibly shaking. She felt Juliet and Rufus staring at her.

"I'm wrong. I must be," whispered Molly. She wanted to be wrong and right, all at the same time. She was certain she knew that face.

Aunty Anne.

Twenty-One

MOLLY'S MIND RACED.

It can't be her, she thought. *I knew she had money, but not this sort of money. Then, again, it would explain the outfits. The lessons. The locket.*

The locket.

Molly's hand automatically reached for the locket beneath her ruff. It was still there. Still safe. The lady, who may or may not be their aunt, laughed, listened, chatted and paid close attention to how the other guests interacted.

If it is her, which it isn't, and she sees me, which she won't, would she even remember me? thought Molly

No one in the room had even glanced up at the Minstrels Gallery, including the lady. However, once Juliet started singing, the woman Molly thought was Aunty Anne did cast a glimpse up at the musicians. Molly immediately realized she was mistaken about the woman's identity.

Much later, after more presentations from the Duke, after more sweet treats and glimmering beverages in shiny glasses, after Molly and Juliet had finished another successful concert and astonished the diners for a second time, they were back at the servants' table eating leftovers from the great feast.

Although there were all sorts of savory options, Molly and Juliet started with the sweetmeats. They had no idea where they would sleep after tonight, so they filled their pockets and pouches with food. Rufus noticed what they were doing and gave his pouch to them.

"Remember kindness," he said, before downing another goblet of ale. "Farewell," he said. "And Fare Well."

With that, he left them alone at the table.

Their pouches full to bursting, they were eating more fruit pies when the door burst open. Lady Exeter swished in, splashing golden liquid from the jug she carried.

"Dear me!" She giggled with each spill. "You've got me all of a gander!"

She reached for empty goblets on the table and poured liquid into them.

"There we go!" she declared, with great exuberance.

She slid one goblet to Molly and another to Juliet. Then, she refilled her own.

"To celebrate your wonderful success!" she tittered. "It'll be excellent fun to have you living here! In the servants' quarters, of course. Drink!"

Molly and Juliet stared at her, not sure what to make of her odd behavior.

"Drink!" she declared again.

"No, thank you," said Juliet, politely.

"No? No?" Lady Exeter's demeanor changed. She became stern, even cruel. "You do want me to speak highly of you to the Duke, do you not?"

"Yes," said Molly. She kicked Juliet beneath the table.

"I don't want to drink that stuff," Juliet moaned to her sister.

"Where will you sleep tonight?" asked Lady Exeter in mock concern.

The girls were mute. A chill ran through Molly. Now that they could no longer use the folly, where *would* they sleep?

"I can recommend you to the Duke. *If* you are nice to me. I can also suggest he throw you out. It is quite cold outside tonight." Lady Exeter made a mocking *brrrr* sound, pretending to be cold. "So, why not take a sip? It'll be fun!"

Uncomfortably, Molly brought the cup to her lips. The liquid smelled strong, too strong. She took the tiniest sip. It burned the inside of her mouth and throat. Molly coughed and spat.

"Urgh!" Molly said, deeply upset. "Why did you make me do that?"

"Uh, uh, uh," Lady Exeter admonished."You're both very handsome and *very* talented. Especially *you*," she said, grabbing Molly's hand. Molly tried to pull her hand away but Lady Exeter held it tightly.

"I don't want you sleeping on the streets," continued Lady Exeter sweetly. "So, let's drink, eat and be merry."

"Lady Exeter!"

Lady Exeter spun around. At the door stood the lady whom Molly had mistakenly identified as their aunty.

"Oh, Lady Southwark, I didn't see you there," said Lady Exeter, all innocent and buttery. "I'm getting to know these fine musicians. We want to make sure the Duke makes the right decision, do we not?"

"We do," answered Lady Southwark. Lady Southwark matched Lady Exeter's buttery-ness. "Pardon the interruption, Lady Exeter. The Duke asked for you personally. Something about room arrangements?"

"Thank you, Lady Southwark," answered Lady Exeter, who curtsied swiftly, took the jug of liquid from the table, and left the room.

Lady Southwark? thought Molly. *She's definitely not our Aunty!*

Lady Southwark closed the door with a click.

"Ah. Isn't that better?" asked Lady Southwark.

"Have you come to assess us, as well?" said Juliet, bitterly.

"Assess? Nonsense! Your artistry is sublime. Especially you." The woman pointed at Juliet. Molly felt a pang of jealousy, but she pushed it back down. If Juliet's voice kept them fed and housed, that was a good thing. Her day would come.

She hoped.

One day.

Maybe?

Lady Southwark swept around the room to ensure no one could possibly be eavesdropping. Molly wondered at the amount of facepaint she wore.

Once satisfied they were quite alone, Lady Southwark asked, "Where will you go after this?"

Molly shrugged her shoulders. She really didn't want to think about being homeless again.

"I thought as much. You're both too talented for anything the Duke has planned for you here. You don't want to end up like Rufus," she said, sadly.

She leaned in closer.

"Gather your things," instructed Lady Southwark. "Don't let anyone see you. Most of the guests are staying overnight. I'll meet you out front. To the left of the front door, there is a row of trees. Wait there. When you see my carriage, get in. In the meantime, gather up as much food and drink, and eat 'til you're stuffed like pigeons. We've a long journey ahead of us."

Lady Southwark twirled around to return to the guests.

"Wh-where are you taking us?" stammered Molly.

"Yes!" said Juliet, wanting to say something.

Lady Southwark spun back around to face them, her dress swishing a few seconds behind her.

"To London, silly," she said.

Twenty-Two

"WHERE AM I?"

The boy lay under a tree at the side of a rough mud road. A thick oak arched over him and through the branches he saw the crisp, blue sky above.

Sky?

Why wasn't he looking at the ceiling?

He had been prodded awake by a family of hogs, snuffling around the base of the tree for truffles, their tiny tails waggling with excitement. Mama hog had clearly not expected to see a human here, but she continued on with her noisy scrabbling.

The boy's head hurt. His mouth was dry. His clothes were a mess. He dragged himself up and promptly rolled into a narrow ditch. He lay there for a while. He felt stiff from sleeping on the frigid ground, in the cold winter air. How long had he been lying here?

He had no idea.

He remembered he had a second pair of breeches back at the house. Which direction was that? Why wasn't he in his house now? He took a minute and tried to piece things together.

He figured he was somewhere between Bitford and Coddlington. He remembered something about...about...running to see a doctor? And then? The doctor was sick so he headed home.

What had happened after that?

Something, someone had hit him. Had it been a cart? Was it robbers on the road? Instinctively, he checked his pockets but there would have been nothing to take. He had been hit by *something*, and fell down.

Yes, that was it. He remembered dragging himself to the side of the road...

...rolling into this ditch...

...pulling himself out and under the tree.

Everything after that was a blank.

He stood up and checked himself. He was okay to walk. He brushed off the leaves, twigs and mud that had dried upon him. The Mama Hog grunted a warning, but the boy couldn't help himself. He picked up a hoglet and snuggled it into his face. The little pig squealed with delight and anxiety. Mama Hog snorted another warning even though she was, frankly, more interested in her delicious mushroomy lunch.

"There you go, little one," said the boy, affectionately returning the baby hog to its snuffling. "I wish you could tell me where I am," he said.

He looked both ways along the road. On the far horizon in one direction, he saw a church steeple. Was that Coddlington? If so, then the other way must be Bitford but when he turned to face Bitford, he couldn't see anything. He was confused. Was he completely lost?

He decided to follow the river in the direction of, what he hoped, was Bitford. Perhaps, the buildings were obscured by trees and they would come into view, as he got closer. At least, a river would eventually bring him to other people who could help him get home.

He wanted to get back quickly. His family needed him.

Twenty-Three

IT FELT like they were doing something wrong.

Has the promise of London made me reckless? Have I put Juliet in danger? worried Molly.

Lady Southwark clearly wanted them to sneak away without alerting the Duke. They didn't change out of their fancy clothes and Molly still clutched the lute the Duke had given her. Was that stealing?

"Don't worry. I'll sort it out with him later," Lady Southwark told her.

Although Molly accepted this glamorous, wealthy woman could not be their aunty, the stranger definitely had their aunt's infectious, daring-do attitude.

London.

She was on her way.

Molly had swooned with delight at stories of London since she was a little girl. Every Yuletide, their father would build a bunch of glamorous shoes to sell in the big city. He returned chock full of money, stories and something delicious to eat. He once brought home a single, round fruit called an *orange*. Molly still remembered its sweet juices.

Her father said people went to London to reinvent themselves. The city was filled with bakers and builders, water boys and ferry men, wealthy and poor, all of whom aspired to be someone else.

Another thing he shared about London were tales about the theater. How stories played out upon a stage enchanted everyone, from delivery lads to Dukes.

Her father said, "You see, Molly, *everyone* needs to be entertained. Everybody wants to escape their lives, if only for a moment. And entertainers? They get to mix with everyone. That poet from Stratford? He hobnobs with the Queen of England. Imagine that."

Molly did. She did imagine that.

Her mother stopped her father's stories with, "Walter! Don't put ideas into the girl's head!" and "Just because it happened to that poet, doesn't mean it happens to everyone and it won't happen to a girl!" At which, Molly's dad would wink at Molly and tap his nose, as if to say, "you mark my words, Moll. You mark them."

So she did.

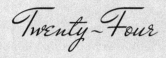

Twenty-Four

THE HORSES WERE BLACK.

The coach was black.

Molly wondered if they might completely disappear once they stepped inside the coach. The opposite was true. The wooden bench was too hard and uncomfortable for anything other than an immediate sense of now. The vehicle rocked with every gallop of the horses and bounced with every

single

bump

on the road.

And there were many bumps.

Still. It was better than walking.

No one spoke. Lady Southwark settled in for the journey. Juliet tried to sleep, but any attempt was repeatedly interrupted by each BUMP! She would doze, then wake with a start, over and over again.

Molly, on the other hand, was too overwhelmed to speak. She appreciated the silence. She did not want to fill the air with meaningless chatter, signifying nothing. And, besides, what was there to say? The girls had thrown in their lot with Lady Southwark. They couldn't go back now.

A loud pounding at the front of the carriage broke into the silence. Molly became fiendishly alert, and Juliet jerked awake. She gripped Molly's hand hard. Molly felt helpless. They were in a moving vehicle, wearing borrowed clothes and riding in the carriage of a stranger. She still had the Duke's lute, and no way to prove it had been a gift. And, after the Duke had shown them such kindness, they had run away.

"HORSE!!" cried the coachman.

Lady Southwark opened a small slat in the wall behind her.

"From whence comes the horse?" asked Lady Southwark.

"Our rear, Ma'am," said the coachman.

"Hmm. He's likely coming from the house. Perhaps the departure of our fine musicians has been detected," said Lady Southwark.

"The horseman is gaining on us, Ma'am," the coachman announced.

"Let him. The Duke does not own these gentlemen. He should have thought of the consequences before showing them off to his London friends. You can hardly steal the tenants if they have not yet signed the lease," said Lady Southwark.

Tenants? thought Molly, confused.

"Besides," continued Lady Southwark, with a twinkle, "If I am removing them for their own safety, it's not poaching at all."

Juliet silently looked at Molly.

Have we been in danger and not known it? thought Molly.

"Thank you, Thomas," said Lady Southwark, as she

closed the little window. Then she whispered to the girls, "We must hide our baubles, in the unlikely event he's a highway robber."

Lady Southwark took out a small brocade purse, removed her jewelry and placed it inside. She did not take off her necklace.

Lady Southwark explained, "Always leave some jewelry about your person when you're about to be robbed. If you denude yourself completely, you give away the game. Leave something easy for them to snatch, like a bracelet or necklace. Never earrings. If earrings are pulled, it hurts like hell's fire burning on both sides of your head. And let us pray it's not the infamous Gamaliel Ratsey. He has far too much fun robbing the wealthy and the last thing we want is him to force you to play that lute before he steals it. Talking of which, hide the lute under this cloth and hand over all your valuables."

Molly and Juliet looked at each other. Were they being robbed right now?

"We don't have anything," said Juliet.

Lady Southwark smiled.

"Well, your talent is your jewelry," she said. She pulled back a thick rug beneath their feet and unlocked a tiny door in the bottom of the carriage.

"Thieves are often as terrified as you are," continued Lady Southwark. "As long as they get something, they're satisfied. They only force you out of the carriage if you give them nothing. Thus-.." She adjusted her necklace to be more prominently displayed upon her bodice.

"Are you sure you don't have anything you would like to keep hidden from the potential marauders?" she asked somewhat sympathetically.

"The locket!" Juliet exclaimed.

Instinctively, Molly reached up to her throat.

"We don't want anyone to take that!" said Juliet.

Suddenly, Molly wasn't sure of this. What if Lady South-wark was a thief? The Lady picked up on their consternation and smiled.

"Very well. If you'd rather keep it hidden on your person, then do so. Hopefully, my necklace will suffice," reassured Lady Southwark.

"No, no, you are right," Molly said. After all, it did make sense to hide the most precious thing they owned.

Molly reached beneath her garments to find the locket. It was tricky. These were unfamiliar clothes with so many layers. After some fumbling, Molly handed the locket to Lady Southwark. The older woman took it in her hand and ran her fingers over the filigree design.

"Beautiful," Lady Southwark said, a faraway look in her eyes. "Someone must love you very much."

"Yes," said Molly. She fought back a surprising tear. This was not the time or space to show vulnerability. They were about to be robbed! Another bang on the front panel made the girls jump. The coachman announced, "Ma'am, the horseman is almost aligned with us."

"Thank you, Thomas," replied Lady Southwark, bracing herself.

"He appears to be alone," said Thomas.

"That's good. Although we can't be too careful," warned Lady Southwark.

"Yes, Ma'am," replied Thomas, who had an edge to his voice.

Lady Southwark turned to Molly and Juliet and said, "Thomas is a very experienced coachman. He's trained in defense. Also he's armed. We're in safe hands."

Juliet wrapped her arms around Molly's waist. Lady Southwark gently placed the locket within her jewelry pouch and lowered it into the hidden wooden chamber. She locked it and placed the key in another compartment, tucked beneath the seat. Lady Southwark, threw the dark rug back over the floor to disguise the hiding place further. This was tucked in to give the appearance of permanence.

Soon, the mysterious horseman was riding alongside them. The man said nothing, just kept pace with the carriage.

"State your business," ordered Thomas, to which the horseman did not reply.

"Are you simply wanting to race?" teased Lady Southwark. "I can say for certain, you'll win," she added, with a cheeky smile.

"My business is with one of your passengers," stated the horseman.

"I'm right here," declared Lady Southwark.

"Gracious Lady, my business is not with you," declared the horseman.

"Be direct, Sir. I am required in London," said Lady Southwark.

"Here!" said the horseman. He threw a small package into the carriage. It landed at Molly's feet. She reached for it, but Lady Southwark stopped her.

"Who sent you, Sir?" asked Lady Southwark.

"The Lady Exeter returns your companion's ring. She has nothing but disdain for his insolence. She instructs the gentleman never to speak with her again. Good night!"

With that, the horseman rode back to the Duke's estate. Lady Southwark lay back in her seat, her mouth turning into a sly grin.

"I,I,I," Molly stammered.

"What's going on?" asked Juliet.

"You tell me," said Lady Southwark.

"These clothes don't even belong to me!" declared Molly, not making much sense.

"Well, there it is. Your returned insult from Lady Exeter," said Lady Southwark.

Molly picked up the package. It felt red hot in her hands, even though it was as cool as the February air outside.

"I'm scared," said Molly, honestly. Why had she been singled out in this way?

"Go on. It won't bite you. Then again, knowing Lady Exeter, it could be a tiny rodent. Is it moving?" asked Lady Southwark.

"No," said Molly, a little nervous.

"Well, go on then. Open it. Don't keep us all in suspense!" urged Lady Southwark playfully.

Molly held the package in her trembling hands. "What the horseman said makes no sense," she stammered. "I didn't give her a ring. Does she mean I stole a ring from her? I would never do that!"

"Yes, yes, yes," said Lady Southwark. "She did not accuse you of robbery. She accused you of slanderous behavior."

"You what?" stammered Molly. "I wouldn't know slanderous behavior if it hit me in the face!"

"And yet it has," joked Lady Southwark. "I'll open it for you, if you like."

Molly hesitated. Is this what all rich people were like? Confusing and a little bit mad?

"No," said Molly. She felt terrifyingly alone. "This is my problem. I'll deal with it."

"It is hardly *your* problem. To my eyes, you're the unwilling object of Lady Exeter's odd attention," said Lady Southwark, cryptically. "And yet, we cannot reach conclusions until we know what the mysterious package contains."

Lady Southwark snatched the package and ripped it open. Everyone gasped. Between Lady Southwark's slender, knobbly forefinger and thumb she held a golden band with a snake-like pattern engraved within it. The snake's eyes were two big, red stones.

"It *is* a ring!" gushed Juliet.

"Very nice," said Lady Southwark, "although a little gauche."

"I, I, I left no ring with her!" blurted Molly. "And even if I did have a ring, which I don't, I would NOT give it to Lady Exeter. It doesn't make any sense! Lady Exeter is not being honest!!"

Molly looked at Lady Southwark, hoping for answers. The woman was eccentric, but she had protected them from Lady Exeter before.

"My dear Walter, it is Walter, isn't it?" asked Lady Southwark.

"Yes," said Juliet, when Molly did not answer.

"Walter. It would appear you have an admirer," explained Lady Southwark.

"A what?" asked Molly. This was all too much.

"An admirer," said Lady Southwark.

"What's an admirer?" asked Juliet, tentatively.

"Someone who admires you," explained Lady Southwark with a glint in her eye. "Someone who thinks you are talented and, in this case, who wants to give you gifts."

Juliet and Molly looked blankly at her. Lady Southwark burst out laughing.

"You're still young. But you'll learn. The way we get on in this world is through admiration. Of one kind or another," smiled Lady Southwark.

"I don't want an admirer!" complained Molly.

"Well, you have one, whether you want one or not. As I said, learn to use this power to your advantage," Lady Southwark said.

"That sounds horrible," said Juliet.

Lady Southwark burst out laughing again.

"Let me tell you a little secret. This..." Lady Southwark pointed to the carriage, to the coachmen, "All of this comes from being admired."

"It does?" asked Juliet, doubtfully.

Lady Southwark burst out laughing again. "Yes, indeed," she said. "Everyone has admirers. The trick is to know what to do with them."

There was silence for a few minutes. Molly turned the ring on her fingers.

"Will she accuse me of robbing?" asked Molly, still scared.

"Sensible question. Lady Exeter is a bit of a dissembler. It is wise to stay away from her web," advised Lady Southwark.

"But this is her ring!" said Molly, even more worried.

"Well, she said it's yours; that *you* gave it to *her*. And that was, in front of, let's see... three-" she pointed at the coachman, "four and five including Lady Exeter's horseman. Five witnesses to attest she said it was yours," said Lady Southwark.

"But what should I do with it?" Molly asked.

"Keep it," said Lady Southwark.

"I don't want it," said Molly.

"Then sell it. It's gold inlaid with rubies. It's worth quite a bit," said Lady Southwark.

"Shouldn't I give it back?" asked Molly.

"On *no account* must you see Lady Exeter again. If you return it, *then* she could accuse you of robbery. No. I'll handle Lady Exeter. *That* will be a pleasure."

There was a moment's silence.

"You've got an adm*irer*!" teased Juliet. Molly hadn't heard Juliet tease her in a long while.

You've got an adm*irer*!" Juliet teased in a sing-song voice.

"Stop!" said Molly, smiling and annoyed at the same time.

"You've got an adm*irer*," Juliet continued.

"She's right," said Lady Southwark.

"Stop! Both of you!" insisted Molly, now laughing.

"You've got an adm*irer*!" trilled Juliet.

"Oh, God!" laughed Molly. "Are you going to do this all the way to London?"

"Yes!" giggled Juliet.

"Don't worry. We'll put a hundred miles between you and Lady Exeter," said Lady Southwark.

"Good riddance!" smiled Molly.

"We make a good band, us lot," beamed Lady Southwark

That's what Aunty Anne used to say, thought Molly. *Maybe it's a sign. Maybe it means we'll find Aunty Anne in London. Oh, please. Please let that happen.*

Twenty-Five

HE STOOD within a series of house skeletons.

Collapsed roofs lay crashed to the ground, as if trodden flat by giants. Here and there, stone clues hinted at what the building once was.

The boy picked his way through the remains of his former home, looking for he didn't-know-what. A remembrance, a remnant, a scrap of something, anything, which could prove his family had once lived here; that he had once lived here.

What had happened to Bitford? Where was everyone? Were they all...dead?

I should died with them, he thought.

His body shook as rage coursed through his veins from his toes to his head. How could this have happened? Why did no one try to find him?

"AAAAAAARRRRRRRGGGHHH!!" he screamed.

A deafening silence answered his passionate roar.

He didn't know what to do. He felt useless.

He sat in the remains of his old home for he didn't know how long.

His mind froze.

His heart numbed.

The cold wind had no impact on him.

His rage kept him warm from the inside.

It wasn't until the sun started to set that his brain began to think again. There were tools. In his father's workplace. He would get them.

I can make shoes. Even the new fashions. There's nothing I can't build out of leather. I'll go to Stratford and get a job. Maybe, even, move to London. I could make shoes for the gentry and, and, and, not just shoes, maybe I could sell my pouches and, Oh! The ideas I have!

He stood.

He walked.

Then he ran.

He did not look back.

Yes, he thought, *Ben Shipton is alive for a reason.*

Book Two

LONDON

Twenty-Six

THE STENCH HIT THEM FIRST.

They had all jerked awake when the coach hit a big hole in the road and, as if in a dream or nightmare, they had woken up in London.

Instantly their senses were bombarded: the clatter of carts, shouts of hawkers selling wares, town criers announcing news, children screeching, everything and everyone at the loudest volume possible.

And the buildings! Molly and Juliet had never seen such grand mansions lined up, like fancy dishes, all in a row.

But it was the assortment of strong, sweet, and stinky smells which were the most overpowering. In one moment, it was a mixture of aromatic spices, followed by the sulfurous smell of horse dung, followed by the distinctive whiff of fish, followed by the rotting smell of garbage. There was an almost constant, sickly, stinging smell of decomposing cadavers. This was the foul base note upon which the city played its odiferous melody.

And there were so many people! People from every corner of the earth, doing people things, everywhere, in every place and all the time.

The coach bounced through another hole and the passengers jolted. Molly felt the lute slide beneath her. As she picked it up, the events of the previous night blurred into focus. Lady Southwark watched them, already wide awake.

They approached London Bridge. It was the only way to cross the enormous river by wheeled vehicle. The bridge was loaded with buildings, some of which were partly built over the side, like eager passengers hanging off a boat's flank. Molly was amazed the bridge didn't collapse under all the weight.

The coach pulled onto the bridge. The horses clopped along the most packed and crowded street Molly had ever seen. About halfway across, the carriage stopped. The horses huffed and stomped the ground impatiently, but there was nothing to be done.

They were stuck in traffic.

Twenty-Seven

THE CARRIAGE JUST SAT.

The horses' power and strength were now rendered useless by the sheer amount of foot and cart traffic around them. The coachmen yelled, the people yelled, but nothing moved.

This is London? thought Molly. *All this energy and nowhere to go with it.*

She noticed a small alleyway between two buildings leading to the side of the bridge. Before she knew it, she had clambered over Juliet, opened the carriage door and jumped outside.

"Walter!" cried Lady Southwark, but Molly was off.

"All is well," she heard the Lady reassuring her sister, "we'll be here for some time," but the voice felt distant as Molly pushed her way through the crowd. On one side of the alley was a perfumer; on the other a leather goods workshop. Molly vaguely noticed a couple of lads working the leather, but she was more curious about the alley. Molly ignored the wafting fecal smells, and dodged the lumpen sources of the odor as she pushed her way to the edge of the bridge.

There it was!

The river.

The biggest river she had ever seen in all her life.

"The Thames," said Lady Southwark, who had stealthily followed after her. "Isn't she glorious?"

Molly was awed by the sheer amount of life on the water. Boats, ferries, people, birds - so much life!

"London doesn't stop at the water's edge," said Lady Southwark. "London spills over into every nook and cranny; wherever London's energy can flow, it will go."

On the north bank, Molly could see how the grand houses saved their true splendor for the river view. On the south side, the buildings were rougher, smaller, and more tightly packed.

"That's our destination." said Lady Southwark, pointing to the south bank. "It's the true Heart of London: Southwark." She pointed to a large white building which stood proudly above the rest.

"You see that big, beautiful building?"

Molly nodded.

Lady Southwark continued, "That building is for bear-baiting. They make bears fight dogs for sport. And that, my dear, is London in a nutshell. Big, beautiful, but with bite."

Lady Southwark laughed. "Would you like to know my impossible dream for London?"

"Yes," said Molly.

"I desire to build a magnificent theater. Right there," said Lady Southwark, pointing to a spot between the bear baiting pit and the bridge. She headed back toward the coach.

"Make sure you look up as we pass under the south gate," smiled Lady Southwark. "You'll see something gory," she said, raising her hands into pretend claws.

"They stick the heads of traitors on spikes!" she continued, unable to contain her delight.

"Why do they do that?" asked Molly.

"For the spectacle!" enthused Lady Southwark.

Molly followed Lady Southwark back to the coach. Juliet had come out and was staring in at the shops. The carriage had barely moved. Molly opened the door and climbed back into the coach, breathless with exhilaration.

Lady Southwark could see London's power work its way into Walter's very soul. On the other hand, Julian was overwhelmed and tired.

There was something about these two lads. They felt strangely familiar to Lady Southwark, even though she barely knew them. She had hoped the older one was her nephew, Ben. She hadn't seen him for so long. Her heart had sunk when he said his name was Walter. Still, she was glad to have saved them from the Duke. Now she had to formulate a plan. How to introduce them to the London scene? She needed to get it just right. They had to be appealing but hard-to-get. She observed her two charges: one ready to soar like a stone from a catapult; the other fearful and unsure.

What a fascinating adventure this is going to be, thought Lady Southwark.

What a fascinating adventure this is going to be, thought Molly.

Twenty-Eight

"I HAVE MARVELOUS NEWS!" said Lady Southwark.

Molly and Juliet had been staying in Lady Southwark's mansion for a few weeks. Molly felt safe for the first time since leaving Bitford. Hundreds of miles buffered them from Mr. John Barnes, the Duke of Armington and Lady Exeter. Lady Southwark had settled everything with the Duke and sheer embarrassment would keep Lady Exeter at bay. Lady Southwark had ordered fresh sets of clothes for her wards and had shown them around the neighborhood.

"Tomorrow, I'm hosting a fantastic feast," Lady Southwark declared. "Would you be so kind as to play your magnificent music, to entertain us?"

Whenever Lady Southwark was excited, she used splendid superlatives. Everything was marvelous, or fantastic, or superb. And, when Molly stopped to think about it, everything was.

"Of course," said Molly. This was a perfect way to return Lady Southwark's kindness, even though she knew she didn't have a choice.

"Would love to!" piped in Juliet, wanting her voice to be heard.

"Perfectly perfect. Walter, I would appreciate it if you might memorize a couple of splendid speeches," added Lady Southwark. "I suspect they'll be well received by my impressive array of guests. I have one particular speech in mind. What tremendous fun this will be, my darlings!" exclaimed Lady Southwark.

Molly and Juliet looked at each other. Lady Southwark behaved more like Aunty Anne every day: her mannerisms, her boldness, her make-things-happen-ness. They had never seen her without her thick, white make-up, so it was impossible to tell. Juliet hoped to be as glamorous as Lady Southwark, one day. Molly hoped she would become their legal guardian.

Molly had come to find out that Lady Southwark was a widow. She was, therefore, free in society to manage her own money, her own land, and her own affairs.

Lady Southwark embraced her freedom.

With gusto.

Twenty~Nine

THEY WERE LOUD.

Very loud.

Molly and Juliet cautiously peeked into the dining room. The men wore so much jewelry, Molly thought they must be pirates.

Necklaces, bracelets, and gigantic rings sparkled. Earrings dangled or hooped from ears. The men appeared larger than their physical size because their personalities were enormous.

They were not pirates.

They were actors.

The charisma of Lady Southwark's guests was matched only by the loudness of their speech and clothes. Their irreverently colored capes splendidly adorned the entrance. They talked loudly and all at once. They babbled and chatted and cajoled and jeered and expounded and pontificated, words tumbling, flowing, like many streams pouring over bubbling rocks, converging, then diverging, then converging again.

They spoke at such a pitch and pace, Molly wondered if they were actually conversing at all. Then, they would all burst into boisterous laughter, all at the same joke, so they were clearly able to speak loudly and listen at the same time. Perhaps it was a unique skill these super humans possessed.

The men were filled with the latest news and gossip: court gossip, political gossip, street gossip and the latest about the notorious Mary Frith, a London Lass who dressed in breeches, smoked a pipe and swore like a sailor.

"She's been arrested again!" exclaimed a guest.

"For dressing like a lad?" asked another.

"Nah. For robbing," said the first.

Then, in more hushed tones, they discussed the Queen's new favorite: Robert Deveraux, the Earl of Essex, but it was treasonous to talk about such things.

Molly was drawn to them like a moth to a flame. She wanted to join them more than anything else in the world.

Presiding over it all, like Queen Elizabeth herself, sat Lady Southwark.

Unlike the Duke's orderly table, this table was chaotic. There was a fun informality about the entire affair. There was none of the accepted social norm of leaving a little food in the dish for the servants.

No.

Every single scrap of food and drink was guzzled by these human-sized giants. The actors ate as if they were starving. Lady Southwark had ensured her staff took their share of the food *before* serving the *theatricals*.

"Come in! Come in!" called Lady Southwark, jovially. Molly and Juliet shuffled into the room like mice at the feet of giant cats. The raucous merriment abruptly silenced, as if Lady Southwark had signaled an intermission.

"Gentlemen, these young men are my wards," she said. "They are our entertainment. *Be kind*."

The actors applauded appreciatively while assessing the two youths.

Not knowing what else to do, Molly and Juliet set up to play. Lady Southwark had had them perform in some of the local inns to build their "London sound" and to get used to London audiences. Londoners had a reputation for being tougher, and less outwardly appreciative, than those in the provinces. Molly checked the tuning of her lute, Juliet cleared her throat and ran a couple of scales. Molly strummed the first chord, and they began:

Spring flowers
Newly open
Full of promise.

We made it
Made it through
The darkness.

Another spring
Is upon us
Another year.

Time for wishes
Spirit of Spring
Be kind to us.

Be kind to us.
Spring.

A man at the table instantly pointed his finger in recognition. He dramatically moved back and forth - now facing the musicians, now facing the table, not wanting to interrupt the music but almost bursting with wanting to speak.

At the first speck of silence, he exploded, "It's you!"

Turning back to the table, he told the crowd, "They were outside my house!" Then back to Molly and Juliet, "Brought me to tears, you did, you scurvy knaves!" His joy infected the entire table and everyone laughed.

"They're quite talented!" exclaimed the largest man at the table.

"You should see that one do my *Venus & Adonis*," said the first man, pointing vaguely in Molly's direction.

"Then, let us see it!" demanded the big man.

"I believe he has something to equally delight you," interrupted Lady Southwark.

She nodded at Molly for her to begin.

"Very well," said Molly, nervously. She took a deep breath.

She proceeded to recite the speech she had heard the Duke of Armington perform at his dinner. The actors watched in respectful silence, as Molly spoke these words:

Now is the winter of our discontent
Made glorious summer by this sun of York;
And all the clouds that lour'd upon our house
In the deep bosom of the ocean buried.

Juliet strummed the lute, causing the audience to applaud.

"If you weren't so young, I'd be worried for my part!" laughed the big man.

"Darlings, *this* is Mr. Richard Burbage," said Lady Southwark. "He played Richard III in the original production. He was rather marvelous."

"Oh!" said Molly, embarrassed.

"You are too kind, m'lady," said the big man, raising a glass to acknowledge his host.

"And this is Mr. William Shakespeare. He wrote *Richard III*," added Lady Southwark. "They are the stars of the London Stage!"

"Hangabout, you can't see the stars without the rest of the night sky," said Will Kempe.

"Yes, yes," said Lady Southwark. "This is Mr. Will Kempe, the genius comedian," she said.

"Genius comedian. You heard the lady. *Genius* comedian!" said Kempe, making the entire table laugh again.

"These gentlemen, my dears, are the best theatricals in all of London," said Lady Southwark, smiling. "They're called the Lord Chamberlain's Men."

"You, young man," said Burbage, as he gestured grandly towards Molly, "have natural talent. I know it when I see it." He pointed to Juliet. "You, my lad, sing sweeter than the heavenly Cherubim themselves."

Juliet smiled shyly.

Burbage continued to Molly, "*You* will join my apprentices at once. The two of you will sing at our show tomorrow afternoon."

"He's not being generous, or anything like that," said Will Kempe, undercutting Burbage's dramatics. "Nathanial Giles just stole our boy singer."

Burbage hit Kempe on the arm.

"That is beside the point," said Burbage. 'I simply will not leave this house until you say yes. Even if it means I have to sleep on this rather splendid floor. You start tomorrow. Come, watch and learn."

"Or," quipped Kempe, "come, clean and don't earn."

Everyone laughed.

"I hope the play's a hit," worried Shakespeare.

"It will be!" declared Burbage. "So, you'll come?"

"Tomorrow?" asked Lady Southwark.

"Um...yes?" said Molly, unsure.

"YES!" declared Juliet, brightly.

Lady Southwark smiled. This had gone far better than she could have possibly imagined.

Thirty

MOLLY WAS THE NEW BOY.

This meant she had to do the worst jobs, like clean up stinky fake blood and empty the poop bucket.

As an apprentice for the Lord Chamberlain's Men acting company, she was surrounded by a cast of larger-than-life characters. The theater was called *The Curtain*, but there were no curtains of any kind. The stage stood on the long side of a wide, rectangular room.

There were four other apprentices along with their teacher, Richard Burbage.

Lady Southwark said he was quite famous.

She said he was the finest actor in the country.

And, most excitingly, he had performed for the Queen.

When Molly watched Mr. Burbage act, she was amazed and confused. Before her very eyes, he transformed into an entirely different person. As Romeo, he became seventeen. *How was that even possible?* As Richard III, he transfigured into the hunchback King. When Burbage was on stage, it was impossible to take your eyes off him. Molly vowed to be as good as him if she ever got the chance.

"He's a great actor," chirped Alvin, every time he watched

Mr. Burbage perform. Alvin Pople, the senior apprentice, was about to join the professional company.

Alvin hailed from Wales. He had been a very successful builder in London. Then, one afternoon, he saw a play at The Theatre and knew he *had* to be an actor. He was tall and gangly, with a shock of red hair and freckles all over his nose. He was a hard worker and very loyal. He had recently been very funny as Flute, in the inaugural production of *A Midsummer Night's Dream*.

Harry Spleen, another apprentice, showed delight in Molly having to do the worst jobs. Harry was a willowy blonde with creamy skin and piercing green eyes. He had a heart-stopping smile, but was bitter and resentful. He believed being an apprentice was beneath him. He envied Alvin. Harry thought he deserved to go straight into the professional company, although he had done nothing to warrant such a promotion.

Harry would loom out of dark corners, and *accidentally* knock over a container of liquid, or a pile of props, which Molly would have to clean up. It felt as if he wanted her to be as miserable as possible, so Molly made sure she was always cheerful around Harry.

"Joy is the best revenge," Aunty Anne had taught her.

The apprentice with whom Molly connected the most was Raymond de Cevil. He had soft curly black hair, dark brown skin and sparkling brown eyes. He beamed positivity and infectious charm.

"You may call me Raymond, because I like you," he had told Molly. He insisted others address him by his full name. His Moroccan grandmother had been Lady-in-Waiting to Queen Catherine of Aragon. Raymond spoke six languages. He was politically savvy, so while in England, he favored French. He intended to become a famous actor-manager, just like Burbage.

Raymond's unabashed self-confidence nourished Molly,

like water to a plant. Whenever he had an unpleasant chore to do, he would shout, "This brings me one day closer!!"

The fourth apprentice was Alexander Rostoff. He was pale and delicate, with translucent skin and watery, blue eyes. He descended from a family of Russian actors. They had been traveling players who settled down in the fast-growing City of London. Company members shortened his name to Alex, but he told Molly he preferred the traditional nickname, Sasha. He had a quietly expressive acting style; the opposite of Burbage's declamatory delivery. He had played Clarence in their recent production of Richard III and elicited great applause and praise from the crowds. Burbage disdained Sasha's subtle acting style as, "too Russian."

Molly longed for an opportunity to act professionally. Unlike Harry Spleen, she put in the work even though it was hard and, sometimes, confusing. One day, Molly was on all fours, cleaning up sheep's blood from the stage floor after a dramatic battle scene. A bloody stabbing was created by the actor tucking a sheep's bladder filled with blood under his shirt. When he was stabbed, he squeezed the bladder and the sheep's blood burst everywhere. Audiences loved special effects - the bloodier the better. Cleaning it up, though, was hard work. Molly was fed-up. The sheep's blood was stinky, sticky, and never-ending. She decided to try Raymond's technique. As she scrubbed the floor, she shouted, "This brings me one day closer!"

"What was that?" boomed a voice from off stage.

Oh, no! thought Molly. *Is Mr. Burbage still here? Did he hear me?*

The big man entered.

"Did you speak?" he asked.

"No, I mean, yes, I mean, not really, Sir, sorryfordisturbingyouSir," blurted Molly.

Mr. Burbage looked out at the empty theater. He breathed in, opened his arms wide, as if taking in the applause he would surely receive after his next performance. He gestured, *I humbly thank you for acknowledging my greatness.*

After his reverie, he turned back to Molly, who had finally - *finally* - cleaned up the blood and packed away the cleaning tools.

"William-" he began.

"Walter," Molly corrected.

"Walter," said Burbage, without missing a beat. "I admire your ambition. You have talent and charisma. It causes you to burn bright. And *that's* what keeps audiences coming back."

His words were kind and unexpected. Molly blushed.

"Thank you, Sir," she beamed.

Burbage continued, "You missed a spot at the front of the stage."

"I did? I'm sorry, Sir," said Molly, put right back in her place.

Burbage gestured, *It's hard when you must do everything yourself* as he swept out.

Once she got to the place on the stage, she saw the wood was perfectly clean.

Why had he done that?

Thirty-One

MOLLY WAS IN AN UNUSUAL POSITION.

As the lowest-of-the low apprentice, she cleaned up after everyone and readied the theater in the early mornings. Then, as a professional musician, she performed on stage in the afternoons. Audiences delighted in *I Menestrelli Segreti* and, especially, Juliet's voice.

One day, Juliet excitedly made an announcement to Lady Southwark and Molly.

"I wrote a madrigal!" she declared.

Molly played the piece. It was excellent.

"You must show this to Mr. Burbage," Molly suggested, her stomach tightening.

Burbage loved Juliet's song and included it in the very next performance. Molly's stomach tightened further. Was Juliet going to be the great success of the pair?

Day after day, Juliet charmed audiences with her lark-like voice. Molly wrote madrigals, but they felt dense next to Juliet's melodic grace. Molly feared her own disappearance; that she would only ever be regarded as Juliet's accompanist. Would she ever be taken seriously as an actor?

~

NATHANIAL GILES WAS a famous organist and choral music writer. He headed the Choristers at the Chapel Royal. If any boy in London had a beautiful voice, Nathanial Giles had the legal right, by royal warrant, to add that boy to his Choristers, whether the parents gave permission or not.

The Lord Chamberlain's Men had been surprised when their previous boy singer, John Carlisle, had left them to join the Chapel Royal. Nathanial Giles had tricked young John with the promise of a decent salary, featured solos and regular performances for the Queen. What young Carlisle didn't learn until it was too late was, once you joined the Chapel Royal, you could never leave. Unless Mr. Giles decided you could.

Burbage had a gentleman's agreement with Giles: the Chapel Royal would never poach from the Lord Chamberlain's Men and the Lord Chamberlain's Men would never poach from the Chapel Royal.

Nathanial Giles broke this agreement when he took John Carlisle. Burbage was furious. Giles gave Burbage his word: He would never, *ever* do that again.

Thirty-Two

BEN HEADED STRAIGHT FOR LONDON.

His dad's former partner had moved to London a few years earlier. Ben sought him out.

Mr. Charlie Littleton had set up a leather goods and shoe-making workshop on London Bridge. He had haunted eyes and a gaunt frame. He had planned for his family to join him in London. The Plague got them first.

"God punished me for my greed," he said, frequently.

When Ben showed up at his workshop, Mr Littleton gave Ben a job on the spot. Then he hugged the boy so tightly, Ben feared a rib might crack.

Ben proved himself skilled and very popular with the customers. They would request specific and more intricate work from him. At first, Mr. Littleton took credit for Ben's abilities. He charged a premium for Ben's delicate stitching and imaginative brocade. The customers weren't having it. They knew Mr. Littleton's capabilities and his shortcomings. Mr. Littleton quickly moved Ben from being an apprentice to a full-fledged employee.

Ben had ideas beyond Mr. Littleton's workshop.

"You need to stay flexible to keep up with fashion," was one of Mr. Littleton's (many) mottos.

Ben thought differently: *Doesn't success lie in getting ahead of fashion? Indeed, to create fashion? Customers don't know what they want 'til they see it.*

Ben tried out new styles of fabric for a shoe with a stronger raised heel, for example. Heels for both men and women, of course. He had purses and pouches with detailed designs and flashes of different colors. He invented a leather clasp with which a person could safely attach a pouch to a belt, *inside* a gentleman's jacket.

Ben was very grateful to Mr. Littleton. Thanks to him, he had a place to work and live in London. He slept above the shop with two other boys who apprenticed there.

He reminisced about his family constantly. He often thought he could see his sisters in the faces of others. Why, just the other week, he saw Molly in the face of a young lad hop out of a carriage and run down the alleyway next to his shop.

His mind was playing tricks on him.

He knew he was alone.

Thirty-Three

MOLLY OFTEN FELT INVISIBLE.

She needed to break free from Juliet's shadow. She wanted to be recognized as an actor, not a lute-playing accompanist and average madrigal writer.

Molly watched her fellow actors, took mental notes and practiced other people's lines. She had memorized almost all the parts in the repertoire. She was determined to learn them all.

The company of actors put on new plays and performed their triumphs in constant rotation. Successful plays kept audiences coming back and the money rolling in. If a show failed after the first couple of performances, it closed. There was never much rehearsal. The play would be written, worked on briefly, then performed. The actors always rehearsed with their new lines learned.

The mornings went something like this:

The apprentices arrived first. They prepared the space for that day's rehearsal and performance. The writer would arrive, anxious about his new play.

FINALLY, the actors would straggle in:

Consistently noisy.

Often smelly.

Frequently hungry.

Eternally LOUD.

They would tease each other and share gossip. Mary Frith was a constant source of shocking tittle-tattle.

"She performed on stage in breeches, smoked a pipe and played the lute!" one said.

"Did she get arrested?" said another.

"Of course!" said the first.

"For dressing like a man?" said another

"Nah! For being a cutpurse," said the first.

All this gave Molly chills, but she ignored them.

Burbage's booted footsteps declared his imminent arrival, and the company hushed in anticipation.

Then, arms open wide, the great actor entered. Oh, how Burbage loved to make an entrance! Even though this was a private rehearsal, an entrance was *always* an entrance. The actors applauded.

Molly wasn't sure if it was to acknowledge the performance Burbage had given the day prior, or because they all wanted to keep their jobs.

AND THEN THERE was Mr. Shakespeare.

Molly admired him the most.

He and Burbage were good friends and fantastic colleagues. They were equals. They both hailed from humble beginnings and had made their way to money and standing through hard work, talent, and endless self-belief. Shakespeare knew the greatness of which the actor was capable, and Burbage loved being stretched by the writer. They were passionate about everything.

If he wasn't at his home in Stratford or at an alehouse, Will

Shakespeare was always at the theater. His desk, in the corner of the theater, was littered with sheets of paper, quills, and inkpots. His fingernails were frequently stained black from ink.

Today was the final run-through of Shakespeare's latest history play. The apprentices had to haul an enormous and heavy trunk from the storage space at the theater - called *The Theatre* - next door. (Even though they owned The Theatre, the company could not perform there because of an issue with the landlord). The trunk was filled with swords, armor, various other props and costumes for their historical plays. Although Alvin was no longer an apprentice, he still helped out. As if by intuition, Harry arrived the moment the job was complete

"Nice of you to show up," quipped Alvin. "Lubberwort."

"Hey!" said Harry. "I do my share."

"Mate. You don't," said Alvin, walking behind the stage.

Shakespeare observed, listened, and drew inspiration from the people around him. He noticed Harry's frequent absences.

Molly wanted to learn Shakespeare's skill of quiet determination. While many successful writers got into drunken alehouse brawls, *this* writer had a family in Stratford to support. He focused, almost entirely, on his work.

Molly hovered around Shakespeare's desk, learning and observing. Mr. Shakespeare was always kind to her and never ordered her about. He confided in Molly that he didn't simply want to write plays. He wanted to "shape theater" itself.

Molly planned to be there when it happened.

Thirty-Four

"BEFORE WE BEGIN!" announced Burbage.

They were setting up for the final run-through of *Henry IV, Part 2*. Burbage struck a dramatic pose, arms and feet open wide like a starfish. Everybody stopped.

Even Shakespeare, who was used to Burbage's dramatic pronouncements, returned his quill to its pot and turned his bemused attention to his colleague on the stage.

"As some of you may know, this is Alvin's maiden voyage into the professional company!"

Burbage gestured *celebration*. Everyone clapped.

"Let's hope he doesn't sink!" quipped Kempe. Everyone laughed, while some affectionately jostled Alvin. Molly smiled. She loved this camaraderie.

Alvin smiled, embarrassed. On the one hand, he really didn't want a big fuss. On the other hand, he quite liked the attention.

"This leaves me bereft!" continued Burbage, striking a gesture of *dramatic sadness*. Shakespeare smiled, indulgently. "It means I have now lost my most excellent assistant," said Burbage. "That role must be filled...immediately! Alvin will advise you."

BURBAGE WAS the only actor in the company who had a dedicated apprentice. It was a highly sought-after, prestigious job. Now Alvin had joined the professional company, this position had become available. Harry Spleen desperately wanted it and had worked hard to get it.

He had:
1. Spread false rumors about Sasha and Raymond de Cevil.
2. Lavished praise on Burbage, to the point of tediousness.
3. Made a great show of fulfilling his apprenticeship duties. These were the regular jobs the other apprentices just got on with.

"MY NEW APPRENTICE WILL BE...." Burbage gestured *anticipation*. He paused to build excitement. Sasha looked down at his hands; he knew it wouldn't be him. Raymond squeezed Molly's arm. He wanted this position. He knew it would help him achieve his dream of becoming an actor-manager, just like Burbage.

"My new apprentice will be...." Burbage struck another pose gesturing *high drama*. Shakespeare rolled his eyes and smiled. Ever the consummate performer, Burbage milked the moment for all it was worth.

"...."

He posed with a new, very dramatic gesture of *playing God*. He hovered his outstretched hand over the crowd and pointed his finger. He was not pointing at Harry.

"Monsieur Raymond de Cevil!" announced Burbage.

"Mon Dieu!" exclaimed Raymond. He hugged Molly and

kissed her on the cheek. Molly blushed. Sasha applauded and smiled. Raymond was the perfect choice. It allowed him to watch Burbage up close, to prepare for his future career as an actor-manager.

Burbage shook Raymond's hand. Then, Alvin walked him off stage to show him the setup. Raymond turned back and smiled at everyone before excitedly disappearing to do his new task.

Once Raymond was out of sight, Harry Spleen sneered. Molly vowed to support Raymond, no matter what Harry said or did.

"Places everyone! Let's start without delay!" declared Burbage, gesturing *exhaustion*. Exit Burbage, with a dramatic flourish.

The actors launched into their run-through of *Henry IV, Part 2*.

Molly watched, riveted. What a story! Before she knew it, they had finished the first half. She snapped into action, helping the actors as needed. Shakespeare had already given the actors' new lines which they memorized on the spot. Now, he thumbed through a bunch of papers at his desk. He appeared to be writing a new play.

Suddenly, the actors started behaving oddly. They straightened their bodies and tidied their clothes. They bowed at odd times; some bumping into each other. Molly turned to see a woman—a *woman* — enter the theater. She carried a leather basket, covered by a simple cloth.

"Winifred!" said Burbage. He became instantly younger and giggly.

"That's his lady friend," whispered Sasha.

"Hello," said Winifred, blushing.

"For those of you who don't know, this is Winifred Turner. She's my, rather lovely, neighbor," Burbage gushed.

Winifred placed her leather basket on the foot of the stage.

"A very splendid basket you have there, Winifred," babbled Burbage, foolishly.

"I could make a joke, but I won't," joked Kempe. "Not with ladies present."

"Thank you, Sir. I bought it at a little leather shop on London Bridge," she explained. "Mr. Littleton has a new employee. He makes such interesting things."

There was an awkward silence. No one really knew what to say, or who Mr. Littleton was, or why there was a woman in rehearsals.

"I made some treats for you," explained Winifred. "For everyone to share," she added, not wanting to make appear rude.

"Were they made by your own fair hand?" asked Burbage, cooing like a turtle dove.

"Certainly, kind Sir," answered Winifred, blushing sweetly.

"Fellows, this young lady cooks with the hands of angels!" Burbage beamed, smacking his belly.

"I'll be the judge of that," said Kempe, stepping forward to help himself to a wild berry tart. He took a bite and savored the confection. Everyone awaited his verdict.

He turned to the actors and said, "DO NOT RAMPAGE!"

He turned back to Winifred.

"Madam, this is absolutely," he turned back to the actors, "NO RAMPAGE!" then back to Winifred, "- divine. These tarts are fit for the Queen."

"Oh!" Winifred blushed. "Thank you, Mr. Kempe. Oh! Well. I'll leave them here."

Flushed and breathless, Winifred gathered her skirts and turned to leave. Then she turned back and asked, shyly, "Would you care to join father and myself for dinner, Mr. Richard?"

"Wild horses could not stop me!" declared Burbage.

"I'm free too," quipped Kempe.

"Watch it," said Burbage. Kempe made a funny backing-down gesture.

"I'll return the basket," said Burbage, gushing.

Winifred blushed again.

"Oh! Thank you," muttered Winifred. Not knowing whether to curtsey or just leave, she made an awkward exit and dropped her handkerchief on the way out. Harry Spleen held the door open for her, bowing deeply as she left.

The moment she departed, the actors charged for the leather basket, roughly grabbing the delicate tarts with their grubby fingers. They stuffed their faces, as if they had been starving until this moment. Only Molly noticed as Harry straightened himself from his bow, Winfred's handkerchief had disappeared.

Thirty Five

"ALRIGHT, truffle pigs! Places for the second half!!" declared Burbage.

The actors got into position to start the run-through of the second half of the play. Molly noticed Shakespeare staring at her.

It wasn't a regular stare.

It was as if he were looking at Molly while, also, trying to catch something in his mind. After a while, he dipped his quill into the inkpot to capture the idea onto paper. He paused, looked up, found Molly again, squinted his eyes, moved his lips as if talking to an imaginary person, then scratched the ideas onto paper. He shuffled back through earlier papers, copied down text from there, then repeated the entire process again.

Confused, Molly joined Raymond off stage.

"Mon dieu! I haven't a clue what to do, Walter," said Raymond.

"Burbage believes in you, Raymond. And so do I," Molly said. "Plus, Alvin will help."

"I'm worried about Harry," he whispered.

"We're all worried about Harry," said Molly.

They set up Burbage's costumes and props for the second half. When Molly re-entered the auditorium, there was Shakespeare staring straight at her, silently mouthing words as they ran through his brain. His body appeared to be in this world, but his mind was somewhere else. He twitched and moved, as if two people were having an argument in his mind. Then, he wrote it all down. After that, his eyes would seek out Molly again. He looked half mad.

I've got to take a chance, thought Molly. She walked right up to Shakespeare's desk, unsure but determined.

"Oh!" the writer snapped out of his reverie. "Was I staring? I apologize. I, um, I study to write," he mumbled, embarrassedly shuffling papers around.

"Thank you. In advance. If you do," gushed Molly. "Write a part for me, that is. I think you're a wizard with words. I'd perform any part you gave me in a heartbeat!"

With that, Molly quickly walked away.

Did I just make the biggest mistake of my life? she thought.

She briefly turned back to see the playwright smile, shake his head and return to his writing.

"BEGIN!" Burbage commanded.

The actors plunged into the second half of *Henry IV: Part Two*.

Thirty-Six

THERE WAS A STRANGE SOUND.

Molly grabbed her chest.

The sound was coming from her.

She was sobbing.

Loudly.

In the most snotty, ugly way.

"That poor old man!" she wept. "What an impossible situation!" She fell to her knees, but didn't want to miss anything, so she stood right back up. In her periphery, she saw Shakespeare smile.

The actors were coming to the end of *Henry IV Part 2*:

Wild in his youth, Prince Hal, had smartened up in order to become King Henry V, played radiantly by Burbage. Will Kempe played Prince Hal's low-life best friend, Falstaff. Falstaff loved Prince Hal like a father loves his son. Falstaff and his friends were playing the fool, when King Henry entered. His Lords and Chamberlains dismissed the ruffians, but Will Kempe's Falstaff greeted his former friend with *"My King! My Jove! I speak to thee, my heart!"* The newly crowned King Henry turned toward his former friend. Molly watched a range of emotions cross Burbage's face: recognition, deep love, sadness, dismissal and, finally, derision. Then, he said, contemptuously: "*I know thee not, old man.*"

Exit Burbage, as King Henry V.

How could he do that? Molly thought, tears pouring down her face. *Wasn't Falstaff a loyal friend? But then again, now he's King, he can't have ne'er-do-wells hanging around. But then again-*

Raymond smiled at her. With his new promotion as apprentice to Burbage, Raymond knew the company could see his talent. The Lord Chamberlain's Men didn't waste time. If you had talent, discipline and motivation, they moved you quickly into the company.

Kempe, as Falstaff, stood alone on stage. Kempe was a genius comic actor.

"To master comedy," Kempe taught the apprentices, "you must master tragedy as well."

Here was a perfect example of Kempe's brilliance. Even as Falstaff's heart was breaking, he smiled and made a joke. This devastated everyone in the audience, including Molly.

Raymond made a silent cheer with his hands in the air. He was so impressed by Kempe.

"We're surrounded by la crème de la crème of theater, Walter! C'est ca! Here, we learn from the best!" he would say.

The run-through ended. Everyone cheered and applauded. Alvin beamed so hard, his smile reached his ears. Cast members slapped him on the back. Alvin opened his mouth wide to the apprentices, in a *is this really happening?* way. Still clad in tear-stained, heavy stage make-up, Burbage shook Alvin's hand.

Just moments prior, they had been breaking Molly's heart. Now the run-through was over, the actors were *out of character*. Where once they had been Kings, Dukes or low-life rapscallions—right here on this stage - now, they were just an ordinary troupe of actors.

Molly was gob smacked.

Thirty-Seven

MOLLY AND JULIET were the first ones to enter the theater that day.

They were not alone.

Lying on the stage were two mighty men: Burbage and Shakespeare. They lay on their backs, shouting, too tired to even look at each other. Around them were scattered upturned pots of ale, scraps of paper and spilled ink, which Molly knew she would have to clean up.

"I can bear this vile rectangle no more, Sir Jacksauce!" slurred Shakespeare.

"I have nine-hundred and ninety-nine problems and you want me to contemplate POLYGONS!!" blasted Burbage.

"Fustulent Bombast!" said Shakespeare, making up an insult, "I need my wooden O!"

"Thou Scurvy Knave!" answered Burbage, spitting out his consonants, "We cannot have our Wooden O, because the landlord seized our Wooden O, and he won't renew the lease on the land of our Wooden O!" Burbage gestured dramatically.

"But that is OUR wooden O!" answered Shakespeare, frustrated.

"It certainly is!" answered Burbage.

The two men promptly fell asleep.

MOLLY WASN'T ENTIRELY sure what the great men had argued about. She and Juliet got on with their jobs, preparing the theater for the afternoon performance. As Molly's fellow apprentices arrived, they worked around the two sleeping (and snoring) giants.

Of course, when performance time came, despite having been up all night and slept all morning on a hard wooden stage, Burbage was still brilliant.

Thirty-Eight

HENRY IV, *Part Two* was a massive triumph.

For the opening performance, Lady Southwark sat in the expensive seats. Alongside her sat the Master of the Revels. He worked for the Lord Chamberlain. It was he who vetted all productions to decide if they would please Her Majesty, Queen Elizabeth of England. If he thought a popular production was suitable, he would invite the company to Court to perform for the Queen.

On the other side of Lady Southwark sat another extremely well-dressed man. Molly had no idea who he was, but she could tell from his clothing that he must be very high up in the Court.

The Lord Chamberlain rarely attended the theater himself. He relied entirely on his Master of Revels. He waited until a production came to Court and viewed it at the same time as the Queen. On this occasion, however, he had been persuaded by a *friend* to attend.

He could not speak of such things.

Such things were spoken of in secret only.

The Lord Chamberlain was curious to listen to a young boy singer who had garnered quite a reputation in London.

This singer was said to have the voice of an angel. The boy singer was frequently accompanied by his accomplished, lute-playing brother.

When the play ended, Molly snuck a glance at Lady Southwark. Tears had tracked down through the Lady's white make-up as she clapped heartily. Her companions applauded and smiled.

Burbage stood beside Molly, taking in the crowd.

"Looks as though we'll return to Court!" he whispered.

He slapped Molly on the back, a little too hard, then strode forward, arms open wide, to take his own very special bow.

Thirty-Nine

ONE DAY, Burbage entered the theater in a foul mood.

He expressed his emotions so perfectly, Molly could almost see a threatening gray cloud above his head.

His mood infected the entire company. No one said a word. The actors knew, from experience, the best strategy was to wait until the great actor spoke. If anyone tried to break the tension, they would be laid low by a tirade meant for the subject of his ire. Molly followed their lead and stayed quiet.

Burbage had argued with Shakespeare, yet again, about the fate of The Theatre. Burbage owned The Theatre, but was unable to use it due to the greedy landlord.

Eventually, Burbage stood up and shouted, "DAMN HIM!!!" He arose with such force that his chair fell down behind him. Alvin, quiet as a mouse, ran around and righted his chair.

"You are the only one, the *only one*, my lad, to do anything useful," railed Burbage, gripping Alvin, a little too hard, on the shoulder. Alvin said a quick "Thank you, Sir?" as he grimaced and bent slightly, under the force of the clench.

"Look at them, *look* at them, sitting on their backsides, doing nothing to help!" Burbage stared at the poor actors with derision. Of course, he was being completely unfair and a part of him knew that.

The actors knew they had to respond, but no one wanted to go first. In the end, it was Kempe who spoke. Brave Will Kempe, as fearless in life as he was on stage.

"Let me guess…" he said, in his cheekiest voice, "the landlord?"

"DAMN HIM!!" yelled Burbage.

As if this were one of his inventive, comic turns, Kempe turned to the actors and said, "It's always a woman or money. If you're unlucky, it's both. Personally, I'd take money, every time."

The actors laughed, awkwardly. Kempe was expertly diffusing the situation.

"RURRAAAAGGGGHHH!!' shouted Burbage, lifting his chair, running across the room and smashing it onto the stairs next to the Pit. He knew enough not to mess with the edge of the stage.

"GILES ALLEN!! Will no one rid me of this *minimus*, this withering piece of knotgrass made, this excrement on any actor's shoe…this, this…"

Kempe, not being able to help himself, said, "Yep! Definitely the landlord."

The actors were relieved. Molly played catch up, fast.

"What's wrong with the landlord?" she whispered to Sasha. Burbage, who had pitch perfect hearing when needed, answered her.

'*EVERYTHING!!*' he yelled.

Molly felt a hand gently grasp her shoulder. It was Kempe.

"Let me explain," he said, giving a quick glance at Burbage for approval. Burbage slumped on the stairs at the side of the stage, in a perfect gesture of *frustration*. He still managed to give Kempe a nod of approval to go ahead with the drama.

"You know the fella who owns the land over the great stone wall, north of the houses, north of The Theatre?" said Kempe, launching into a theatrical presentation.

"*Our* theater!" boomed Burbage, gesturing *despair*.

Molly nodded.

"Let me present to you, Giles Allen," said Kempe, holding out his arm. He knew an actor would jump in and join him. Henry Condell obliged.

"Aha! Giles Allen is the landlord of The Theatre. Burbage's very own father built The Theatre! But now, thanks to Giles Allen, we have to rent the theater next door. Problem is, this theater, the Curtain Theatre, is rectangular. Our theater - *The* Theatre - is a lovely octagon," said Kempe.

"So much nicer," whispered Thomas Pope, another actor in the company.

Condell hunched his shoulders and wrung a piece of cloth, as he spoke: "Gotta get me rent. Gotta get me rent. As much as I can *squeeze* out of the actors. They can't do nothin' with their nice fancy theater without paying me the *rent!*"

Molly smiled. Even though she knew this was all a clever ruse to calm Burbage, it was very nice to have the finest actors in England put on a show, just for her.

The actors could sense Burbage returning to himself. Kempe twinkled triumph in his eyes. Condell continued, "I'm the King of my land. The KING!"

Burbage stood up, ready to take part.

"Excuse me, landlord, what purpose does our theater serve if it is closed?" asked Burbage, hat in hand, gesturing *meekness*.

"It matters to me not a jot!" said Giles. "You own the theater, I own the land. As long as The Theatre is on my land, which will be forever, you must pay me rent. And that, Sir, is that."

"And SCENE!" Kempe called. Everyone burst into applause.

Molly's mind whirred.

"And that, my lad, *that* is the problem we face," said Burbage, completely back to himself. "We must rent the Curtain theater, when we *own* a perfectly good theater, right next door. But his new lease? It's too damn high. I refuse to sign it!"

"Why don't you move The Theatre?" blurted Molly, before she realized the words were out of her mouth. Everyone turned to face her. She felt awkward and embarrassed. What to do next? She could choose:

1. Stay silent and look foolish.
2. Speak up and still possibly look foolish.

Which was worse? At least, by saying something, she would look foolish for doing something than for doing nothing. Perhaps?

"Well. My thought is, here's my thought…"

I'm off to a bad start, thought Molly. *Oh, no. Everyone's looking and listening to me. I think it's a good idea, but will they think so? I have to say it now, oh, oh, here I go…*

She said, "If you own the building but the landlord owns the land, well, why don't you move the theatre?"

"What did you say?" said Burbage.

"I, I-.." she looked around for support. The actors looked back at her, aghast. Raymond smiled, encouraging her to keep going.

"It was just a question," continued Molly. "If you built The Theatre, can't you take it back down and move it somewhere else?"

"Move The Theatre —that's a good one," said Kempe, joking and monitoring Burbage at the same time.

"Move The Theatre?" said Burbage. He gestured, *pondering.*

Harry sniggered.

Oh, no, thought Molly. *I've said the wrong thing. Career over. Before, it's even begun.*

"Move The Theatre-.." Burbage gestured to his mouth and to his temple, to demonstrate *reasoning*. Burbage was famous for his gestures. He once told Alvin the gestures helped him think and feel.

Everyone silently watched as Burbage walked and thought (and gestured). Molly wondered if she were being mocked. Burbage now stood, left hand on hip, his right hand completely covering his upturned face, his fingers drumming his forehead in a repeated rhythm.

"Move the….Move the…" he muttered.

He struck another pose. This time he gestured *deep in thought.*

"Move the, move the, move the, move the, I HAVE IT!!" he announced, arms open wide, hands outstretched, smiling.

"You, Walter, are a genius!!" he said, slamming his hand down hard onto Molly's shoulder. She winced at the force, but appreciated the appreciation.

"Company! I have news."

He hesitated - dramatically, of course. "None of the words I am about to speak must leave these walls," he announced. The actors nodded their assent.

"Swear!" he bellowed.

"We swear!" said the actors, quivering with excitement.

Shakespeare scribbled down notes.

"With the help of a friend, I have secured land on Bankside, just south of the bridge," said Burbage. Molly wondered if the friend might be Lady Southwark.

"We will build a theater there. Sir Will is my co-conspirator in this," said Burbage. "This new theater will be the greatest theater London has ever seen! Due to, ahem, financial issues, we have yet to afford the building materials. I propose, based on this young man's suggestion, that we take down the old theater and use the materials to build a new theater!"

Burbage struck a pose gesturing *genius*.

The company fell silent.

Juliet piped up, "I think it's a fabulous idea, Mr. Burbage!"

"It's certainly a bold one," said Kempe.

"Are you in, Kempe?" asked Burbage.

"Fortune favors the bold!" answered Kempe.

"How do you propose to do it?" asked Henry Condell, ever practical.

"Where there's a Will, there's a way!" joked Kempe.

"Funny," said Will Shakespeare, drolly.

"Hey, I'm a Will, too!" Will Kempe quipped.

"When the landlord is away, the mice will play. More than that, I *will* not say," smiled Burbage. "I want to know who of you is brave enough to attempt something never done before? An act of defiance that will define us as a theater company. An "up yours" to the landlords of the world! An act of rebellion by actors against the establishment! For London! For England! For Theatre and St. George!!" cried Burbage.

Molly stood up. "I'm in!"

"I'm in!" declared Raymond.

After that, the entire company rose to their feet, cheering. Juliet jumped up and down. Molly stood on her chair clapping. How she loved this wild, crazy, irreverent group of talented people!

Striking a gesture of *victory*, Burbage exclaimed, "We will, at a time I cannot disclose right now, MOVE THE THEATRE!!"

Forty

JULIET HEARD EVERYTHING AS MUSIC.

Burbage was a trumpet. Kempe was a crumhorn. The actors' interchanges were madrigals. A play was a series of musical compositions. Only Molly's voice was spoken.

The company had just completed a run-through of a play written by Ben Jonson, who had already retired to an alehouse. Burbage and Shakespeare conferred on stage. This often happened after a run-through. The actors checked in with each other—was there anything they could do to make their performances better?

As they talked, Burbage and Shakespeare continued to cast glances over at Molly. The writer would shuffle through papers and hold up lines for Burbage to look at. Eventually, they decided.

"You, lad… William!" called Burbage

For an actor who carried hundreds of lines in his head at one time, Burbage had a poor memory for names.

"His name's Walter. Sir," smirked Harry.

"I know that, Hubert," snapped Burbage. "Walter. Approach."

A frisson fizzled through the group. Harry sneered. Was

the new apprentice about to get fired? A little daunted, Molly joined the two men on stage. Burbage still wore his costume from the run-through, makeup and all.

"Sir Will here," said Burbage, "has something he'd like to try." There was an intake of breath. Harry's jaw tightened.

Will handed Molly a sheet of his writing. "I, *we*, would like you to read this."

"Come along," said Burbage, bounding to the center of the stage.

Where does he get his energy? thought Molly, rushing to keep up.

Molly stood on stage with the greatest actor of all time. In front of her, in the Pit, the actors watched closely. Her entire body trembled. She looked down at the paper. She saw her cue lines, followed by her text. Burbage gave her directions: "They hate each other but, deep down, they love each other. Is that right, Will?" he asked.

"Somewhat," said the writer. Molly observed how attentive Burbage was to Shakespeare's direction. "They want to hate each other, but they're drawn to each other. Like moths to the moon."

"Aha! I understand," said the actor. "Ready?" Burbage asked Molly.

"I think so," whispered Molly, barely getting the words out of her mouth.

"Darling, we can't hear you," sneered a voice in the crowd.

It was Harry.

"Is this better?" said Molly, much louder. The audience laughed. Alvin playfully, but not that playfully, shoved Harry.

"I'll gesture like this, as if I have just spoken. Then you begin" said Burbage.

Inside Molly's head, she screamed: *OH, LORD! I'M BEING DIRECTED BY MR. RICHARD BURBAGE!!!*

On the outside, she merely said, "Yes, Sir."

Molly had nothing to lose, so she gave it her all. She cut Burbage off with her first line.

"I wonder you will still talk, Signior Benedick: nobody marks you."

The audience automatically cheered, shouting 'Ooooh,' and 'get her," and 'how's he going to come back from that?"

Shakespeare smiled. This was exactly the reaction he desired.

Burbage paused for the perfect amount of time, before answering,

"What, my dear Lady Disdain! Are you yet living?"

The audience burst out laughing. Burbage was a master of timing. Could Molly replicate it? She jumped in with her retort.

"Is it possible disdain should die while she has such meet food to feed it as Signor Benedick? Courtesy itself must convert to disdain, if you come in her presence."

The audience loved it. Burbage, as Benedick, replied:

"Then Courtesy is a turncoat. But it is certain I am loved of all ladies, only you excepted: and…truly, I love none."

"A dear happiness to women,"

That was it. The audience went wild. Shakespeare smiled. Molly continued:

*"They would else have been troubled by a pernicious
suitor."*

She hit on the word pernicious, to which Burbage
gestured *outrage*. The audience burst into laughter again.
Molly continued:

*"I had rather hear my dog bark at a crow than a man swear
he loves me."*

Again, the audience yelped enthusiastically. Someone
cried, "top that, Signor Benedick!" Another said, "He can't.
The lass wins."

Molly watched as Burbage did something really interesting. He acted hurt and cut to the quick but loving the sport
with this woman.

His reply: " *Well, you are a rare parrot-teacher."*

She said: *"A bird on my tongue is better than a beast of yours."*

He replied: *"I' God's name; I have done."*

"Is he giving up?" someone called.

Exit Burbage. The audience burst into vigorous and enthusiastic applause. Burbage and Shakespeare bounded back
onto the stage.

"What do you think?" Shakespeare asked, expectant-
ly. "I'm still working it out, but-"

The actors applauded again. Shakespeare laughed. He
turned to Molly.

"What do *you* think?" he asked.

The great writer was addressing her! Asking her opinion!
Molly took a deep breath and said, "I like it. A lot. It's funny."
She reached for a harder word."And poignant."

"Do you think it will be a hit?" he asked.

Before Molly could answer, the company yelled out, "Definitely! Of course!"

Burbage and Shakespeare conferred privately. Molly stood

awkwardly to one side. Should she even still be on the stage? After a moment, Burbage bounded back. He always bounded.

"Gentlemen, gentlemen," he announced. The company quieted down. "This decision usually takes much consideration and some, ahem, auditions."

Harry Spleen breathed in and smiled. Was this his moment? He pushed himself to the front of the Pit and looked directly up at Burbage.

"Sir Will and I have decided to do things a bit differently today. You just witnessed the audition!"

Harry Spleen turned his face toward Molly. His smile was stuck fast, but his eyes were icy green daggers.

"Walter?" asked Burbage.

"Yes, Sir?" answered Molly.

"Walter...what?"

"Harcourt, Sir."

"Walter Harcourt. A splendid name for an actor. Gentlemen, please welcome to the great professional company of the Lord Chamberlain's Men: Walter Harcourt!" declared Burbage.

"What?" Molly doubled over in disbelief as the acting company gave another resounding round of applause. Raymond leaped up and yelled, "OUI!!" Alvin and Sasha cheered. Juliet jumped up and down at the back of the room. Loud drums and trumpets and clavichords clanged in her head, all at once.

There was one person Molly could no longer see.

Harry had disappeared.

Forty-One

BURBAGE HAD A NOSE FOR SUCCESS.

He could smell it.

Henry IV, Part 2 had been a storming triumph. The Lord Chamberlain's Men had been invited to perform *Henry IV Part 2* at Court in front of Queen Elizabeth. This was the greatest honor a theater company could achieve.

Shakespeare's new play, opening today, was called *Much Ado About Nothing*. Burbage was certain this play had even more potential for success. The Lord Chamberlain's Men were on a roll.

Shakespeare told Burbage that the young actor, Walter, had sparked life into this new play. It was only fair to cast him in the part he had inspired. Burbage was doubtful. Walter was still untried in a leading role. What if he fell apart once he got in front of an audience?

Burbage couldn't take the risk.

Burbage demoted Walter to the smaller part of Hero. The run-through went well and Burbage was confident about the performance.

Molly, on the other hand, was a bundle of nerves. What if she forgot her lines? What if the audience could see she was a girl playing a girl? All night long she had been plagued by the same nightmare: She was center stage, with no costume and couldn't remember a single line. Alvin said this was a common actor's nightmare; it meant Walter was thinking like a professional. He said that dream was a good omen.

HARRY HATED that Raymond had a major part in this production. His resentment grew like a spiraling serpent, swirling in his gut and curling up his spine into his brain. Once there, he could only think negative thoughts about his fellow actors and blamed them for his misery.

Harry hoped their rival company, the Lord Admiral's Men, would cast him in their upcoming production.

I just want my talent to be recognized, he thought bitterly.

JULIET WAS SINGING in the production, of course. She was also Molly's dresser.

It felt strange for Molly to wear a dress again. And what a fancy dress her costume was! There were so many layers. It meant they had to start getting into costume before the other actors came into the shared tiring-house. Molly's farthingale made her gown stick straight out at the waist. It looked as if she wore a table around her middle. Once fully dressed, she swished her restrictive-yet-voluminous skirts. She looked at Juliet and burst out laughing.

Juliet, a few tears in her eyes, whispered "*My sister.*"

Raymond entered. He had come in early to set up and prepare. He looked very dashing in his costume. He held two small yellow flowers. He gave one to Juliet and the other to Molly. Molly gripped her stomach.

"I feel as if I have a hundred butterflies fluttering inside here," she said.

"Ah! The butterflies!" declared Raymond. "Butterflies are good. They mean you care."

"I want to do well!" Molly blushed.

"Then do what you do best and you'll be fantastique!" said Raymond. "And if you make a mistake, make it LOUD-LY!" He laughed, then left to triple check Mr. Burbage's props and costumes.

"Are you ready?" asked Juliet.

Molly breathed out. "Yes," she said.

They hugged. It was a challenge as Molly's farthingale stuck out so far from her waist.

"Hey Moll," whispered Juliet. "Look at us. Here we are."

Molly released Juliet from the hug and looked deep into her eyes. She took a breath, pressed her hand against her bodice.

"Here we are," she smiled.

Forty-Two

BEN WAS LEARNING to love everything London offered.
Except:

He didn't like bear-baiting.
He didn't like cock-fighting.
He didn't like courtiers who acted like they owned the
place.
He didn't like courtiers who wore rapiers strapped to
their waists.
He didn't like the stinky stench.
He didn't like the crowds.
He didn't like feculence in the streets.
He didn't like the noise.
He didn't like the fishy smells.
He didn't like being forced to wear a wooly hat on
Sundays.
He didn't like Southwark.

What he did like was...
The *theater*.

THE ROSE THEATRE was the closest to his work. He would head south off London Bridge, walk through the gate with the heads on pikes - he didn't like the heads on pikes - and into seedy Southwark. He would only go to this God-Forsaken part of town to watch a production by The Admiral's Men. Mr. Edward Alleyn, their lead actor and theater-manager, was enormously talented. Ben had also been to the Blackfriars Theatre and to the Curtain Theatre.

Ben did not like the Blackfriars Theatre.

The Blackfriars Theatre acting company was entirely made up of young boys, about his age and slightly older. He did not like that.

Ben loved the last production he had seen at the Curtain Theatre. It had an odd title, though: *Henry IV, Part Two.*

What happened to Part One? he thought.

He much preferred going to The Curtain Theatre as it meant he didn't have to go to horrible Bankside, in horrible Southwark. He thought Richard Burbage a better actor than Edward Alleyn, though they were both very talented. The Lord Chamberlain's Men had a new play opening. It was called: *A Lot of Fuss About Nothing.*

He did not like that title.

That Stratford poet needed to write better titles.

The fuss-about-nothing play was advertised thusly:

See the play before it is performed for the Queen!

He planned to see it next.

He had worked late into the night and completed all of his orders ahead of schedule so he could take the afternoon off.

Ben dreamed of owning his own business so he could make his own hours. Oh, the ideas he had! His mind burst to the brim with ideas of new creations to be made from a piece of leather. All he needed was the equipment.

And a good location.

And some money to set it up.

Well, he could dream, couldn't he?

Forty-Three

MOLLY WAS TAKEN ABACK by the loud applause.

Smiling and clapping from the expensive seats perched her beloved patron, Lady Southwark.

Burbage was the master of milking curtain calls. He opened his arms wide, then put a hand to his breast. He looked in all directions, resting his grateful gaze on each section of the audience, lingering over the expensive seats, before lowering into another deep bow.

Somehow, his bows conveyed humility and gravitas all at the same time. Molly tried to do the same. She took in every area of the auditorium. Then, her eyes landed on Sasha, who already held a broom to start sweeping the minute the crowds left the auditorium.

Seeing her friend, Molly's hands flew to her face. As she bowed, her teardrops fell onto the stage. This made the audience clap even harder. Before she knew it, the entire cast was applauding her as well. She didn't know what to do, so she took another bow, burst out laughing, and reached her hands out to her fellow actors, as if she were already a star.

As Burbage took her hand, he whispered, "masterfully done, Harcourt." He smiled at her for a split second before returning his attention to his first love, the audience. He waved, put his hand onto his chest and bowed again, all the while holding onto Molly's hand. He encouraged her to step forward with him. They took their own bow as the cast applauded.

Whew! Bowing is as important as the production! thought Molly.

She was right. The bows were part of Burbage's charm. His bows said to the crowds, *Yes, while I acknowledge I am a great actor, I humbly remain one of you. Keep coming back.*

As Molly and Burbage turned back to the rest of the players, he whispered, "Now, we wait for an invitation from the Queen!" He indicated the smiling Master of Revels, sitting next to Lady Southwark. Once Molly had rejoined the company, Burbage immediately spun back to the audience and swept forward alone. Arms wide, he turned in all directions, as if hugging them all from the stage, adoring the adulating crowd. He bowed deeply.

Then, he turned back to the actors, his eyes hunting out someone. Eventually, they alighted on Juliet. He summoned her forward. She looked completely lost and tiny next to the acting giant.

"Our official songbird," he said. The crowd broke into enormous applause again.

"Take a bow, my dear," he whispered to Juliet. She bowed awkwardly, then retreated. This charmed the audience even more.

Molly smiled proudly at her sister. Sitting on the river bank, almost a year earlier, neither of them could have imagined this.

Burbage turned back to his beloved audience once more. He quieted them down. "Gentles, if you enjoyed the show…" he began. The crowd went wild. He smiled and gestured *humble* and *modest*, as he quieted them down again.

"Gentles, if you enjoyed our new play, please return

tomorrow night and bring two friends. Tell everyone you know. Let's shake up ShoreDitch!!" The crowd cheered again.

Burbage led his cast off stage. Immediately, Burbage strode back center stage for a final solo bow. He was extremely happy. As he returned to his room, he passed Molly, untangling herself from her costume.

"Excellent!" he said, before striding off to his own room. Burbage shed pieces of costume as he walked. Alvin and Raymond followed closely behind. They caught, or tried to catch, the costume pieces as they flew through the air.

"That's good," said Alvin.

"What is?" asked Molly.

"Mr. Burbage said, "Excellent." That's high praise from the master," he explained. "Well done!"

"Parfait, Walter!" said Raymond, giving her a thumbs up.

Molly and Juliet grabbed each other and jumped up and down.

"Aaaarrrrgggh!!!" they screamed.

Forty-Four

BEN WAS GOING to the theater.

Again.

He was excited.

He put on his church clothes. He wore new shoes he had crafted himself. He smoothed his hair with water. With a skip in his step, he strode from the shop and into the crowded thoroughfare of London Bridge. The bridge's busy push and pull had an ebb and flow of its own, like the river below them. He flowed North.

Once on land, he walked straight up Grace Church Street and through the Bishops Gate. Everywhere, everyone was selling something. In London, you could buy anything.

Eventually, he arrived at ShoreDitch. He had learned the correct title of the play. It was *Much Ado About Nothing*. As he entered the theater, his pulse quickened. His hands felt a little clammy. He still didn't think much of the title, but he truly loved the theater.

He pushed his way into the groundlings area, called the Pit, where poorer folks paid a penny to stand right in front of the stage. Behind him sat fancier folks who paid more for a seat. Some paid still more for a cushion. Ben smiled. Everyone came to the theater, just as they came to London herself. He felt alive and happy.

A young man nudged Ben and asked, "Hey, why aren't you back there?"

"Excuse me, what?" said Ben. He turned to a youth with translucent skin and watery blue eyes.

"As you're here, can you help? Take this." The young man thrust a small ceramic pot into Ben's hand. "Do what you can. The play's about to start and I'm sure there's a good few groundlings who haven't paid their pennies."

Ben was confused.

"I, I," stuttered Ben, holding the pot.

"Fine, fine," said the translucent youth, snatching the ceramic pot back. "You should be getting changed, anyway. You haven't given yourself much time. You've got to dress up as a girl! That takes ages. Go! Get into costume! And sharpish!" And with that, he disappeared into the crowd.

After a moment, a drum sounded.

A hush fell over the crowd.

Four musicians entered. One of them, the smallest, reminded Ben of someone. He couldn't place it.

Pipes played in perfect harmony, then the smallest boy sang. His voice was exquisite. As the minstrels played and sang, pairs of actors in masks danced onto the stage. They faced each other, backed away, squared up again, then spun away. A handkerchief fluttered between the different partners. Ben wondered if this was what life was really like at the Queen's Court.

Two couples were featured in the dance. A young couple and a slightly older couple. They would separate, then reunite. It was awkward and funny, and the groundlings chuckled. A groundling next to Ben bit into a cooked chicken leg. Others slurped ale.

The handkerchief came to a stop in the younger woman's hands. The music softened and came to a gentle stop as the dancers cleared. Only the two couples remained on stage.

And so the drama began.

Forty~Five

BEN FELT CHILLS. He was confused.

He looked at a ghost.

How could his sister be on stage?

Did Aunty Anne have a son he didn't know about? He knew girls and women were not allowed to act on stage (*though my sisters acted up, all the time*, he joked to himself). So, he knew the actor had to be a boy playing the part of a girl. And, as a girl, he looked exactly like his sister.

Ben knew Aunty Anne lived in London. His mother had refused to tell them where. His mother was always tense when she talked about Aunty Anne; something about religion and romantic choices. She worried about her sister's influence on Molly and Juliet. She called Aunty Anne 'wayward' and said she had a 'disregard' of society's expectations, especially for women.

An oyster fork brought Ben back to the present. It flew by Ben's ear, landing on the ground in front of him. Ben picked it up and looked for whence it had come. He saw a petulant, well-dressed young man leering at him. That was another thing he didn't like about London—how people threw rubbish everywhere.

Ben focused his mind back on the stage. Within minutes, he was completely lost in the story: Would Beatrice and Benedick declare their love for each other? Would Hero be redeemed? Then, all the actors were dancing again, and the play was over. The boy with the lark-like voice sang a song about love everlasting. Ben cheered and applauded. What a play! (*Still a terrible title though*)

As the company bowed, Ben fancied that the boy who played Hero caught his eye. He was sure of it. It was a flicker of a moment, before the actors left the stage. Burbage returned alone, arms open wide. Ben felt as if he were being hugged by the great man. Burbage made his announcement. "If you like this play, return tomorrow and bring two friends!" Exit Burbage, and it was all over.

The groundlings were rushed out of the theater. "Feel free to gather in the local ale-houses," the ushers yelled. "Hold on tight to your purses, though!"

MOLLY FELT CHILLS. She was confused.

She was sure she had seen her brother in the audience. She knew that was ridiculous. Her brother was dead. Still, she had to find out who the person was. She clawed off her costume - it took forever - all the lacing to be unlaced, all the layers removed. Frustrated, she let the costume fall to the floor and tripped her way out of it. Leaving it crumpled where it lay, she pulled on her street clothes and ran around into the auditorium.

The Pit was empty. Sasha was already sweeping.

"Did everyone leave?" asked Molly, slightly breathless.

Sasha picked up something gooey from the floor. "Can you believe the stuff they bring in?" he asked. "This looks like a rotten oyster."

Molly ran to the door and looked out. The crowds had

already wandered away. Disappointed, Molly returned to the tiring-room, to hang up her costume and set up for the next performance.

~

BEN WAITED outside the theater for a little while. Most of the audience had already left. Some were making merry, with song and raucous laughter, in the nearby alehouses. Others had wandered home or back to work. Alarmingly quickly, Finsbury Fields felt empty, ominous, and unsafe. He still had to walk all the way back to London Bridge. He wanted to get home alive and unrobbed.

As Ben walked, his mind filled with the world of the play.

If I was related to the actor in the play, wouldn't that be amazing? He thought to himself. The closer he got to home, the more he berated himself.

Who do I think I am? Do I honestly think that I, a lowly crafts-man, could be related to an actor in the Lord Chamberlain's Men? They perform for the Queen, for goodness' sake! Talk about ideas above my station. Come back to reality, Ben.

He did, however, resolve to return to the theater as soon as he could make the time.

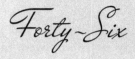

Forty-Six

"I'M BURNING WITH CURIOSITY," said Lady Southwark.

Molly and Juliet were heading out to set up for *Much Ado*.

"How did you come by this lovely locket?" she asked.

Molly faltered. "It was, um, it was given to us," she answered awkwardly.

"May we have it back, please?" asked Juliet.

"Alas, I have a tiny problem with that," said Lady Southwark.

Molly and Juliet instinctively inched closer to each other. Lady Southwark had given them so much. But to keep their locket? That was asking too much. How could they tell her without appearing ungrateful? Or, even worse, being kicked out onto the street? *London* streets, no less.

Lady Southwark deftly popped the locket open and looked at the painting inside. She quickly snapped it shut, tears pooling in the bottoms of her lids. She stared at Walter and Julian. She took a breath.

"I know these people," she said. "In the painting. I know them."

Molly and Julian gasped. Lady Southwark laughed, wiping away tears.

"I know, I'm being silly, but what are the odds? And yet, here we are."

Lady Southwark took a moment.

"I had this locket made. These three children are very dear to me. *Were* very dear to me. I, uh, I was forced to stop seeing them due to, let's call it, a disagreement with their mother. For their well-being, I took myself out of their lives. Now, I look back and wonder if that was the right thing to do."

Juliet turned to Molly, excitement brimming. Molly indicated for her to remain silent.

"Why can't you see them?" asked Molly.

"It's a long story. Suffice it to say, their mother disapproved of, well, *everything* about my life. Once I became Lady Southwark, she refused to-.. Let's say it brought finality to the relationship."

Lady Southwark forced a smile to her lips, covering obvious heartbreak. Molly felt her chest tighten. She couldn't tell her the truth about who she was. Not now! Not after the great reviews she had received for her performance in *Much Ado About Nothing*. And audiences were wild about Juliet's singing. If they told her the truth, it would mean the end of everything.

"I heard the entire village was burned to the ground," Lady Southwark's mouth tightened, "by *Mr. John Barnes*." She looked back at the locket. "This is the only thing left."

"Lady Southwark," said Juliet, carefully. "If you could see them again, would you want to?"

Good question, thought Molly.

"With all my heart," said Lady Southwark. "If you knew how often I lie awake, remembering them. I taught the girls how to read; I wanted something better for them than village poverty; I wanted to prove to them that being female doesn't mean we aren't smart. Of course, society tries to make us powerless. I wanted them to know they had power."

Juliet looked at Molly. She seemed to speak inside Molly's head: *Please, can we tell her? Pleeeeease?*

"I can't tell you how grateful I am to have stumbled upon you two," said Lady Southwark, laughing slightly to move on from the pain. "You have brought more joy into my life than you will ever know. You remind me a little of the boy in this painting. I'm happy to help you achieve your dreams."

Molly shuffled, awkwardly. Was it the right decision to stay quiet?

"I knew I had to rescue you from the Duke. You would have wasted your youth there. And you have far too much talent to waste. But then, you had this locket! It was like a sign. Here, it's yours. You can take it back," she said.

Molly took the locket. She clicked it open, looked at the picture, then closed it again. Although her heart was breaking, she said, "Please. You should have this." Molly handed Lady Southwark the locket, her entire body shaking.

"Are you sure?" asked Lady Southwark.

Juliet looked at Molly, surprised.

"You've shown us such goodness. It's the least we can do," Molly said.

Lady Southwark took the locket.

"Thank you," she whispered.

Lady Southwark opened up the locket. She looked at the picture. She tilted her head back as if memories weighed heavily upon her. Tears rolled down her cheeks, melting track marks down her white makeup.

It took every ounce of strength Molly had to not run to her, to not hug her, to not tell her the truth. Instead, she pulled Juliet brusquely from the room and out the front door, leaving Lady Southwark to her memories.

Forty-Seven

THE FIRST PART of their walk was in stony silence.

Once they were halfway across London Bridge, right by the leather workshop and the alleyway to the water, Juliet screamed at Molly. "You're NOT BEING FAIR TO ME!"

"Quiet down," instructed Molly, aware people were glancing their way.

"Why didn't you tell her?" Juliet continued.

"What if it's a trick?" asked Molly, worried. "Maybe she's trying to find out who we really are."

"That did not sound made-up to me!" shouted Juliet.

"You think I don't want to tell her?" asked Molly, trying to calm her sister.

"YES!! That's exactly what I think!" said Juliet.

A few bystanders noticed them, but quarrels on the bridge were not unusual. One of the leather shop apprentices on a break leaned against the door, enjoying the free entertainment.

"How will we make money? Huh? If she finds out, how will we survive?" asked Molly.

"She'll look after us," said Juliet.

"She left us! Remember?" said Molly.

"But that was...She'd keep us. Wouldn't she?" stammered Juliet, unsure.

"I don't know!" said Molly, shaking.

Juliet fell quiet. Molly watched Juliet work things through. Aunty Anne had abandoned them before - could she do it, again? Molly realized how much she'd toughened in the last year, but Juliet hadn't. Somehow, her little Julie had retained her sweetness, her wide-open innocence, her desire to be loved and protected.

"At least, I have you!" said Juliet, giving her big sister a sudden hug. Molly, taken by surprise, instinctively stepped back and her sister fell. Juliet looked up at her, heartbroken.

"Jules, I'm sorry. I'm *sorry*!" said Molly.

It was all too much. Tears in her eyes, Juliet *ran.*

Molly ran after her, through the crowded thoroughfare of London Bridge. She would lose sight of Juliet, dodge through arms carrying bundles, legs walking, running, pushing carts, small herds of animals, then catch a glimpse of her again. It was like trying to swim fast through a raging sea.

"Julie!" Molly called out. "Wait! Please! I'm sorry!"

On the north side of the Thames, they dodged and bobbed through the narrow streets. Sharp turns and bends meant it was hard to keep up with Juliet. Every now and then Molly saw Juliet's hat weave and dart around a corner, but when Molly got there, Juliet was on to the next.

Eventually, Juliet stopped. She stood on one side of the road. She searched through the crowd and saw Molly coming. Molly chasing after her made her feel good. It reminded her of how much Molly loved her, how much Molly *needed* her. She trusted Molly would never leave her, that she would always come back.

Juliet leant against a wall, on the other side of a crossroads. She gave a little wave. Molly knew it meant Juliet was going to wait for her. She'd made her point. A flood of pedestrians crossed between them. Molly pushed her way through. When she got to the other side, Juliet was gone.

Molly looked all around her. Juliet had signaled a truce. Why had she not waited for her? It was not like Juliet to play games like this.

Molly noticed some men whispering at a nearby archway and alley. They looked at Molly, discussed amongst themselves, looked back at Molly, then walked away into the shaded alley.

Molly realized she was going to be late for work. Hopefully, Juliet would already be at the Curtain Theatre.

She didn't want to leave this spot, though.

Something didn't feel right.

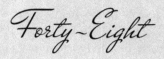

Forty-Eight

JULIET WASN'T at the theater.

Molly had no idea what to do next.

"Salut, Walter! Where's Julian?" asked Raymond. He loved little Julian. His soaring high notes lifted every heart in a room. Word had gotten out. There was a new angel in town.

"I bet they've poached him," said Harry, a nasty grin spreading across his face.

"Poached? Who? What are you talking about?" asked Molly, scared.

"Yep, they've most likely snatched him," said Harry icily.

"Who? **WHO**?" asked Molly, angrily.

"Calm down," said Harry, dismissively.

"Stop it, Harry," warned Raymond.

"WHO? WHO'S GOT JULIET?" shouted Molly.

"Juliet?" asked Harry.

"Julian. That's just… Romeo and Juliet, it's a joke," said Molly, quickly recovering. "Will you, *please*, tell me who's got Julian?"

"I'm just sayin' a songbird voice like that-" teased Harry.

"Harry. If someone has Julian, you need to tell us," said Raymond.

"Why? What are *you* gonna do about it?" taunted Harry.

"I'll go and get him, that's what!" said Molly.

They might poach you, Walter. Look out," taunted Harry. "Second thoughts, probably not."

"Harry!" said Raymond, frustrated.

"I'll poach you like an egg, if you're not careful," said Alvin, who still came in early.

Behind his desk, Will Shakespeare quietly paid attention. Actors trickled in to get ready for the show but were distracted by the drama playing out amongst the apprentices and Alvin.

"Very funny," Harry smirked.

"Stop playing games, Harry. He's only eight, in't he Walter?" asked Alvin.

"Yes," said Molly, quietly.

A flicker of meanness crossed Harry's eyes.

"Eight years old, and lost in London. Oh, dear," he said.

"WHAT DO YOU MEAN?" yelled Molly.

"Spit it out, Harry," said Raymond.

"Who's gonna want a lovely songbird?" teased Harry nastily.

"Not the Royal Choristers?" asked Raymond, hardly daring to say it.

"Nathanial Giles?" asked Alvin, going cold with fear.

"Wait, is that the fella who steals boys for his choir?" clarified Molly.

"Nathanial Giles does what he wants." said Harry Spleen, his mouth twisting into a grimace. "He's got a royal charter. Nothing to be done. Shame."

Just then, Burbage bounded in, a scroll in his hand.

"We have it!" he announced. He gestured *triumph*. "Here, in my possession, is a request to perform *Much Ado About*

Nothing at Court, for Her Gracious Royal Majesty, Queen Elizabeth!"

The actors' response was muted. Burbage looked confused. He had made a fantastic entrance with the most glorious news. Shakespeare whispered the explanation to Burbage.

"I'm sorry, Mr. Burbage. I need to find Julian," said Molly, tears streaming down her face. She charged out of the theater.

"He does not know where to go. I'll help him," said Harry. He ran out after Molly, hoping his heroics would be noted.

"I'd better go after them," said Alvin.

"WAIT!" commanded Burbage. "What's going on? Where's Julian?"

"Harry Spleen says Nathanial Giles got him," said Alvin.

Burbage grabbed his chest in a *stricken* gesture. His face grew fiery red.

"Nathanial Giles has *WHAT?*"

"That's what Harry Spleen says, although how Harry Spleen knows, I don't know," explained Alvin.

"Nathanial Giles? *AGAIN?*" roared Burbage.

"Harry says he's got a royal charter or something," added Alvin.

"I'll tell him where to stick his royal charter! We have a royal charter too, or did Nathanial Giles FORGET?" Burbage bellowed with such force, the actors froze. "I'll give Nathanial Giles a piece of my mind. I am CURSED with Giles! Never, *ever* write a character called Giles. I shall refuse to play him," he instructed Shakespeare.

"Um, that's not-.." started Shakespeare.

"CANCEL THE SHOW!" Burbage dramatically declared. "WAIT!" he exclaimed, almost as quickly. "Condell, what would be our financial loss if we cancel?"

Henry Condell looked gravely at Burbage. Burbage gestured *worry*, placing the palm of his hand across his eyes.

Harry caught up with Molly, who was already storming down Cheapside, past St. Paul's Cathedral.

"Hey!" shouted Harry.

"Leave me be, Harry," yelled Molly, furious and frightened.

"Where are you going?" asked Harry.

"To the Blackfriars Theatre. They might know something," said Molly.

"You have a show, you know," sneered Harry.

"I know that! Please tell Mr. Burbage I'll be back in time for the performance," said Molly.

"I'll do that," said Harry. "I'll head back now and tell him."

"Thanks, Harry," said Molly.

Condell anxiously approached his boss. Henry Condell was the accountant for this production. He kept detailed notes, not only of the money coming in but also the costs of props, costumes, even parts of the script.

Condell and Burbage conferred quietly. The show was very popular. They had received their official invitation to perform for the Queen at Court. Gentry would now travel from all over the country to see this production.

Harry crept back in.

"Where's Walter?" asked Burbage.

"I couldn't find him, Sir, I looked everywhere," said Harry.

"Someone tell that boy the show must *always* go on," said Burbage. "I performed the day my father died," he added, dramatically.

"It's his baby brother," said Shakespeare, compassionately. "He's eight, and he's missing."

"I'm not completely heartless," said Burbage, changing his emotion in an instant. "If only he weren't so damned talented!"

Burbage gestured *deep in thought*, with his hand to his furrowed brow. He paced, head raised one moment, lowered the next. Eventually, he declared, "We'll do the show. The moment the performance ends, I'll seek out Nathanial Giles and bring Julian back. Sasha, do you know Walter's part?"

"Yes, Sir," said Sasha, "but I'm sure Walter-"

"I know it, backwards, Sir!" interrupted Harry.

"Alright. Harry, you play Hero. For today," said Burbage.

"But-" said Sasha.

"Raymond, you'll stay as Claudio," instructed Burbage. "Sasha, you'll sing Julian's songs and help as my apprentice. I'll need to leave the theater quickly. Let's have a celebrated performance. Then I'll *rip* my pound of flesh from Nathanial Giles."

"Yes, Sir," said Harry.

Harry smiled slyly to himself. This had worked out remarkably well.

Forty-Nine

BEN GOT to The Curtain Theatre early.

He hoped to catch the actor before he went in.

There was already a crowd of groundlings gathered in the Pit, eating, drinking and making a day of it. The translucent youth walked around with the ceramic pot, taking the penny entrance fee from each groundling.

"Did you find him?" the pale youth asked Ben.

"Oh. No. Not yet," answered Ben, awkwardly.

Did he read my mind? He asked himself.

"Walter, you can't give up. Mr. Burbage will fix this. He will find Julian," said Sasha.

"Oh? Thanks," said Ben, very confused.

Who is Julian?

Fifty

HARRY REACHED into his sleeve and pulled out Winifred's handkerchief. It was white with delicately embroidered pink flowers in the center.

Secretly, Harry replaced Raymond's prop handkerchief with Winifred's real one. When it was time for the closing handkerchief dance, Raymond rushed off stage, grabbed the handkerchief and rushed back on. As they danced, no one noticed the switch. Frustrated, Harry whispered, loud enough for Burbage to hear, "What a pretty handkerchief!"

Burbage was "in character" and completely focused on the dance. However, Raymond did notice and tossed the handkerchief to the next dancer, as if it were red hot.

"Gentle with the handkerchief!" admonished Harry, trying again for Burbage's attention. This time it worked. When Burbage saw the handkerchief, his face grew red. The handkerchief fluttered from dancer to dancer. Eventually, Burbage grabbed the dainty handkerchief as he danced next to Raymond.

"Where did you get this handkerchief?" whispered Burbage angrily as he danced and smiled at the audience.

"From the prop table, Sir," said Raymond, innocently.

"Did Sasha set your props?" asked Harry.

"I did, Sir," said Raymond. "But I set a different handkerchief. I don't know where this one came from."

The dance continued. Sasha sang Juliet's closing song. The play ended. The audience applauded. The show had gone well, but it wasn't up to its usually excellent standard. Burbage bowed dramatically, then stormed off stage.

Throwing off his costume, he yelled, "Raymond!!" Sasha tried to catch all the flying garments, but it proved a challenge.

"Yes, sir?" said Raymond.

"Tell me again, how did you come upon this handkerchief?"

Harry watched, secretly.

"What are you up to, Harry?" asked Alvin. He always sensed when Harry was up to no good.

"Nothing," said Harry.

"Shouldn't you be thinking about Julian and Walter?" asked Alvin, suspicious.

"'Course I am," said Harry, not moving.

"Well, then?" demanded Alvin.

"Right," said Harry, rushing away.

∼

IN THE PIT, Ben wallowed in disappointment. *Where was the actor who looked like him? What had the translucent youth meant about everything being okay? And who was Julian?*

"I guess it means I have to come back," he sighed.

After a moment, Ben smiled.

He couldn't wait to return to the theater.

∼

MOLLY RETURNED as the company was cleaning up. Burbage was yelling and Raymond was cowering. Harry was sneering and Alvin was staring him down. What on earth had happened?

"Walter!" cried Sasha, running to her.

Everyone went quiet. Quarrels momentarily forgotten, they hoped for good news.

"Did you find him?" asked Harry, pretending to care.

Molly shook her head. Her cheeks were red and raw with salt tears.

"I-I-I'm sorry Mr. Burbage. I asked Harry to tell you I'd be back in time for the performance," said Molly.

Burbage threw an angry look at Harry.

"But when I came back, Harry was already in my costume. Are me and Julian kicked out of the company? Please don't kick us out, Sir, this is our life!" pleaded Molly.

"Walter," said Burbage, "if we learned anything from this wreckage of a performance, it's that we need your brother. And we need you. Now, have you had any luck?"

"I didn't know where to go, Sir, so I went to the Blackfriars Theatre," started Molly.

"That's Henry Evans' place" interrupted Kempe, "He's in with Nathanial Giles. He won't let the boys leave and all that. Please God, our Julian is not there. That would be bad. That would be very bad. That would be very, very-"

"Kempe. Stop," said Shakespeare.

"What?" asked Molly, terrified.

"I'm sorry, Walter. Go on," the writer said, gently.

"I-I knocked on the door," stammered Molly. "A young boy opened it. He said he hadn't seen a Julian but that he might be with the Royal Choristers. But-" She started to cry again. "I don't know where that is."

"Well, I do!" bellowed Burbage.

Molly saw Raymond jump. He wasn't himself at all. Even

from the depths of her despair, she was compelled to ask what was going on.

"What was all the fighting about?" asked Molly.

"A handkerchief," said Alvin.

"Winnie's handkerchief!" roared Burbage.

"That was Miss Winifred's handkerchief? Ah. Now it all makes sense," said Alvin.

"I swear, I never took it!" pleaded Raymond.

Harry smiled.

"Mr. Burbage, I-" Molly took a breath. There was so much going on at once. "I saw Miss Winifred drop that handkerchief as she left the theater, the other day."

"You did?" said Burbage.

"I-I-I believe someone picked it up," stammered Molly. She couldn't quite get it out.

Harry shot her a look.

"Someone? *Someone?* Was that someone *Raymond de Cevil*?" blasted Burbage.

"No! Raymond would never do a thing like that," insisted Molly.

"Elle a raison!" declared Raymond.

From the depths of her hopelessness Molly felt a furious lava of rage gather in her guts, rise up through her spine and explode from her volcano mouth.

"Is it not enough? Is it not enough, young man, that you steal my part when my brother is missing? He's only eight years old. This is *London*!! And then, not only that, you switch the prop handkerchiefs to hurt Raymond? What sort of hateful, spiteful-"

Molly lunged at Harry. She hit him, grabbed his hair, kicked him as hard as she could. He tried to push her off. Alvin, Raymond and the other actors reached in to separate them. Alvin got in a few additional kicks.

As the actors dragged Harry away from Molly, his blonde hair flopped over his forehead. Sweat poured from his face and armpits. He locked his green eyes upon hers and sneered. It was a vicious, cruel sneer. It was a look that implied he knew something new about Molly; something he had not known before. Molly felt hollow.

"YOU!" said Burbage, turning on Harry.

Harry's demeanor immediately changed to meek and submissive.

"Sir, I picked it up, yes, I wanted to give it to you, Sir, to return to your lady friend, but I must have dropped it, I lost it, honest Sir, that's the God's honest truth, Sir!" blathered Harry.

"The truth?" asked Burbage, doubtfully. "You'd better watch your step, Harry, or I'll take you to the Blackfriars Theatre myself!"

Molly fell to her knees. All she wanted was her sister back.

"What if Nathanial Giles doesn't have him? What if Julian is just lost?" she cried.

"I know Nathanial Giles," Burbage spat out the name as if it were dirt on his tongue. With dramatic determination, he said, "He'll be there. I promise you. I'll bring our boy back."

"Thank you, Mr. Burbage," said Molly, quietly

"Don't thank me, thank Queen Bess! We perform for Gloriana in two days! We need our songbird for that! All this will end well, Walter. You'll see. "

"You'll see," mocked Harry, just loud enough for only Molly to hear.

Fifty-One

"I'M A TERRIBLE, HORRIBLE PERSON!" cried Molly.

"Being London's rising star says otherwise," smiled Lady Southwark. She'd seen nerves before, but this was different. "How *exciting* – performing for the Queen in your very first show!"

"It's not that! Well, yes that, but no, no! Everything's a mess and it's all my fault!" wailed Molly. She collapsed onto the floor.

Lady Southwark's skirts ruffled, as she *oofed* and *ahhed* her way to the floor next to Molly. She gently placed Molly's head on her lap and stroked her head.

"I often find problems loom large in the echo chamber of my mind. They grow and grow until I don't see any way out. But shall I tell you a little secret I discovered?" asked Lady Southwark.

Molly nodded a yes. It was easier than speaking.

"Find one person you trust and tell them. It's similar to lancing a boil. Once all the poison is out, you start to heal. You stop worrying about the problem and start looking for solutions. So much more productive, don't you think?

Molly nodded.

"Would you like to try it?"

Molly nodded again. She had to choose her words carefully.

"He's gone," muttered Molly.

"That's a good start," affirmed Lady Southwark. "Now, I need a little more. Who has gone?"

"J-J-Julian" stammered Molly. "How could I have been so stupid?" Molly hit her own leg.

"Walter, stop. Breathe," said Lady Southwark.

Molly took a deep breath and calmed herself. Worrying wasn't going to get Juliet back. She needed to take action. Lady Southwark was the person she needed right now.

"On the way to work, yesterday," said Molly, hesitating, "We-..We had a quarrel."

After a moment, the words tumbled out, falling, one on top of the other. She told Lady Southwark the story of Juliet's disappearance.

∾

"It's not like Julian to not show up for a performance," she explained. "He's very proud of his work."

She took a breath. Lady Southwark rubbed her back.

"Then, then," Molly's mouth twisted with fury. "Harry Spleen. Vile, hateful *Spleen*, he, he, he said–"

She paused.

"Yes?" encouraged Lady Southwark.

"He said…" Molly searched for the courage to repeat the words. "He said Julian was poached. By Nathanial Giles."

"I know of him." Lady Southwark pressed her lips together in disapproval.

"He steals boys for the Royal Choristers and for the Black-friars Theatre," said Molly.

There. She'd said it.

"Surely, that's illegal," said Lady Southwark.

"It should be! But Harry Spleen said Nathanial Giles has a Royal Charter that lets him take whatever boy he wants and there's nothing anyone can do about it!" said Molly. "So, there's nothing, nothing, I can do."

"We'll see about that," said Lady Southwark.

"I'm so stupid! Stupid, stupid, stupid!" shouted Molly, striking her thighs.

"Hey! Self-pity begets nothing." Lady Southwark held Molly's face. "Now listen. I want you to listen. Are you listening?" she asked.

Molly nodded, her cheeks squashed between Lady Southwark's hands.

"Are you sure?" asked Lady Southwark.

Molly nodded.

Then Lady Southwark said the words which would impact Molly for the rest of her life. "There is always a way," said Lady Southwark. "There is *always* a way to get what you want. You just have to work out how."

Molly looked into Lady Southwark's eyes. Her mental fog cleared for a moment, and for that moment, Molly felt hopeful. Then she remembered.

"There's more," Molly said.

Fifty-Two

MOLLY WAS silent for a long time.

She had so many thoughts running through her head, she didn't know which one to catch and direct to her mouth to speak. Each thought felt like a dangerous chess move. No matter which move she made, this wonderful woman who had given her so much, would surely feel betrayed.

Lady Southwark sat patiently. Eventually, she said, "There's usually no right place to begin. It's best to simply start speaking. You'll only get to your destination if you take a first step."

"You'll hate me," said Molly.

"My emotional reactions are for me to decide," countered Lady Southwark.

"I keep making wrong choices," said Molly.

"If you're making choices," countered Lady Southwark, "you're playing the game."

"What game?" asked Molly.

"Life," explained Lady Southwark.

"You'll throw us out," said Molly.

"Now, how would that be received, throwing out London's newest star? The moment he became successful?

Oh, no, my dear. I intend to ride on your coat-tails as long as I can. Besides, it will increase the value of my house once people know Walter Harcourt lived here," said Lady Southwark.

"I'm not Walter Harcourt," said Molly, quietly.

Molly saw Lady Southwark's smile stick as she sensed her body stiffen.

"Oh? Is it a - what do you theater-types call it - a stage name?" asked Lady Southwark, a little too brightly.

"It's a bit more complicated," said Molly.

"In my experience, young people always think things are far more complicated than they actually are," said Lady Southwark, expertly covering her nerves.

"It's-" Molly took a breath. "I'm a girl."

Lady Southwark sat up, shaking a little.

"Is this true?"

Molly nodded.

"But, but, but you're performing for the Queen, when is it, tomorrow?" spluttered Lady Southwark.

"Yes," whispered Molly.

"But, but, that would be treason. We could all hang," gasped Lady Southwark.

Molly scrunched her face.

"There's more," she said.

"More than treason?" asked Lady Southwark.

"Yes," said Molly, quietly.

"Well, you'd better tell me," said Lady Southwark.

"My real name. It's Molly."

Lady Southwark's body tensed so much it shook as if it had been dropped on ice. Her face grew paler than her white make-up.

"Molly?" she asked in a whisper.

Molly nodded.

"As in," Lady Southwark barely dared breathe the words. "As in, Molly *Shipton*?"

Molly was silent.

She saw her Aunty's eyes pleading for a yes.

Molly knew she stood on a precipice.

If she said nothing else, she could continue her secret life. She would do her best to find Juliet alone. That meant she might never find Juliet.

If Molly told the truth, she could lose everything. *Again.*

She had already lost everything.

Juliet.

Could Aunty Anne help her find Juliet?

Juliet.

She longed for Juliet. She must do everything in her power to find Juliet. Even this.

Molly bowed her head.

"Yes," she whispered.

Filled suddenly with fear and desperation, she blurted, "Please don't throw us out! Give us a few days. We'll pay you rent the minute we make real money, which will be soon, I promise."

"Throw you out?" asked Lady Southwark, stunned.

Molly's Aunty threw her arms around her newly discovered niece and held her tight. The force of the hug surprised Molly. She had not been hugged in a very long time. Yes, she had experienced the childish, full-of-love hugs from Juliet-

Juliet

-but no adult had hugged her since her mother had died.

At first Molly strained within the comfort of the older lady's embrace, unable to bear the love, the tenderness, the *safety* it contained. Molly was scared to relax, scared to trust, scared to believe she could be cherished. Her Aunty held her fast and snug, as if she sensed Molly's resistance. In her Aunty's arms, Molly felt like a child again; like there was an adult to look after her, to take care of her.

Molly could fight no longer. Everything she had suffered in the past year washed over her like a giant wave.

She sobbed.

She groaned.

She wept as if every other time she had cried had been a spring shower. Her voice howled like the North Wind itself. Grief gushed through her like a tempest. She could do nothing but be tossed and turned within it.

Almost a year of struggle, endless survival, of always watching out, of always being in charge, of always making all of the decisions, poured from her.

She wailed for the loss of her mother.

For the loss of her father.

For the loss of her brother.

For the loss of her home.

For the loss of her childhood.

For everything she had lost.

For the loss of Juliet.

After some time, Molly settled. The two naturally parted. Then Molly reached and hugged her Aunty again. She did not want this feeling to end. The two of them laughed. Molly sat back on her haunches. Aunty Anne's makeup had smeared away, and Molly clearly saw her beloved Aunty's face.

"I must admit, I did wonder," said Lady Southwark, with a sly grin. "After all, you are the spitting image of your brother, if he were older. But then, you said your name was Walter, and you didn't seem to know who I was."

Lady Southwark teared up again.

"You, my dear, are my Lazarus. You are my second chance. Here you are alive, successful and under my roof. Now I can be redeemed."

She gave Molly a squeeze.

"I wanted to tell you before," said Molly, "but I was scared. Are you angry with me?"

"Angry?" said Lady Southwark. "The only thing to be angry about is my face paint. It's everywhere. My dear, dear child. Today is the most wonderful day of my life! Oh, but I know I look a mess. This moment calls for something better."

She rang a bell. A maid entered, who helped Lady Southwark to her feet.

"But Juliet!" blurted Molly.

"Juliet," said Lady Southwark, with a loving smile. She pointed to her face, "First I'll sort out this, then I'll sort out that. Meanwhile, darling, you have a performance." Lady Southwark turned to leave, stopped, and turned back. "Have you told anyone else? About… yourself?"

"No," said Molly.

"Then I forbid you to do so. As I'm sure you have heard, the show must go on or the theater will close. And they cannot do the play without their young star. Go! Shine bright! I'll repair the rest."

With that, Lady Southwark swept out.

Alone once more, Molly dried her face. She felt as if she had cried the entire River Thames and River Avon combined. She assessed her new situation. Some things had changed, but some remained the same.

Things that remained the same:
1. She had a performance that afternoon.
2. She lived in the same house.
3. Juliet was still missing.

Things that had changed:
1. She had regained her dear, dear Aunty Anne.
2. She might get her head chopped off for committing treason.

Fifty-Three

NATHANIAL GILES HAD *INTENDED* to keep his word.

He really did his best.

He'd heard about the new musical duo at the Lord Chamberlain's Men. He wanted to be honorable. Thus, he refused to see any show at the Curtain Theatre, so he wouldn't be tempted.

One day, he had a visit from a striking young man, with blonde hair and piercing green eyes. The young man mocked Nathanial Giles.

"How can it possibly be that the Royal Choristers do not have the best singer in town?" the youth had asked. "Everyone knows the most beautiful voice in London is performing at The Lord Chamberlain's Men. Just thought you'd like to know."

After that, Nathanial Giles had been unable to resist.

Fifty-Four

EVERYONE WAS ANXIOUS.

No one had seen Burbage since he stormed out after the performance, the day prior.

"Don't you worry. Mr. Burbage will get it all sorted out," Alvin reassured Molly.

"Don't make false promises," sneered Harry Spleen.

No one thought about the show or that, shortly, the audience would arrive. Except for Harry Spleen, of course.

"It'll be okay," said Raymond, reassuringly taking Molly's hand.

"Oh, God, I hope so!" cried Molly.

"Don't speak another word," whispered Raymond to Harry.

"He's coming!" said Alvin. His time as Burbage's apprentice had attuned his ear to every footfall of the great actor.

Burbage entered. He looked ragged and worn, as if he had raged all night. He gestured *despair*. Large globules of salt tears and snot poured down his enormous face. He could not raise his eyes to look at his company of actors. He gestured, *deep shame*.

"He has Julian," was all he said. Suddenly, he charged through the group, up the stairs and onto the stage.

"PLACES!!" he roared, as he stormed off to his room to prepare.

~

A SHORT TIME LATER:

The stage was set.

The theater was full.

The props were lined up.

The minstrels tuned up.

The actors warmed up.

The audience primed up.

The show was about to start.

No one wanted to perform. Everyone was depressed.

"WALTER," a familiar voice said.

Molly turned.

There stood Juliet.

"Oh! Oh!" cried Molly, throwing her arms around her little sister. She held her tightly, ever so tightly. She promised herself she would never be jealous of her gorgeous, talented, sweet, kind, loving little sister, ever, *ever* again.

"He's here? Il est rentré!" cried Raymond. Tears rolled down his cheeks.

The entire company threw their arms around Walter and Julian.

The start of the play was delayed.

Molly and Juliet were carried on a wave of actors to Burbage sitting in his room. He gestured *self-hatred* and talked angrily to himself. At the commotion, he looked up. His face instantly filled with love and joy. He gestured for Julian to come to him. Molly had never seen Burbage this gentle as he brushed Julian's hair back from his face. It was as if Julian were his very own son.

"Nathanial Giles swore to me. He *swore* he would never let you go. Yet, here you are, my darling boy. What happened?" he asked.

"After you left," whimpered Juliet, "Mr. Giles told me to lose all hope of ever leaving."

"Urrrgh! That man!" yelled Burbage. He gestured *hatred*.

Juliet cried.

"Mr. Giles said I would never see you, or any of you, again. Unless it was in an audience. He said I was now a royal chorister, and it was his job to look after me. Then another man showed up. An older man. He gave Mr. Giles a letter with a big wax seal. When Mr. Giles opened the letter, he got furious. Oh, Mr. Burbage, I was so scared. But then he said it was a direct order from the Lord Chamberlain. The letter said he had to let me go on pain of death. That I was needed for a Royal performance, and for all acting performances for his company, forthwith," explained Juliet.

"The Lord Chamberlain himself, eh?" smiled Burbage. "Why didn't I think of that?"

"So, it wasn't you that did it?" asked Juliet.

"I went straight to Nathanial Giles. That took guts. Whoever went to the Lord Chamberlain? That took brains. And connections. An audience with the Lord Chamberlain usually takes weeks," explained Burbage.

"Then, how?" asked Juliet, mystified.

"Someone got to him and told him what had happened, I suppose," said Burbage.

"But who?" asked Juliet again.

"My dear boy, sometimes it's better to be grateful and not ask too many questions," said Burbage.

Molly wondered - surely it couldn't be Aunty Anne? Could it? She sat next to the Lord Chamberlain at the performance. How was her Aunty so well connected?

"Now, this is the most important question: Do you think you can sing in today's performance? Or do you need to rest?" Burbage asked.

"I'm always ready to sing, Sir," said Juliet.

"Splendid. Well then...Once more unto the breach, dear friends... PLACES."

Fifty-Five

HE WAS SHAKING ALL OVER.

Ben had decided:

Today was the day.

He would return to the Curtain Theatre and introduce himself to Walter Harcourt, no matter what. He was nervous. Were there even any Harcourts in the family? He didn't think so.

What he knew was that he could not sleep until he found out. The idea that he might have a living family member thrilled and terrified him. He finally decided that:

1. If Walter Harcourt *was not* related to him, he would have lost nothing. He would still be the only surviving member of his family. Aunty Anne could be anywhere, so she didn't count.

2. If Walter Harcourt *were* related to him, they might not even like each other. Perhaps the actor had tons of relatives and had no need of another. He would only know if he asked.

3. If Walter Harcourt *were* related to him and liked him, then that would be a good thing. Right?

4. If Walter Harcourt *wasn't* related to him, he would look foolish. He realized this was the most likely option. How

could a mere craftsman possibly be related to a professional of the theater?

He decided potential humiliation was a small price to pay for knowledge.

He was determined to arrive at the theater earlier than last time. Hopefully, he'd catch the actor going in. If he wasn't there, he planned to leave a message with the translucent boy with the watery eyes.

Yuletide meant the workshop was flush with customers. They even had visits from Court envoys, looking for pouches, and knick-knacks, and "something specials." Ben built a neat sideline in the tiny coin purses, which slipped easily onto the inside of a belt. They were miniature works of art. Each was decorated with embroidery-like patterns he had learned from his father. Apparently, one of his pouches had caught the eye of Sir Walter Raleigh, the famous traveler and favorite of the Queen. He had sent an envoy for Ben to design a larger pouch. Ben fantasized about it being a gift for Her Majesty. Now, wouldn't that be something?

Imagining the impossible, again, thought Ben.

Ben had trouble keeping up with his orders and keeping it a secret from Mr. Littleton. In the end, he decided to be honest and offered Mr. Littleton 10% of his takings. Mr. Littleton never said no to money. Especially when he had done nothing to earn it.

Given that he was bringing in additional income, Ben negotiated more time off. He planned to use that time to go to the theater.

A lot.

He strolled north across London Bridge, then along, the now familiar, Grace Church Street, through Bishop's Gate, across Moor Fields and into Finsbury Fields. He walked into the theater to find the translucent young man alone, sorting through a series of chests and boxes.

"You're keen, aren't you?" the boy laughed. "Doors don't usually open for another hour."

Ben whipped his hat from his head and creased it several times in his hands. "I wondered if I might, if, well... Is Walter Harcourt around?"

"Are you related to him?" asked Sasha.

"I don't know," said Ben.

"You look just like him," observed Sasha.

" Is he around at all?" asked Ben, nervously

"They're all in Greenwich," said Sasha.

"Greenwich? How do I get to Greenwich?" asked Ben.

"You don't just get there, my friend. You are invited. Do you have an invitation?" smiled Sasha.

"I don't," answered Ben, humbly. "Is there something special about Greenwich?"

"Special? It's as special as it gets, mate! They're at Greenwich Palace. They're performing for the Queen of England," said Sasha.

"Oh," said Ben. How did he keep getting this wrong? "Why, uh, why aren't you with them?" he asked.

"Someone has to stay here and sort out this mess," said Sasha. "Plus, Burbage thinks my acting is too *subtle*. He didn't cast me in the play."

"That's a shame," said Ben.

"It's rotten, but what can you do? It's his company, not mine. Now, when Raymond starts his own theater company, it'll be different," said Sasha, hopefully.

"Who's Raymond?" asked Ben, finding it hard to keep up with all the names.

"Raymond de Cevil is a fabulous actor and future actor-manager," replied Sasha.

'Oh," said Ben, not really understanding.

There was a moment of silence. Ben shifted from foot to foot, not knowing what to do with himself.

"When in doubt, help," his Aunty Anne would say.

"Would you… like some help?" asked Ben.

"Would I?" asked Sasha, pushing a trunk towards Ben. "Can you tell the difference between a costume and a prop?"

"Is a costume a thing you wear and a prop a thing you hold?" asked Ben.

"More or less," said Sasha.

"I think I can manage that," joked Ben.

They both laughed. Then they got to work.

Fifty-Six

SHE WAS SHAKING ALL OVER.

Less than a year ago, Molly had been sitting outside the burning wreck of her childhood home. Now, she was about to perform for the Queen of England. How had her life come to this?

She took a breath.

Will I remember all my lines? she wondered, nervously.

Harry Spleen had contrived a way into this major event. He had managed to get himself a tiny part, as well as being in charge of some costumes. He wanted to move to the Admiral's Men, the biggest rival theater company in London, and he hoped a Royal Court performance would get him noticed.

Burbage gave them a rousing speech.

"This is the greatest honor of our lives." He gestured *great honor*. "Whereas we always give our best, today we must give even more. Call upon your muse, let us bring Good Queen Bess, the greatest of pleasure!"

Rather more mundanely, he added, "And remember! Always check your props."

Exit Burbage, to do his personal preparation.

Apart from Burbage, all the actors had one tiring-room in

which to change into their costumes. Juliet scouted out the darkest corner she could find. There, she arranged Molly's dresses and underclothes. While others were checking their props, Juliet held up the skirt as a make-shift screen, while Molly quickly whipped off her own shirt and put on the costume's linen undergarment. It had been washed especially for this performance and was tighter than usual. It was hard to pull it over the bandage wrapped around her chest. Just as she was getting it down, Harry Spleen entered.

"Why are you all the way over there?" asked Harry, suspicious.

Quickly untangling herself, Molly couldn't think of a suitable answer.

"Just making room for everyone else," said Juliet quickly. Molly smiled. She loved her sister so much.

"Successful actors take space," said Harry, setting up in the center of the room.

Burbage entered.

"Harry, move to the side," he said. "Make space for the lead actors."

Shamed, Harry sheepishly gathered his stuff and put it in the opposite corner. Molly finished pulling down her shift and hoped no-one had paid attention. Juliet handed her the farthingale.

"Julian," said Burbage. "We'll start with your ballad, *All's Fair in Love*. It will set the right tone for the entire afternoon."

"Thank you, Mr. Burbage," said Juliet, smiling broadly.

"What ballad is that?" asked Molly.

"I'll tell you later," said Juliet, hurriedly.

"Your brother came to me with a ballad he penned," smiled Burbage. "It's good. I'm glad it's us and not Nathanial Giles playing it at Court."

"I wouldn't have given it to him," smiled Juliet.

"My brother is very talented," said Molly, playfully punching her sister on the arm. Inside, she was terrified. Now

Juliet was performing her own musical piece for the Queen of England.

That doubled their chances of being caught.

That doubled their chances of being hanged for treason.

She sent up a silent prayer that it would all work out.

Fifty-Seven

IT WAS five times as large as the Duke of Armington's feast. At least.

And this time, Molly was a guest.

One of the best things about acting at Court - apart from the pleasure of performing for the Queen of England - was the enormous party she threw for the actors afterwards. This included a massive meal, music and much merriment. If the Queen really enjoyed the play, she might even give a speech from the balcony. She might even stay for the first dance. The Master of Revels was very careful to scrutinize each production, prior to coming to Court, so the Queen was never disappointed.

The theatricals were much more fun than the Queen's usual guests and the head butler loved them. He always went overboard with the dishes for the revelers. He knew the actors would eat every morsel. The enormous feasting table was so heavily laden with platters of food, Molly wondered how it stayed upright.

The butler had great pleasure pointing out food from a place he called, the *"new world"*. There were squishy orange tubers called *sweet potatoes* and red things called *tomatoes*.

There was a platter of something called *peanuts* and several roasted birds called *turkeys*.

Molly spied a bowl of orange balls with a thick peel, similar to the precious one her father had brought home from London. How could there be so many altogether, all at once?

The butler made an announcement.

"Gentlemen of The Theater," he began. Molly smiled at Juliet - they were *Gentlemen of the Theater*!

The butler continued, "To express Her Majesty's gratitude for bringing your wonderful work and artistic talents to their palace today, Her Most Gracious and Generous Majesty has provided a special treat for you all. Before you all are seated, please try this New World delicacy. Her Majesty secretly secured it from the Spanish. Shh. Tell no-one. Except the Spanish Ambassador"

This last sentence caused resounding laughter. Everyone knew of the animosity between the Spanish and the English, especially since Sir Walter Raleigh defeated the Spanish Armada.

A footman brought in a shallow dish covered in a gold cloth, which the butler removed with a flourish. On the plate were several tiny gold cups filled with a brown liquid. Each cup was shaped into either a tiny flower or an acorn.

"This is cho-co-late," the butler explained. "The Aztecs reserved it for priests and kings. Her Majesty now reserves it for their very special guests. Please, try some."

Molly took a sip of the brown liquid. Instantly, she felt as if her brain were previously a bud now opened into a flower. She couldn't stop smiling. She was filled with love for everyone, even Harry Spleen. When she looked at her fellow actors, they were all grinning.

"Please, be seated," said the butler, jovially. It still made him chuckle to watch guests try this elixir for the first time.

❧

THERE WAS MUSIC, merriment, and dancing.

The actors ate.

And ate.

And ate.

They must have been full, yet still…

They ate.

They drank, and drank.

And ate.

New platters were brought out, piled high with fruit, delicately miniature fruit pies, comfits, and all kinds of other delicious sweetmeats.

As this was Molly's first time performing at court, her fellow actors kept celebrating her. They would hug her around the shoulders, playfully tap her, and tease her mercilessly. Harry asked if she would like to dance.

"Oh, no. Thank you, Harry," smiled Molly.

"I must insist," said Harry.

"I have two left feet," laughed Molly. Harry was oddly intense and it made Molly feel uncomfortable.

"I'm certain you'll be fine," insisted Harry.

"There are ladies of the Court with whom you could dance," said Molly, looking around the room. Plenty of courtly women were in attendance.

"I'd like to dance with *you*," said Harry.

"Harry, I've said no. Why must you be incessant?" said Molly, annoyed.

Harry threw himself down into the empty chair next to her.

"Because, I strongly suspect you know the female part," said Harry, viciously.

"The only dances I know are those we learned for the play," insisted Molly.

"Then you *do* know the ladies' part," sneered Harry.

Taken aback, Molly stammered, "The-the-the company dances, yes."

"Not just those dances," spat Harry.

"Why are you being like this?" asked Molly.

"I saw the wrap around your chest today," said Harry, triumphant.

Molly had spent a long time preparing for this moment she hoped would never come. She reached for a fig to give herself a moment. She said, "I wear a bandage to protect my spine. Ask a physician. And it's none of your business."

"I don't know…Is there anything worse than being a girl?" taunted Harry.

The table around them went quiet. An ignorant statement at the best of times, making that statement here, in the Queen's palace, was an even greater insult.

Molly's volcano of anger surged through her.

"I'd say Her Majesty has done pretty well for a *girl*, wouldn't you?" she said. "London is the center of the world! We beat the Spanish Armada! Our glorious Gloriana, our sublime Majesty, turned our emerald island into the envy of the globe!"

The table burst into thunderous applause. Shakespeare scribbled a quick note.

"To Her Gracious Majesty!" declared Burbage."May God keep and save our good Queen Bess!"

"May God keep and save good Queen Bess!" chorused the company.

Hidden to one side of an upper balcony, having prepared to make a speech, Queen Elizabeth smiled. She liked to secretly observe her guests. She was intrigued by this new, young actor and, very much, enjoyed his defense of her. Of course, her butler would ask the rude young man to leave. She made a mental note for an addition to her upcoming portrait. She would have the artist cover her dress in eyes and ears, to demonstrate she was always listening and always watching.

Everything.

"Well, obviously, I-I-I don't mean Her Majesty," blurted out Harry, completely changing his tune. He'd only meant to privately threaten Molly. He had not meant to get caught.

"I'm not sure the Ambassador's Men should take you. In my very humble opinion," said Kempe, sarcastically.

"How do you know about that?" asked Harry.

"Ours is a small world, Harry. Everyone knows everything about everybody," Kempe replied.

"The Ambassadors don't want him," said Condell.

"Is that so?" said Harry, sarcastically.

"Makes sense," said Alvin.

"Gentlemen! This is not a common alehouse! Have you forgotten where we are?" blasted Burbage.

The butler entered and whispered in Harry's ear. Harry stood, flustered. His face turned blood red. He grabbed a fruit tart and pointed it aggressively at Molly.

"You've not heard the last of this, Walter *Harcourt*!" Harry stormed out of the hall.

Molly looked at her hand. It was shaking.

The fig was completely crushed.

Fifty-Eight

BEN'S bad luck had led to something good.

He had made a new friend in London: Alexander Rostoff, otherwise known as Sasha. Together they sorted out the costumes and props into category, size and style. They further divided these into:

1. Those in need of repair.

2. Those beyond hope of repair.

As Ben always carried his tools with him, he made some on-the-spot repairs to belts, sword sheaths, and leather buttons.

Sasha was impressed.

"You should come and work for us," Sasha said.

"I'm not an actor," said Ben. He'd never considered the theater as a place of work

"It's mostly us apprentices who do the repairs. And we change things around, depending on the play. See this cloak? It's black, and black cloth is expensive. We were given it for a Court performance. We use it for *everything*. For a king, we add a dash of purple; for a Duke, we might add a fur trim. For witches, we could splash a bit of mud on it. We use the same stuff all the time, so everything always needs mending," explained Sasha. What had looked incredible to Ben on stage now looked ordinary.

"There are witches in the theater?" asked Ben, wide-eyed and a little fearful.

"Let's face it, Ben. There are witches everywhere," said Sasha.

They both laughed.

"But not in London," said Ben, needing reassurance.

"Who knows? There's a lot of strange things in London," said Sasha, joking. "But we could definitely use someone who's handy with tools and can repair the big stuff. You're perfect," he continued.

"Does it come with housing?" asked Ben.

"Not unless you want to sleep in here," said Sasha, indicating the theater. "Some of us do, though. Sometimes."

"How much does it pay?" asked Ben.

"I'd have to check," said Sasha.

"Thanks, but I do pretty well at my workshop. I make gifts for the fancy folks at Court," said Ben. "But, if you ever need anything fixed, I'll try to help."

"That's very nice of you," said Sasha.

"Can I ask a favor?" said Ben.

"Here we go," said Sasha.

"What?" asked Ben, genuinely.

"There's always something," said Sasha.

"No, no, I didn't mean it like that," protested Ben. "I meant what I said about helping."

"What is it you want in return, then?" asked Sasha.

"It's not like that," said Ben.

"It is what you say it is," said Sasha, smiling. He really liked Ben and especially enjoyed joking with him. "I'm just teasing you, mate. Spit it out."

"Oh," said Ben, feeling foolish.

"You really are from the sticks, aren't you? I guess I've

been in the city too long. What do you need, Ben?" asked Sasha.

"You know the actor, Master Harcourt?" asked Ben.

"The one who looks like you?" clarified Sasha.

"I'd like to meet him," said Ben.

"Oh, would you now?" teased Sasha.

"How can I do that? I've tried all sorts. Even coming here today. It seems impossible," added Ben.

"It's not usually that hard," said Sasha. "They're all at Court today, which means they'll be back here the day after tomorrow. Come back then, and I'll introduce you to Walter."

Ben's face went dark, and he looked down.

"What is it?" asked Sasha.

"I have to negotiate all my time away from the shop. I'll do my best to come the day after tomorrow, but I can't say for sure," explained Ben.

"I see," said Sasha, thoughtfully.

"I'd better get back, especially if I'm asking for more hours off in one week," said Ben.

"Listen, come back just before the end of the performance, the day after tomorrow, and I'll let you in. I'll make sure you meet Walter. I promise," said Sasha.

"Thank you. Thank you so much!" said Ben, hugging Sasha.

"That is fine," said Sasha, laughing.

"I hope he wants to meet *me*," said Ben.

"That I can't help you with," smiled Sasha. "But I can let him know that there's a nice, young man who would like to make his acquaintance; someone who bears a striking resemblance to himself. Is that about it?" asked Sasha.

"That's it, exactly," said Ben, smiling.

"Now, you best be off, so you can work to come back," said Sasha.

Ben packed up his tools to leave.

"Oh, and Ben?" said Sasha.

"Yes?" asked Ben.

"Thanks for today. I'll mention you to Mr. Burbage. Just in case a job ever comes up. You never know, right?" he added.

"I doubt it but, you never know," said Ben, smiling.

With that, Ben left the theater and headed back to work. He was suddenly aware of a tightening in his chest and a flurry in his stomach. It felt familiar and unfamiliar all at once, bubbling up, sparking his mind and making him smile.

He stopped.

What was this feeling?

It was hope.

Fifty-Nine

"YOU'VE ALWAYS REMINDED me of my son," said Shakespeare, his eyes tearing slightly.

Molly sat across from him, not sure why the writer had asked for this meeting.

"They say time heals all wounds," he continued, shuffling his papers. "I would argue time brings acceptance, but the wound never heals. It may not remain the gaping gash of loss, but there is always a lesion. The tiniest reminder may open the wound back up at any, unexpected moment. The loss is always, well, a loss. Time just makes it less immediate."

Mr. Shakespeare stopped speaking for a moment. Then, dipping his quill into an inkpot, he scribbled a note of what he had just said.

"I understand," said Molly quietly.

"Hmm? What was that?" said Shakespeare, still scratching his words onto paper.

"I know some of the loss of which you speak," she said, her eyes turned downward. Was she ready to talk about this?

"I had an inkling," he said, putting his quill into its holder and folding his hands together on the desk. "There are two clubs," he said. "If you have not lost a family member, you have no awareness of the clubs or that you are a member of one. But once you lose someone, you become acutely aware you may never leave the other club. For the club of loss is a club from which no traveler returns," said the writer.

There was some silence.

The writer grabbed his quill to capture what he had said. "No traveler returns," he muttered. He stopped and looked back at Molly.

"Go on," he prompted.

Molly tried to find the words. The writer waited patiently.

"I lost everyone, Sir," said Molly, her voice barely more than a breath. "except Julian. My mother, my father" She paused. "Ben."

"Ben?" inquired Shakespeare.

"My twin," whispered Molly, barely getting the words out.

"Ah," the writer answered. "My Hamnet was a twin. A boy and a girl. Fraternal. Which were you?"

"Identical, Sir," Molly whispered. She didn't like lying to Mr. Shakespeare but it was necessary.

"Ah," he said.

Molly nodded. "My aunty had stopped coming to visit. We were all alone…"

Mr. Shakespeare picked up his quill from the inkpot and scratched some more notes. Once he had finished, he returned the quill back to its post.

"A day doesn't pass when I don't think about my boy, my Hamnet," he said quietly. "Lost to the undiscerning Plague."

"That's. That's what happened with-" Molly couldn't talk anymore.

They were silent for a good, long time.

"Mr. Spleen made an accusation against you," said the writer, gently. "Is there anything you need to tell me? In confidence, of course."

"I-" she began, sheepishly. It felt wrong to not tell the

exact truth to Mr. Shakespeare, but she wanted to stay acting. "I wear a bandage. To support my spine," lied Molly.

"Ah," he said. "Anything else?"

"No, Sir," said Molly, keeping her eyes lowered.

"I hope you feel you can be honest with me," he said.

"Yes, Sir," said Molly.

"The last thing we want is another *Molly Frith* situation," he said.

"I understand, Sir. I agree," said Molly.

"Are you able to do fight scenes? Swordplay? Rapier and dagger? Tumbling?" asked Shakespeare.

"There's nothing I can't do," said Molly, relieved. "I can even take down theaters," she joked.

The writer laughed. "We'll soon see about that."

He sat back in his chair.

"Spleen put us in an awkward position. He's gone, of course. To the Blackfriars. But, if there were even a whiff, a suggestion, a *hint* of something improper, especially as egregious as a girl acting on stage, the Puritans would have us all hanged from Tyburn Tree in the twinkling of an eye. Ooh! There's another one…"

He muttered, "twinkling of an eye…" as he scratched down the words.

"Surely no one believes him? He was drunk," offered Molly.

"Spleen's green eyes turn wild with jealousy, sometimes. He becomes a monster," he said.

Shakespeare snatched the quill and scratched a note. He muttered as he wrote, "green… eyed… monster." Then he said, "Oh! That's perfect! What was I talking about?"

"What are you working on, Mr. Shakespeare?" asked Molly, diverting away from the earlier topic.

"Oh! Will, please. I'm working on a few things. I'm formulating a play about a noble Moor driven mad by a jealous English captain. He uses a handkerchief to deceive him."

"That sounds intriguing," said Molly. *Is he writing it for Raymond?* she wondered.

"Well, that's my intention," said Will. "Alas, audiences can be as fickle as females. Oh, that's-" He scratched down the phrase. "Ha! They're pouring from me today!" He returned his quill to its holder. His fingertips and the underside of his nails were stained black with ink.

"I'll tell you a secret," he said. Molly leaned in closer. "This Spleen incident has enlivened me and my writing. It's so immediate. It has given me excellent material. I've started work on the follow up to Henry IV. I'm calling it Henry V. I want it to be a glorious battle play."

"Oh!" said Molly.

"I'm working on another Roman play, too," he continued.

"A duke once told me the English love all things Italian," enthused Molly.

"A duke?" questioned the writer.

"Yes," smiled Molly. "He gave me the lute."

"A duke. I'm intrigued," said Will. He wrote a note.

"How do you do it?" asked Molly, moving the attention away from herself. "Write all these plays, I mean."

"Necessity is the mother of bold creativity. It forces us to be inventive," he said. "It compels us to take risks."

"I understand that," said Molly.

Will fixed Molly's gaze. She squirmed under the attention.

"I've another play in mind," he said. "In this one, a girl disguises herself as a boy to survive."

"Oh?" said Molly, a little too tightly.

"She's so well disguised that the man who loves her doesn't recognize her. And a woman falls in love with her as a boy. What do you think?" he asked.

"It sounds wonderfully confusing," said Molly,

"That's exactly what I want. Humor from confusion; wit from danger. I might even set it in Italy," laughed Will.

"I would like to play that part, Sir," said Molly, surprised at her own boldness.

"Oh? And why is that?" he asked, as if fishing for unspoken information.

"I think I'd be good in it," smiled Molly.

"Necessity has made you bold as well, I see," said Will.

"It sounds like fun. That's all," said Molly, trying to keep it light.

"I'm intrigued by you, Walter. Of all places, you chose this unfamiliar country, the *theater*, in which to land and make a name for yourself." Will laughed. "You remind me of me."

"I love the theater, Sir," Molly gushed. "Honestly, I don't know what I'd do if I didn't have the theater." Molly felt a swelling in her chest. She was speaking from her heart.

Will's eyes brightened.

"Yes," he said. "No other profession can do what we do. We take people out of their pelting, petty lives for a little while - Oh! That's good - we allow audiences to forget themselves, if only for a moment. They can live someone else's pain, someone else's risk, someone else's love, without consequence. And actors, well - we can mingle with Queens and common men, and everyone in between."

Will returned to his writing. Molly waited.

"Ach! What did I just say? Pelting..petty lives?" he muttered.

"Pelting, petty yes," said Molly. Will scratched it down.

Molly grinned. She was in love. Not with a person, but with a world.

The theater.

She was home.

Sixty

THE STENCH of blood was overwhelming.

No one, in the entire history of England, had ever taken down a fully built theater before, especially in order to rebuild it. Burbage assured everyone that what they were doing was well within their legal rights. Besides, they didn't have a choice.

"Blame the greedy landlord!" declared Burbage.

Everyone cheered.

If this is strictly legal and legitimate, thought Molly, *why are we doing it at night?*

It felt illegal, even if it wasn't. And thus, it felt exciting.

Half of *The Theatre*'s storage barn was taken up with *Stoughtons' SlaughterHouse*. The sweet, acrid smell of cattle carcasses stung the inside of their nostrils.

"Remember this for our next bloody battle scene," Burbage said. "Pay attention to your body's reaction. Is this how Henry felt at Bosworth Field? Or King Richard, when he begged for a horse?"

"Yes, yes," quipped Kempe. "I'll remember this, the next time I have myself a cut of beef."

"Whenever that will be," Condell jibed.

"Do they serve steak at Newgate?" bantered Kemp.

"Enough nonsense talk," ordered Burbage.

"Is it possible? That we'll be thrown into Newgate prison?" asked Molly, wide-eyed and worried.

"Absolutely not!" said Burbage. "Remember, Allen owns the land. We own the theater. And as it is *our* theater, we can move it!"

Peter Streete was an investor in the Lord Chamberlain's Men. He also was the best carpenter in all of London. He brought his team of builders to help with the endeavor. They uncoupled the main timbers of the outside structure and the actors carried them all to the cart. Molly warned Juliet about getting splinters. No one wanted that.

Word spread about the theatricals' daring-do and a crowd gathered. They cheered and applauded each time a large timber clattered down. Some of them tried to help, but that just got confusing.

"An audience is essential," muttered Burbage, "but they must know their place."

Every aspect of life was a form of theater for him.

Even Lady Southwark showed up.

"I can't miss this!" she explained. "You are the most exciting theater company in all of London!"

Lady Southwark didn't stay long. It was muddy and dark and not the place for Ladies (or long dresses). She brought comfits and sweet tarts for the company, handing them out like the queen distributing alms. She suggested this battle with the landlord was their very own Agincourt. With a wink at Molly and Juliet, she headed home.

Word eventually reached the landlord, Giles Allen. He did not want to leave his family Yuletide gathering, so he sent his lawyer to put an end to the mischief. By the time the lawyer arrived, red-nosed, flustered, and roughly dressed, they had transferred most of the theater onto carts.

"Cease! At once!" declared the lawyer, unheeded.

Thomas Pope cried out, "The first thing we do, let's kill all the lawyers!"

Everyone laughed. It had been his line in *Henry VI: Part 2*. The actors were not going to stop now, not even for a lawyer.

"Well, I never did!" exclaimed the lawyer.

"You never did and you never would," quipped Kempe.

"You simply cannot, you simply must not-" blustered the poor lawyer, completely out of his depth, "You must desist!" His voice was drowned out by another creak and crash of timber.

Once *The Theatre* was completely dismantled, Burbage wiped his hands and walked over to the floundering lawyer.

"What may I do for you, Sir?" he asked as he gestured *congeniality*.

"You must, must, must stop!! You're not allowed to do this!!" blurted the lawyer. In his world, he was only treated with deference or fear.

"In all my life, I have never encountered anything like these, these, these disregarding, self-possessed, overly confident, annoyingly rude *actors* before!" he burst.

"You'd like us to stop?" asked Burbage.

"Yes! Yes! Yes! You must cease forthwith!! At once!!" shouted the lawyer, a button popping on his outsized chest.

"But, Sir, we have stopped," said Burbage, sweetly.

They turned to the space where *The Theatre* had been.

"Put everything back! You-you-you must put everything back! Right now! Everything! Rebuild!" said the lawyer.

"You've got to be joking," said Kempe.

"I never joke! I'm a lawyer!" said the lawyer.

"Good one. You catch that, Will?" Kempe said. Will nodded.

"I simply cannot ask them to do that," said Burbage.

"Then, then, then, then, then you are breaking the law!" declared the lawyer.

"Funny," said Kempe.

"Here's a copy of the lease," explained Burbage. "You'll see it says, Mr. Allen, your client, owns the land. Have we taken any land? Have we taken any land, boys?" asked Burbage

'No," cried the company in unison.

"Mr. Allen owns the land. Mr. Cuthbert Burbage—that's my brother, he's right over there—say hello, Cuthbert," Cuthbert waved, Burbage continued, "and Mr. Richard Burbage - that's me, I'm an actor, very nice to meet you - own everything built *upon* the land. Thus, we are merely taking what is, rightfully, legally, ours." Burbage ended with a small bow, gesturing *mock reverence.*

"I-I-I shall see you in court!!" said the lawyer. As he stomped out, his shoe stuck in a mud slip and he sank to his ankle. He pulled his foot out but his shoe stayed mired in the mud.

"Here, let me help you," said Burbage, pulling out the shoe for him. Its bow had been completely flattened by mud. The lawyer snatched his shoe and wobbled as he placed it back on his foot. He lost his balance and fell splat.

Bottom first.

Into the mud.

Legs in the air.

Papers everywhere.

Burbage, Kempe, and Molly helped him up, trying very hard not to laugh. The lawyer shook them off and stamped away, stumbling on the muddy ground as he went.

"Where I come from, we say *thank you*," said Kempe.

"In court!" was the lawyer's parting shot. The lawyer angrily clambered into his fancy carriage, trailing mud and goop everywhere. The carriage jerked forward, then trundled away across Finsbury Fields.

"Can he see us in court?" asked William Sly.

"He can, but he won't. He has no grounds," said Burbage.

"Well, that's all he has – his grounds!" joked Kempe.

Burbage laughed. "Very good, Kempe! And that's why we paid a king's ransom for smart lawyers to draw up our lease."

All that remained in Giles Allen's courtyard was a low mound where the Pit had once been. Mr. Burbage stood in the center. Gesturing triumph, he planted a makeshift flag on the ground and raised his arms, victorious, into the air.

"Friends! Colleagues! Actors! Remember this day! On this day, we rise victorious from the depths of despair, from the clutches of greed, from the ire of Puritan non-theatricals. On this day, we are reborn. Soon, very soon, we will build the greatest theater London has ever seen!" cried Burbage.

The crowd roared and cheered, throwing their caps in the air.

The actors, builders and carpenters strapped themselves to the wagons and hauled the wood to a spot just north of the Thames. When the weather turned warmer, they would take the timber across the water to their reserved spot in Southwark.

Molly smiled.

Nothing can be better than this moment. Ever, ever, ever, she thought.

Sixty-One

SHE LOOKED AT A GHOST.

Molly stared, mouth agape, at the visitor before her. He, too, was silent, twisting his woolen cap between his hands, his weight shifting from foot to foot.

Have I gone completely mad with grief, like Constance in King John? Am I seeing ghosts as real people now, wandering the ramparts of my life in this theater? Is this a spirit come to warn me of my unexpected and impending doom? An angel come to protect me as the world flops upwards? What schism does this heavenly mortal represent in my life? God's teeth, I'm even thinking in the language of Mr. Shakespeare, thought Molly.

"Uh..." said Ben. He did not know what to say. He was stunned. In front of him, like a mirrored reflection, was his exact replica. It was as if the Creator had carved his double out of stone and brought it to life.

Ben took a breath. He'd better say something.

Molly took a breath. She'd better say something.

They spoke at the same moment:

"I'm sorry to bother you," he said

"I thought you were dead!" she said

They were both silent again.

"Do you two know each other?" asked Sasha.

They answered simultaneously.

"No," said Ben.

"Yes. I don't know," said Molly.

"Intriguing," said Raymond, who had joined Sasha for this performance.

"It is?" asked Ben, completely befuddled.

"Give me a minute. I want to…" Molly indicated she had to finish getting changed. She turned to go, stopped, and said, "Don't go anywhere. You promise?"

"Uh… yes, Sir?" said Ben.

"*Sir*," smiled Molly. She winked at Sasha and Raymond, as she pointed her thumb at Ben. "Get him."

She turned to leave. She ran into the wall. She straightened herself up. She turned back to Ben.

"I meant to do that!" she said. Ben smiled. Molly almost bumped into the wall again.

What's going on with me? She thought. *I've walked this route a hundred times!*

"It's *this* way!" joked Raymond, as he headed behind the stage with ease.

Molly turned back to Ben and said, "Stay right there."

"Yes?" said Ben, getting confused.

"Swear!" said Molly.

"I swear," said Ben, smiling at the absurdity of the situation.

"I'll make sure he doesn't leave," assured Sasha. "Stay, boy!" he instructed Ben, as if he were a small dog.

Molly ran back to the tiring room, barely missing the wall a third time.

"What's wrong with me?" she said out loud.

Ben turned to Sasha, who shrugged. This had been the best theater he'd seen in a long time, and it wasn't even by Mr. Shakespeare.

Sixty-Two

MOLLY HAD CHANGED into her street clothes at lightning speed. Without telling her why, she had instructed Juliet to do so as well.

"Hurry, I've something to show you," Molly had said. Grumpily, Juliet obliged.

"Why do you think you can still order me about?" grumbled Juliet. "I make my own money and my own way."

"You'll be pleased, I promise!" said Molly, almost ready. She hurriedly thrust her costumes onto their hooks, set up her props for the next day, and ran back out.

She rushed out too fast. She returned to drag her truculent sister out with her.

"Come on!" said Molly.

"Don't pull so hard!" said Juliet.

Just before they went into the Pit, Molly looked Juliet squarely in the eyes.

"In a minute, you'll probably want to shout and jump about and say things, but don't. Do you hear me? Just stay calm. At least, until we're a long way from the theater."

"Fine!" said Juliet, now even crosser with her sister.

Molly took Juliet's hand, took a deep breath and drew

back the curtain. The minute Juliet saw Ben, she yelled, "That's a ghost!"

"Let's walk," said Molly, painfully aware of her brother's potential to unwittingly unmask them. Juliet tried to act nonchalant. She coughed, put her hands into her pockets, but she grinned from ear to ear. Ben was very confused. Why were they acting so strangely? And who was this other boy? And why did he look so much like his little sister but a boy?

Molly gripped Ben's arm and pulled him out of the theater.

Sasha walked with them.

"Oh, Sasha. This is private," said Molly,

"Can't I come? I want to know how this ends!" he pleaded.

"You are the *best*, Sasha. We just need some time. I'll tell you all about it tomorrow," promised Molly.

"Very well," said Sasha, disappointed. "I wouldn't want to be a third wheel. Or fourth, in this case. You have a nice night. Remember, you're like family to me." he said, sounding lonely. Molly gave him a hug.

"Thank you, Sasha. I love you, too," she whispered in his ear. Then the three of them left.

Molly needed to make sure they were somewhere they could speak freely and not be overheard; a place where she could see several feet around them, so no one could spy on them. They sat on the steps near the stubby tower of St Paul's. It had enough noise to cover their conversation and enough space to be secret and unobserved in public. They munched small pieces of fruitcake Molly purchased from a street seller. Yuletide meant delicious, seasonal foodstuffs were sold everywhere.

After some silence, Ben blurted out, "Are you my cousin?"

Molly said nothing. With all her heart, she wanted to tell

Ben the truth, but she was terrified. Obviously, he was friends with Sasha. Juliet, though, had had enough.

"Walter, may I speak with you? Privately?" Juliet said, crossly.

"Uh. Yes?" questioned Molly.

"Stay there, monsieur," said Juliet, as she pulled Molly aside.

"Monsieur?" said Ben and Molly, simultaneously.

"I'm being fancy," said Juliet.

Once they were out of Ben's earshot, Juliet let loose.

"I want to tell him," she said.

"We can't!" argued Molly.

"He's our brother!" raged Juliet.

"I know that!"

"He thinks he's all alone in the world when we're right here!"

"It's too dangerous," said Molly, worried.

"Sometimes, Moll, you have to take a risk. You just have too!" said Juliet.

"Julie…" said Molly.

"I'm going to tell him, whether you like it or not!" said Juliet.

"Jules, don't be like…" but Juliet had already stomped back to Ben.

Slowly, Molly returned. She sat on the other side of Ben. Juliet looked at Molly, eyes wide, and said, "Go on, then."

"Go on, what?" asked Ben.

"You must swear to keep it to yourself," said Molly.

"I've been asked to swear a lot today," answered Ben, uncomfortably.

"Do you swear?" asked Molly.

"I swear," said Ben, unsure but smiling.

"I'm Juliet!" blurted out Juliet.

"No, you're not. You're a boy," insisted Ben.

"I'm still your sister," she said, smiling.

Ben took in Juliet's face for the first time. He put his hand to her temple, stroked down the side of her face to her chin. As he stared at his little sister, his eyes pooled with water.

"It *is* you," he whispered.

In a daze, Ben dropped his head and covered his face with his hands. Tears ran down his nose and onto the floor.

"Ben-" started Juliet, but he raised a hand to stop her.

"I'm sorry," garbled Ben. "Please, a moment, I, give me, I just, I don't-"

Ben wept quietly.

"I thought you were dead," he said. "All of you, dead. I thought I was alone."

Juliet cast a glimpse at Molly, who looked away.

I'm not ready, she thought.

Ben had felt unanchored ever since leaving Bitford. Now, seeing his sister, he felt as if he had landed on a new shore. Life, which had taken everything from him, had finally given something back.

Juliet placed a gentle hand on Ben's shoulders. Ben, his head down and body hunched with grief, turned into his little sister. She hugged him as he sobbed.

"You're not alone. Not anymore," whispered Juliet.

Molly was stunned by how grown up Juliet was in this moment. Molly felt awkward and childish. She could not move. Her heart ached too much. More than anything in the world, she wanted her brother back. Her twin. Her other half. But how could she?

Eventually, the reunited siblings untangled themselves from each other. Ben kept his gaze on Juliet. He feared if he took his eyes from her, she might disappear again.

"But *why* are you a boy?" he asked.

"Ben, be smart. How could I make it as a girl in London? I couldn't be a musician, for a start," she said. It had never occurred to him how much more challenging it might be for girls to make a living. Her musical talents would not have been realized, for sure.

Molly carelessly broke off tiny pieces of the cake and let them crumble for the birds. She was no longer hungry; she was terrified. Once she told her brother the truth, there would be no way back. Everything would be different.

But would it be a good different or bad different?

Sixty-Three

THE THREE SIBLINGS walked back together along Cheapside, bedecked with its musical market sellers. They turned right onto Grace Church Street. Straight ahead of them stood the busy thoroughfare of London Bridge. This was where they would say goodbye to Ben.

For the entire walk, Juliet and Ben chattered away like birds, their arms tightly wrapped around each other. Ben was so full of joy, he pushed away obvious questions such as "What happened to Molly?" and "How did you get to London?" and "How did you survive in London?" and "Why does this actor look so very much like me?"

Molly was scared. She had no desire to go back to point-less occupations and adjusting her behavior to please whichever man or boy happened to be in the room. She liked her independence. She liked making her own money. She liked her freedom. She did not want to give that up.

On the other hand, he was her *twin*. She wanted to hug him so tightly she would swallow him up.

As they pushed and shoved their way across London Bridge, their pace slowed. They did not want to say goodbye. Eventually, they came to the workshop, with the alleyway to the water next door. "This is where I first saw Southwark," said Molly.

"I think I saw you," said Ben. "But I thought I was daydreaming."

They stared at each other.

Juliet said, "Uh... Walter? May I speak with you for a minute?" She pulled Molly into the alley and spoke in an urgent whisper. "Why are you being so cruel?"

"I'm suffering too," retorted Molly.

"He thought we were dead! And you won't tell him?" Juliet said.

"What if he tells Mr. Burbage or Mr. Shakespeare? My career will be over," said Molly.

"Your career? Always your career!" mocked Juliet.

"Yes!" said Molly, ardently.

"He's your *brother*," said Juliet. "Do you honestly think he would give you away?"

"Not on purpose," said Molly, feeling badly.

"Not anyhow!" said Juliet.

They were silent for a moment.

"I want to take him to Aunty Anne," said Juliet.

"No!" said Molly, without thinking.

"She's his aunty, too. Honestly, I can't believe you're doing this," said Juliet.

"I know, I know. I feel-. I'm so-." Molly wrestled with herself, her body twisting, her arm at her forehead.

Ben had joined them in the alleyway.

"I know who you are," he said.

Sixty-Four

AUNTY ANNE WAS BESIDE HERSELF.

"All my family under my roof. Molly, Juliet and now, Ben! Oh! I'm going to spoil you all and spoil you rotten!!" she had said. Almost immediately, the maids had brought in an array of comfits, tiny fig tarts and other sweet delights.

Every time Juliet popped a sugar-coated almond into her mouth, she said, "Thank you."

"Thank you," chew, swallow.

"Thank you," chew, swallow.

"Thank you," chew, swallow.

The others watched her for a moment.

"Are you thanking each almond comfit?" asked Aunty Anne, bemused.

"Absolutely!" smiled Juliet. "Sugar-coated almonds led us to Aunty Anne. I ate too many of them in the folly; that got us caught by Lady Exeter. Because of that, the Duke of Armington had us play at his party. That's where you whisked us off to London. And now look! Without these sweet, sweet almonds, we would never have seen Ben again, ever."

"You are right!" laughed Aunty Anne. "I shall have them

made for every meal, forever more. Bless you, humble almond."

"And your sweet, sweet coating," said Ben, licking off the outside. He'd never eaten such irresistible confection in his entire life.

Molly nibbled at the sweets – how could she resist? - but she looked down and away from the group. She was worried.

"How did you know it was me?" she asked. "Could you tell?"

"Molly! If I could tell by looking, I'd have been round the back of that theater the first day I saw you on stage. Nothing would have stopped me. I still can't believe it!" said Ben. "Even right now, I can't tell by looking at you. Even though I know you're Molly. You look like a boy!"

"Are you sure?" Molly asked.

"Moll, would I tell you anything but the truth?" said Ben.

"No," said Molly.

"It's not just your clothes, it's your hair, the way you move, it's your...manner. I don't know. You're different from the Molly I know," said Ben.

"I'm still the same Molly, you know. I'm just different," laughed Molly, popping a comfit into her mouth.

"Now," said Aunty Anne. "Tell me, do we need to do anything about the suspicions they have about you being a girl?"

"I convinced them," said Molly.

"They convinced you they're convinced," said Aunty Anne. "They are actors, after all."

"Mr. Shakespeare just asked if I could do stage combat," said Molly feebly.

"No one thinks girls are capable of any sort of combat, my dear," said Aunty Anne.

"He asked because of my back!" said Molly, getting upset.

"Your back?" Aunty Anne asked.

"Yes! Harry Spleen says he saw my bandage," said Molly.

"Why do you need a bandage?" asked Ben, confused

"I wrap it around my chest," said Molly.

"What? Why?" asked Ben, not understanding.

"It helps her look more like a boy," explained Aunty Ann, kindly. Juliet giggled and popped an almond into her mouth.

"Thank you!" she said.

Although Ben still didn't get it, he smiled as if he did. This made Molly burst out laughing!!

"We have some differences, you know!" she laughed.

Ben squirmed.

"Hmmm." Aunty Anne mimed putting a hat—or crown - onto her head. "I've put my thinking hat on," she said. "There's a solution here. We just need to work out what it is."

"Aunty Anne," said Ben. "I missed you."

"Don't get all soft on me, Ben. I adore you, but not right now. I need to think," said Aunty Anne. "Could you please put your thinking hats on, too?"

Juliet, Ben and Molly all mimed putting hats on to their already hatted heads.

Sixty-Five

A FEW DAYS LATER, Ben and Aunty Anne were working on a solution to a problem only Aunty Anne could see brewing on the horizon.

"How unusual is it for fraternal twins to look as much alike as you do?" asked Aunty Anne.

"Very unusual," said Ben.

He popped a comfit into his mouth. Aunty Anne made sure sugary almonds were always available and Ben couldn't get enough of them. He'd eaten so many, his gums started to ache. He wondered if it might be related to the sweets. Then again, they said the Queen brushed her teeth with honey, so who knew?

"I still have my thinking hat on, Ben. Do you?" she asked her nephew.

Ben involuntarily put his hand to his head. "Uh... I think so?"

"Make sure it is. This is a serious problem waiting to happen-"

Molly burst in.

"He's gone to the Lord Chamberlain!" she cried.

"Who? Spleen?" asked Aunty Anne.

"Yes!"

"I knew it! He's a scoundrel!!" said Aunty Anne.

"There's going to be an investigation! Am I going to be hanged?" cried Molly.

"Let's take a moment to calm ourselves," said Aunty Anne, who had learned, from bitter experience, never to take important action when in a heightened emotional state. She sat still, and took a deep breath.

"Breathe in, hold, breathe out, hold," directed Aunty Anne. Molly really did NOT want to breathe! Didn't Aunty Anne understand the severity of the situation? Didn't she understand how they needed to take action, and fast?

Aunty Anne persisted. Molly had no choice but to join her. As she slowed her breath, she felt herself relax. She glanced at Ben, who grinned at her.

At that point, Juliet twirled in. She looked different. At first, Molly couldn't place what was different.

Then she realized.

Juliet was wearing a dress.

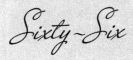

Sixty-Six

"AUNTY ANNE SAYS I can wear it in the house. Aren't I pretty?" said Juliet. She swished her dress around her.

"You-you-you can't wear that!" said Molly, frantically.

"Why not?" asked Juliet.

"You know why not!" said Molly.

"Actually, I don't," said Juliet.

"Because.... because you can't!" said Molly.

"It's so swishy," said Juliet. "With Ben and Aunty Anne and everything, I want to feel myself," said Juliet, shyly.

"You look very nice, Julie," said Ben.

"Doesn't she?" agreed Aunty Anne.

"You look… grown up," said Ben, a little sadly.

"No! No! Stop this!" said Molly. "Juliet, you sold another ballad! You're recognized for your talents. You sang for the Queen of England! You want to throw all that away, so you can wear a dress?" asked Molly in disbelief.

"No one can see," said Juliet.

"What about the people in this house?" asked Molly.

"My housekeepers are sworn to the utmost secrecy," said Aunty Anne. "Aren't you?" she called out.

"Yes, Ma'am," came a woman's voice.

"My housekeeper has to stay within earshot at all times, in case I have need of her," explained Aunty Anne. "Don't worry! If you knew the secrets held within these walls... Oh, I could tell you a few stories... Isn't that right, Mrs. Blackhall?"

"Yes, muh-Lady," came the reply.

"My staff have been tested to the end of the world and back, and they have proved honorable. Plus, they may have secrets of their own. I couldn't possibly comment," she continued with a cheeky grin.

"Yes, muh-Lady," came a cheeky reply.

"Well, Juliet?" Aunty Anne continued. "How do you like the dress?"

"I love it!" said Juliet, swishing and swirling her skirts.

"I put one on your bed, too," Aunty Anne said to Molly. "If you want to wear it."

"Do any of you actually care that I might be hanged? Or have my head chopped off? Anyone? Anyone at all?" shrieked Molly.

"Molly, dear, it's just a bit of fun," said Aunty Anne, "And only in the house."

Molly slumped into a chair, hands on her chin, staring straight in front of her.

No.

No!

She did not want to wear a dress.

She did not want to go back to her old life, to the restrictions, the expectations. More than that, she wanted to keep on acting. She loved what she did, more than anything else in the world. She did not want to be forced to give that up. No one could deny her capabilities. Plus, she loved the camaraderie. She loved how the company accepted her for who she was.

No.

She did not want to lose any of that.

On the other hand, there was going to be a hearing. If it went against her, not only would she be punished, but the people around her would be punished, as well. The people she loved most in the world. By refusing to conform, she put her loved ones in danger.

Just when she had found them all again.

Sixty-Seven

"I *THINK* I HAVE A SOLUTION," Ben said.

They had been silent for a long time.

"Marvelous! What is it?" said Aunty Anne.

"Fraternal twins as identical as me and Molly almost never happen. But Molly really looks like me. Especially now. So, why don't we give the Lord Chamberlain the science about twins. We tell him Walter is an identical twin, and then I come in. I'm a boy, so that means she must be a boy, too. What do you think?" he asked.

"Do you know what, Ben? That is a marvelous idea and it might very well work. At the very least, it will give the cover everyone is craving," said Aunty Anne. "I, also - ahem - had a word with some people I know who are - ahem - invested in this situation."

Everyone looked at Aunty Anne. Even Mrs. Blackhall popped her head round the corner, smiling. "As you were, Eve," said Aunty Anne, playfully. "I could tell you stories. HA!" she laughed. "But I won't. At least, not now. We have more pressing issues."

Aunty Anne and her stories.

They were always fabulous and mostly true. She lived a life larger than most, and she had the joy and scars to prove it. It also meant she had contacts in high places.

Very useful.

Particularly now.

Molly's mother had always said her sister Anne's stories would lead her children astray.

And here we are, thought Molly, *trying to avoid treason. Maybe Mom was right?*

"My friend," explained Aunty Anne, "has been very clear with me. What we need to do is nip this rumor in the bud; stop the gossip before it starts," Aunty Anne was on a roll now, "In fact, we need to generate gossip about that knave, Spleen! Oh, yes, this is it, family. We will turn this into a story about his jealousy. How he went mad with bitterness. How he concocted wild stories about his fellow actors! The people will eat that up."

Molly jumped up.

"He stole a handkerchief to make believe an actor was having an affair with the manager's lady friend!" she blurted.

"We'll call her his betrothed!" said Aunty Anne. "What else?"

"He never showed up on time. He didn't do the work he was supposed to do. He tipped stuff over when he knew I'd have to clean it up," Molly said.

"Scoundrel. Anything else?" said Aunty Anne.

"He lied to Mr. Burbage. He told him I wouldn't be back for a performance when he knew I would be. Then took my part," said Molly.

"Excellent. Anything else?"

"He always spread gossip about the other actors, hoping he'd get promoted. He was always envious of anyone else's success," she said.

"Perfect. A jealous apprentice who takes revenge on everyone promoted ahead of him," said Aunty Anne.

"Do you think it will work?" Molly asked.

"It must," said Aunty Anne.

Sixty-Eight

IF IT WERE DISCOVERED that a girl had acted professionally in front of Her Royal Majesty, there were several possible outcomes.

All of them were bad.

Some of them, deadly.

1. Molly.

She could be found guilty and possibly punished for treason. Even though she had only spoken of loyalty and fealty to the Crown, her actions would be considered treasonous.

2. Richard Burbage.

As the principle actor-manager of the Lord Chamberlain's Men, it was he who brought Walter Harcourt on as an apprentice. Was it not then he who, either knowingly or unknowingly, had allowed this travesty to occur?

3. The Shareholders of the Lord Chamberlain's Men.

It was against the law for women to act on stage. Therefore, if discovered, had they not potentially carried out a crime in public? Before hundreds of hapless theater goers, no less? Audiences who had, unwittingly, paid for the privilege? They were all potential witnesses and accessories to a crime. They would doubtless want their money back.

4. The Actors.

If the actors knew, did they cover it up? If they had not known, how had they not known?

5. The Landlords of the Curtain Theatre.

They had rented their space to the Lord Chamberlain's Men. They had, wittingly or unwittingly, allowed a crime to occur in their building.

6. The London Theater World.

Did the Puritans not repeatedly warn against the sins of the theater? Against the heresy of actors pretending to be royalty? Against boys dressing as girls? Against the eating of oysters during performances? Against brawls breaking out in nearby inns? This was PROOF that all theaters must be shut down! Immediately!

5. The Lord Chamberlain Himself.

The company bore his name. He was their patron. That meant that he, personally, vouched for them. If this rumor proved true, his reputation would be mud. Perhaps even his head would roll.

6. Her Royal Highness, Queen Elizabeth.

No doubt, it would make the Queen of England look extremely foolish and expose her to ridicule. If she had been duped by a mere *girl*, then why not by every spy in the world? Or the Emperor of Spain himself? Indeed, after all of her tremendous feats and triumphs, her wealth and even her defeat of the Spanish Armada, this would be the one thing which would be remembered about her reign. Just like her mother, Anne Boleyn, who was mostly remembered for having her head chopped off.

7. Harry Spleen.

If Molly were found guilty, he would be regarded as a Puritan hero. Without doubt, this would mean he would never act again.

Sixty-Nine

"YOUR LORDSHIP."

Aunty Anne dropped into a very low, very elegant curtsey. Her voice flowed like melted butter.

"Lady Southwark," said the Lord Chamberlain, from his podium. "It is a pleasure to see you, albeit in a somewhat unusual circumstance."

"Your Lordship is *always* kind and gracious," answered Aunty Anne, in her butteriest voice.

The Lord Chamberlain coughed. He explained the presence of a woman - a *woman* - in the hearing room. "This anomaly will all make sense once you hear the case."

"Thank you, my Lord," purred Lady Southwark.

"Everyone knows the complaint," stated the Lord Chamberlain. He used his 'let's get this over with' type of voice.

"My Lord," began Aunty Anne, "I move to throw out this specious complaint. It was brought forward by one Harry Spleen. He is nothing more than a petty, jealous, former apprentice actor."

At this, Harry stood up, outraged. He blustered and waved his arms about.

"Young man, sit down. This helps neither you, nor your case," patronized the Lord Chamberlain.

Harry Spleen slumped back down heavily and crossed his arms. Molly watched Alvin, Sasha, and Raymond nudge each other.

"My lord, Master Spleen, had a problem with young Master Harcourt, the moment our young man stepped foot into the theater," explained Lady Southwark.

Again, Harry Spleen jumped up. He was clearly furious and out of his depth.

"Remain seated, Master Spleen! You help not your case with such rash behavior!" commanded the Lord Chamberlain.

Again, Harry threw himself back onto his seat.

"Evidently, Spleen is a hot-head who was jealous of the unusually fast rise of Master Harcourt. He was envious from the start and his-.." Aunty Anne looked down at a scratch of paper, "his green-eyed monster of jealousy took hold."

The folks in the gallery gasped. The Lord Chamberlain chuckled. Aunty Anne cast a quick, almost imperceptible, glance up at Mr. Shakespeare and Mr. Burbage sitting in the gallery. Molly noticed the writer smile ever so slightly. He appeared to enjoy how his phrase, "the green-eyed monster" captured the audience.

Audience. Must I think of everything in terms of theater? Molly thought.

Molly put her hand to her chest. Her heart was beating so fast, she was sure the entire room could hear it.

Aunty Anne continued: "Spleen worked diligently to undermine Master Harcourt. He told lies about Master Harcourt. He tricked him. He misplaced props. He removed costumes, or dropped them from hooks."

Harry Spleen was up on his feet again. He yelled, "None of this is true!!"

"He poked fun at him," continued Aunty Anne. "He criticized him. He didn't show up to help with group tasks. He started rumors. The great Mr. Kempe overheard some accusations."

Mr Kempe smiled and gave a little wave to the crowd.

"At Her Gracious Majesty's Palace, no less!"

Gasps erupted from the crowd.

"Harry Spleen lied so he could take over Master Harcourt's role in a performance of *Much Ado About Nothing*," she continued, "when he knew Master Harcourt's brother had been kidnapped!"

More gasps from the crowd.

Harry stood up, then sat back down.

Aunty Anne gave special attention to the pamphleteers and gossip mongers in the crowd who scratched notes onto paper with their quills.

"Harry Spleen even attempted to turn Richard Burbage against another rising star with the use of a misplaced handkerchief. This demonstrates a pattern of jealousy."

Here, Aunty Anne put on her own acting performance.

"Walter Harcourt. A young man who wanted nothing more than to make a new life for himself in London. He was alone and bereft after his family had been murdered!"

Aunty Anne paused for dramatic effect.

"By whom were they murdered, you ask?" she said. "No, no! Ask not by whom, but by *what*?" She paused. Molly watched Shakespeare scribble notes.

"They were killed by the Devil and his plague!" she preached.

Gasps and exclamations burst from the crowd. Quills wobbled like birds across several notation pads. Aunty Anne had them eating out of her hands.

"Thus, young Harcourt came to London with nothing but the clothes on his back and a dream. I ask the good people here today: Is it wrong to dream?"

"No!" answered the crowd.

"Order," said the Lord Chamberlain. He tried hard not to smile. Lady Southwark was doing a fine job.

"Through sheer hard work and determination, Master Harcourt made his way to the very heart of the London stage. The jewel of Her Great Majesty's entertainment. His talent was immediately recognized by England's finest actor, Mr. Richard Burbage!"

Mr Burbage gestured *modesty* and for being flattered *far too much.*

"Mr. William Shakespeare, London's greatest writer, recognized Master Harcourt's talent and wrote plays with him in mind," she continued.

Shakespeare smiled. Burbage gestured *awe and gratitude* to Shakespeare, who gestured *'Oh, stop.'*

Theater to the last, thought Molly.

"Thanks to your Lordship and Her Majesty, long may she continue to grace us with her kindness," crooned Lady Southwark.

The Lord Chamberlain gave a small nod. That was the most gesturing he could muster.

"I intend to prove that Harry Spleen spread lies and gossip with malicious intent. His desire was to destroy the career of a talented young actor."

Again, Harry stood up.

"SIT DOWN!" barked the Lord Chamberlain.

The apprentices pulled Harry back down. This was not how he intended this to play out. Harry knew Walter wasn't a girl. All he wanted was for Walter to be kicked out of the company.

"And now, my Lord Chamberlain, my evidence," declared Aunty Anne.

"Evidence?" asked the Lord Chamberlain, confused. He had thought the discrediting would be enough.

"My Lady Southwark, this is somewhat unexpected," he flustered.

"My Lord Chamberlain," smiled Lady Southwark, calming the room with her voice. "Conclusive evidence has come to light. It will close the book on this chapter, once and for all."

"Affirming evidence?" asked the Lord Chamberlain.

"Exactly so," reassured Lady Southwark. "I intend to prove beyond any doubt or question that the Lord Chamberlain's Men have neither transgressed nor broken any law. I plan to show that the Lord Chamberlain himself is beyond reproach. I desire to demonstrate that Her gracious Majesty has only been protected, loved and revered by her Lord Chamberlain. I will prove that the rumor and insinuation of one jealous young man is just that - rumor and insinuation; that his accusation is based on nothing but his own jealous and fevered fantasy."

Harry was alarmed. All he wanted was a chance to play some good parts! His entire life he'd had to scrabble to survive: at home, on the street, in the orphanage and now here. Maybe, this time, he'd gone too far?

"Your Lordship, I'd like to call my first witness," buttered Lady Southwark.

"Witness?" whispered Harry Spleen, angrily. "I thought this was an investigation, not a court of law!"

"It's the Lord Chamberlain's investigation," corrected Alvin.

"Then why's there a witness?" asked Harry, panicked.

"You complained to the Lord Chamberlain. You work it out," whispered Sasha.

"My first witness, My Lord, comes all the way from Bitford. He will identify this young man and give you evidence to back it up," said Lady Southwark.

"I'd like to call in Mr. John Barnes."

Molly froze.

Seventy

A RUFFLED and grumpy Mr. John Barnes entered the room.

He was not happy to be there.

Not happy at all.

Lady Southwark threatened to tell everyone the real reason Bitford had burned to the ground. Unless he showed up today, that is.

"Thank you for coming. Mr. John Barnes," smiled Lady Southwark. She walked towards Molly and Juliet. "Do you recognize these two people here?"

"Aye," said John Barnes.

"How do you know them?" she asked.

"Offered them a job, didn't I," he said brusquely.

"This job would be where?" asked Lady Southwark.

"On my estate," he answered.

"And what sort of work would that be on your estate?" asked Lady Southwark.

"Laborer, gardener, that sort of thing. I'm building an orchard," he said.

"Is this work usually done by lads or lasses?" she asked.

"Lads, of course," answered Mr. John Barnes. "Stupid question."

The Lord Chamberlain coughed. Pointedly.

"To be clear, would you ever offer laboring or gardening work to girls?" asked Lady Southwark.

"They'd only make a mess of it," he said.

"Is that a no?" asked Lady Southwark.

Mr. John Barnes leaned forward aggressively. A mean scowl spread across his face. He was filled with hate. He hated this woman. He hated being questioned by her. He hated that she knew the real reason for the fire. He hated that she considered herself his equal.

"Aye," he spat. "Lasses are good for two things and two things only: cooking and making babies. If you want anything important done, ask a lad."

A chill ran through the room.

Lady Southwark took a moment. She stepped away from Mr. John Barnes. She took a breath and calmed herself. *What a hateful man*, she thought. On the outside, she smiled, swished her skirts and resumed questioning.

"I would say Her Majesty is good at rather more than that," stated Lady Southwark.

"Aye, well, I don't mean her, obviously," said Mr. John Barnes, shifting uncomfortably.

"This is a warning," cautioned the Lord Chamberlain. "If you *dare* mention her gracious Majesty again, then do so with respect."

"Aye, Sir," said Mr. John Barnes, chastened.

Lady Southwark continued."Did you offer laboring work to these two people here?"

"Aye," said Mr. John Barnes.

"Why did you offer them work?" she asked.

"I wanted to help the lads out." Mr. John Barnes shuffled uneasily, in an unconscious gesture of *lying*.

"Did they need help?" asked Lady Southwark.

"Aye!" he spat.

"Why did they need help?" asked Lady Southwark, a glint in her eye.

"Their village burned down, didn't it?" said Mr. John Barnes.

"And why did their village burn down, Mr. John Barnes?" asked Lady Southwark, ever so sweetly.

"The Plague," spewed Mr. John Barnes. He was furious.

"The Plague," repeated Lady Southwark, the slightest hint of doubt in her voice. "Did they seem capable of the work?"

"Of course," he said.

"Of course?" she clarified.

"Aye! I wouldn't have offered them the work otherwise, would I? 'Specially that one," He pointed at Molly.

"That one there?" confirmed Lady Southwark, pointing to Molly.

"I said so, didn't I?" he exploded. "Do you always repeat what the man says? Going on and on. Lasses have straw for brains."

"Sir! That is quite enough!" barked the Lord Chamberlain.

"Is what I say not true?" asked Mr. John Barnes. Some of the crowd assented. Most were shocked by his rudeness.

"SILENCE!" bellowed the Lord Chamberlain. "Apologize."

"I apologize, your lordship," muttered Mr. John Barnes.

"Not to me, you loggerhead. To the Lady!" said the Lord Chamberlain.

"Apologize? To her?" gasped Mr. John Barnes.

Lady Southwark smiled innocently.

Mr. John Barnes coughed.

The crowd waited.

"I apologize, your ladyship," he mumbled.

There was a momentary silence.

"Did he *say* something?" asked Lady Southwark gently.

"Louder," instructed the Lord Chamberlain.

"I apologize, your ladyship," he said, a little louder.

"I couldn't quite-" Lady Southwark pointed to her ears, gesturing *I can't hear*.

"I'm sorry, your Ladyship!" he gruffly said, finally audible.

"Thank you, Mr. John Barnes. You may go," said Lady Southwark.

Mr. John Barnes stormed out of the room.

An awkward silence followed in his wake.

"Are all your witnesses equally unpleasant?" asked the Lord Chamberlain.

"Certainly not," assured Lady Southwark.

"That was hardly substantial," he chided.

"Exactly!" shouted Harry Spleen.

"Yes!" said some onlookers.

"Order!" ordered the Lord Chamberlain.

Molly shifted in her seat.

Lady Southwark reassured the room. "Your gracious Lordship, that was simply the first step. Come with me on the entire journey. I promise, the landing will be all you imagined and then some."

"Do not waste our time, Lady Southwark," scolded the Lord Chamberlain. He had taken an enormous risk letting Lady Southwark present here today. Had he made a mistake?

Burbage and Shakespeare looked worried. Had they risked too much? Should they have cast the young actor adrift?

Harry Spleen smiled to himself.

Perhaps this would all work out in his favor, after all.

Seventy-One

"MY LORD, I'd like to call my next witness."

Molly shuddered.

What was Aunty Anne doing?

Lady Exeter glided into the room. An exultant intake of breath rose in the crowd. Her skirts fluttered, like gossamer, behind her. Her face was painted pale white, in the style Queen Elizabeth had made popular. Her hair was styled and studded with tiny teardrop pearls. Burbage lent forward and gestured *true admiration*. Even Shakespeare stopped writing for a moment. He took in the lady's grace and elegance. Lady Exeter was a moving work of art.

Unconsciously, Molly put a hand to her neck.

Lady Southwark guided Lady Exeter to her place. Lady Exeter didn't seem to stop. It was more as if she settled into a repose.

She's good, thought Lady Southwark. She knew so much more about Lady Exeter than this performance suggested. *All the better for my argument.*

"My Lady Exeter," said Lady Southwark. "Thank you so much for coming here today."

Lady Exeter ignored Lady Southwark and addressed the Lord Chamberlain.

"Your Lordship is always gracious," said Lady Exeter. Her voice was as buttery as Lady Southwark's had been.

Is there a school where ladies learn to talk buttery? wondered Molly.

"My Lady Exeter, thank you for coming. Please direct your attention to the Lady Southwark," admonished the Lord Chamberlain.

"Lady Exeter, almost one year ago, there was an incident at the Duke of Armington's home. Do you remember it?" asked Lady Southwark.

"There have been many events in my life," answered Lady Exeter dismissively. The crowd listened attentively.

"I do not doubt that, Lady Exeter," said Lady Southwark, laying it on thick. "You are known to live a rich and illustrious life. Cast your mind back to a dinner at the Duke of Armington's estate. He introduced *I Menestrelli Segreti.* They entertained his guests that weekend. The lute player caught your eye."

"Lady Southwark, I do not pay attention to *lute players,*" spat Lady Exeter. She said *lute players* as if they were dirt beneath her perfect nails.

"No doubt," buttered Lady Southwark. "However, do you recognize this *particular* lute player?"

Molly squirmed as Lady Exeter narrowed her gaze upon her.

"Yes," said Lady Exeter, quietly.

"The incident to which I refer, involves a ring," said Lady Southwark.

"I know," said Lady Exeter, even quieter. Her cheeks reddened.

Lady Southwark could feel the crowd leaning in. "Would you care to continue?"

"That young man!" Lady Exeter exploded. "That young

man had the audacity to give me his ring!"

Molly felt queasy. She watched Lady Exeter quake and shiver due to an affront which never happened.

"This young man had the audacity to give you, a Lady, his ring?"

"Yes," said Lady Exeter, visibly trembling.

She's a good actress, thought Molly

"Did anything else happen with this ring?" asked Lady Southwark.

"I had my footman return it to him," cried Lady Exeter, showily dabbing an eye with a handkerchief.

Molly watched Shakespeare scribbling and scratching his quill across paper.

"You gave the young gentleman his ring back?" clarified Lady Southwark.

"He's not a gentleman! He's a knave!" wept Lady Exeter.

The crowd gasped. The Lord Chamberlain hit his gavel.

"Gentle Lady, please refrain from such language. It becomes neither you nor this office," he said.

"I regret my speech, my Lord. I am a mere woman. My emotions are harder to control," said Lady Exeter.

She doesn't believe that for a second, thought Molly.

"To reiterate, this young man audaciously gave you his ring, and you returned it?" asked Lady Southwark.

"Yes," said Lady Exeter.

"The giving of a ring..is this something a young woman would ever do?" asked Lady Southwark.

"Of course not!" exclaimed Lady Exeter.

The Lord Chamberlain smiled quietly to himself. Harry Spleen slumped further into his chair.

"Your Lordship?" said Lady Southwark. She turned to the Lord Chamberlain to see if he had questions.

"Thank you, Lady Exeter. That is all," said the Lord Chamberlain.

"Your Lordship." Lady Exeter curtsied and floated from the room.

Beads of sweat baubled down Molly's face.

How could she survive any more of this?

Seventy-Two

"BEFORE I PRESENT my final witness, I'd like to pose a question to the room," said Lady Southwark.

The Lord Chamberlain's elbow rested on the arm of his chair, his fingers raised to his mouth, smiling slightly.

"That is a perfect gesture of *admiration*," whispered Burbage to Shakespeare. He copied the gesture, determined to use it the next time he played a lord.

"My question is this," continued Lady Southwark. "Can you always tell fraternal twins apart?"

She spun around to face the Lord Chamberlain. "My Lord?"

"Uh, yes?" he blustered. "Yes, I believe you can. Fraternal twins, yes. They are never identical."

"Never identical. *Thank you*, my Lord," said Lady Southwark, with a quick glance at Molly. "In the case of fraternal twins, there is always a distinguishing feature. That's how you can tell them apart." Lady Southwark turned to the crowd once more and said, "How about identical twins?"

The crowd murmured, "They'd be identical, wouldn't they?"

"My Lord?" asked Lady Southwark again once she was sure the crowd was on her side.

"Well, it's in the name," he said, somewhat patronizingly, "*Identical* twins."

"Exactly so. Thank you, my Lord. Identical twins are always identical," said Lady Southwark. "Sometimes, their own birth mother has trouble telling them apart!" Lady Southwark smiled as the crowd tittered.

Molly was full of admiration. What a wonderful performer Aunty Anne was. Molly glanced up at the gallery. Shakespeare was still scratching down notes.

"Could two girls be identical twins?" said Lady Southwark.

"Yes!" said the crowd.

"Could two girls be fraternal twins?" she asked.

"Yes!" said the crowd.

"But would they look exactly alike?" she asked.

"No!" said the crowd.

"How about a boy and a girl? Could they be identical twins?"

"No!" yelled the crowd.

The Lord Chamberlain was bemused. Where was his friend going with this?

"How about two boys? Could they be fraternal twins?"

"Yes!" said the crowd.

"If one identical twin was a boy, would the other twin have to be a boy?" she asked.

"YES!" said the crowd. They were enjoying this show. Even Harry Spleen joined in.

"Gentlemen." Lady Southwark paused. The entire room hushed with expectation. Lady Southwark walked up to her niece. "This young man is not Walter Harcourt."

A frisson buzzed through the room. Molly writhed on her bench. What was Aunty Anne doing? The crowd tittered and whispered. The Lord Chamberlain banged his gavel.

"Order!" he cried. "Lady Southwark, explain yourself!"

"Your Lordship," buttered Lady Southwark onto the toasty crowd. "This gentleman is not the real Walter Harcourt because... This is the real Walter Harcourt."

At that moment, the door opened and in stepped Ben. He was dressed exactly the same as Molly, even down to the woolen cap.

The crowd gasped.

"Identical twins!" declared Lady Southwark triumphantly.

Burbage struck a gesture of *exultant shock*. Shakespeare scribbled so furiously, his inkpot fell and rolled under his chair. The crowd cheered jubilantly. Hats were thrown into the air.

"Order! Order!" cried the Lord Chamberlain, at the delighted crowd. After some minutes, they returned to order.

"Your Lordship, I rest my case." Lady Southwark lowered into a deep curtsey.

There was silence. The Lord Chamberlain suppressed a self-satisfied chuckle.

"My dear Lady Southwark," he said, addressing the entire room. "You have acquitted yourself excellently today. Master Spleen's case has no merit. It is nothing more than fruit bourne from the seeds of jealousy. Jealousy designed to destroy another young man's career."

"Furthermore," stated the Lord Chamberlain, wishing to retake command of the room. He had ceded to a woman for long enough, (albeit an extremely smart and capable one).

"Her Majesty is incredibly perceptive and wise. She would have noticed in an instant if a *girl* had performed before her. Her Royal Majesty knew all along this case had no merit. Her Majesty would never have allowed such a travesty in her presence!"

The crowd applauded, along with cries of "Good Queen Bess!" and "Long Live the Queen."

Shakespeare had retrieved his inkpot and was scribbling again. Molly saw him mouth the words, "seeds of jealousy." He had ink on his face and, even, in his hair. His quill broke. He reached into his doublet and pulled out a leather holder. Inside were fastened an array of quills. Ben had made it for him.

The Lord Chamberlain was on a roll. "Her Majesty expanded trade and dispensed with wayward leaders from other countries. Her Majesty fended off attacks attempted on her gracious personage. Her Majesty dealt with all of these tribulations with a fair, courteous yet strong hand."

There was no stopping him now.

"I ask you, would this same Majesty, this leader of men, be so easily fooled by a group of *actors*? By a troupe of alehouse boilers?" Burbage grimaced at that one. "A menagerie of misfits who strut and fret their two hours upon a stage, telling stories of imaginary people, signifying nothing?"

"NO!" yelled the crowd.

Shakespeare had run out of ink. He reached into a pouch attached to his belt, near his rapier. It had a small stopper and a weighted bottom: another invention created and designed by Ben. Shakespeare dipped the quill into the small hole at the top, returned the stopper, and continued to write. His paper was leaning on a leather-bound hard surface, with a closable cover, in which he could keep his papers safe once he had finished writing. Another of Ben's inventions.

Lady Southwark smiled, indulgently, as the Lord Chamberlain pontificated. *Let him prattle on as long as we are free at the end of it,* she thought.

"I ask you," said the Lord Chamberlain, "would our noble sovereign succumb to an obvious misdemeanor and invite such trouble into her noble court?"

"No!" yelled the crowd.

"Her Majesty is beguiling, not gullible," continued the Lord Chamberlain. "She would never have allowed this corruption of truth, this travesty of justice, to occur in her presence. What they do in the bawdy streets of Southwark may be one thing, but in the Queen's Court? That is entirely another. No! No, no, no! The case has been proved beyond doubt. It is without merit. I am satisfied. No crime has been committed. Walter Harcourt is a boy."

The crowd cheered. Hats flew up into the air again.

Burbage stood up, his arms above his head in a gesture of *surprise victory*. Shakespeare joined him. Ben and Molly hugged. Juliet jumped up and down, then threw her arms around the twins. Lady Southwark smiled benignly at the crowd. She gave a discreet wink to the Lord Chamberlain, who nodded his head, ever so slightly, in acknowledgement.

Before she knew it, her nieces and nephew were hovering around her, their grins almost sliding off their faces. Lady Southwark hugged them to her, casting her eyes upward.

"Thank you," she said. "Thank you."

As they turned to leave the courtroom, the giant frame of Burbage blocked their way. He gestured *triumph and happiness*.

"Come here, you old scoundrel," Burbage said, as he grabbed Molly and ruffled her hair a little too roughly. "I always knew Spleen was wrong. How could a girl be such a fine actor? Impossible!"

Shakespeare stood more quietly to the side, his papers folded into Ben's invention, his fingers completely black with ink. His smile spoke volumes.

"And you!" Burbage turned, "Ben is it? Sir Will, here, showed me your creations. How would you like to work for the Lord Chamberlain's Men?"

"I can't act, Sir," said Ben.

"Not as an actor. God, no! As a prop-maker and stage-hand. We could use your talents. What do you say?" asked Burbage.

"That sounds appealing. I have to check with my boss," smiled Ben.

"Appealing! Listen to the fellow. *Appealing*," laughed Burbage, having fun at Ben's expense. "Today we became the most famous theater company in the entire world! Of course, we are appealing. Is it about the money? Don't worry—I'll make sure you're properly compensated, and I'll deal with your boss. After today, there's nothing we can't do! At least until the next big thing."

Seventy-Three

A REQUEST from the Queen was never a request.
It was a summons.

Seventy-Four

IN REALITY, there was nothing any commoner could do to properly prepare for meeting the Queen of England.

Burbage and Aunty Anne did their very best.

It was rumored that Queen Elizabeth, never having children herself, had a particular interest in the welfare and careers of the young people who performed at Court. She wanted to protect them. She was curious about young Master Harcourt.

Especially now that he had become famous.

Seventy-Five

THE ROOM WAS GRAND, with tall candelabra, and a fireplace at both ends. The walls were dark and imposing, made of deep cherry wood carved into twisted, ornate designs. Molly's chair was high-backed, with arms perfectly placed for resting. She felt dwarfed by the decor. Perhaps that was its intent?

Molly sat at an enormous table. The word enormous was not enormous enough to describe the enormity of this table. It was the length of her childhood home. Each chair was the same as hers, except for the one at the end. That chair was larger, slightly raised, and even more ornately designed. The carvings on the back of that chair were exquisite. A unicorn, a lion and roses were intertwined with trees, leaves and flowers. All these surrounded a beautiful ER for Elizabeth Regina.

Molly's heart pounded so much she feared it might leap out of her chest and take residence elsewhere. No matter what others thought of her, Molly was still the same inside. And now, her royal highness, the great Queen of England, wanted to meet her!

What on earth would they talk about?

What if Molly said the wrong thing?

What if she messed the whole thing up?

Burbage had given her a few lessons in decorum and courtly manners. Aunty Anne had given her a small box to give to the Queen.

"Never meet Her Majesty without bringing a gift. This will do nicely," Aunty Anne had explained with a smile.

The ornate box looked so tiny and trifling on the grand table.

What could possibly be inside it? thought Molly. *And what could Aunty Anne own that would be suitable for the Queen of England?*

Molly turned the box, looking for clues.

She tapped the box.

She flipped the box.

She flicked the box so that it spun.

She stopped it spinning.

She flicked it again.

She flicked it so hard, it flew and "plop" fell off the other edge of the table. Shocked, Molly ran around to salvage it.

She couldn't see it.

It wasn't on the floor.

Where was it?

Hurrying, Molly saw it had fallen onto the seat of one of the chairs. The chair was tucked in so tightly it was hard to reach the box. She knelt down with her head beneath the table and scrabbled to reach the box. Her bottom stuck out and up into the air.

That was the moment Queen Elizabeth, the Royal Queen of England, entered the chamber.

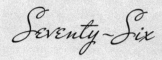

Seventy-Six

"HER ROYAL HIGHNESS, the Queen of England," announced the page.

"Oh, no!" said Molly, out loud. She hurriedly untangled herself, bottom first, from the wooden furniture, tiny box in hand. She stayed on her knees and bowed her head.

The Queen stopped. It was not the job of her royal personage to walk towards her subject. The subject must always walk toward the Queen, then bow or curtsey. If proffered, they are to kiss the Queen's ring.

When no one moved, Molly remembered the protocol. She slapped her own forehead; this was already a disaster! She shuffled forward on her knees, unsure whether it was appropriate to get back up from a kneeling position.

The floor was hard beneath her moving knees and, without realizing, she said, "Ow!" with every knee-step. As she got closer to Her Majesty, Molly proffered up the box, still saying "Ow!" with each step.

How could I mess this up so utterly and completely? thought Molly.

Molly heard a strange sound. She looked up to see the Queen laughing into the back of her hand.

"Thomas, help the poor lad up," she said, waving vaguely toward a page.

Thomas, one of the Queen's pages, helped Molly stand. He bowed to her Majesty, then returned to his place at the side of the room. Molly, remembering, bowed to the Queen. Burbage had run her through this a thousand times. Why did she think she had to kneel?

"I fear you have taken one too many comic acting lessons from the great Will Kempe!" exclaimed the Queen.

"Your Majesty," said Molly, not knowing what else to say.

"Master Harcourt," said the Queen, extending her right hand.

Whew. Molly knew exactly what to do now. All she had to do was step forward and kiss the Queen's ring.

That's all she had to do.

Step forward, head down, half bowing, take the Queen's hand and kiss her ring.

That was all she had to do.

She stepped forward, grabbed the proffered hand a little too roughly, and gave the ring a kiss.

There, I did it. Nothing went wrong! thought Molly.

"Oh!" remarked the Queen.

"Oh," remarked the pages.

Molly realized she had said her inside thoughts out loud. There was a momentary silence. Then, the Queen chuckled as she swished her way to her throne, at the top of the table.

"Oh, my goodness, Master Harcourt. We haven't laughed so much in a very long time!" smiled the Queen.

Molly had been warned:

The Queen always refers to herself in the plural.

Even so, it was confusing. Molly kept thinking the Queen was talking about another unseen person. The pages shuffled Molly back to her original chair.

"Do you have a gift for Her Majesty?" whispered Thomas to Molly.

"Yes! Here!" Molly replied, a little too loudly.

Thomas whispered to Molly. "Walk forward, bow, and present Her Majesty with your gift. Say something like, "I humbly present your gracious majesty with this gift, should you be willing to accept it."

Molly had practiced this with Aunty Anne. How had she forgotten everything now she was here? Molly stopped, took a breath. She straightened her clothes. She stepped forward. Queen Elizabeth was still chuckling.

Molly bowed her practiced bow.

"Your majesty, I humbly-" she began.

"Yes, yes," interrupted Her Majesty, smiling. "We accept. Thank you."

Thomas took the box and placed it on the table in front of the Queen.

"My dear Master Harcourt, you have already given us a much greater gift. The gift of laughter. That is much more precious than any gemstone or, even, gold itself. Gold is hard to the touch and lonely. Laughter is l'eau de vie! It reminds us we are alive. It means we have friends. Do sit, Master Harcourt."

Molly moved to sit in her assigned seat.

"Not so far. Nearer. Right here," demanded the Queen. She showed the seat on her left hand side. There was a slight bristle amongst the pages in the room, as Thomas pulled the chair out for Molly.

Molly moved closer to the chair by the Queen, not sure what to expect. She felt ashamed at having made a complete fool of herself. In her mind, she reached for the lessons Aunty Anne had taught her, but they had all fallen out of her head. Molly took a deep breath. That, at least, was something she remembered from her Aunty. With her breath, she reset her mind. She told herself, *I've been invited here for a reason. I need only be myself and all will be well.*

"Your Majesty," she said out loud. She bowed as she had

been taught, with her right foot stepped back slightly, her left foot forward, lowering her head, with her arms pointing backwards.

"Your gracious Majesty," she continued. It was coming back to her now. "This invitation to meet your royal person is the greatest honor of my life. Anything I can do for your royal highness, I am entirely at your service."

"Thank you, young man. You may sit," said the Queen, as gracious as had been described.

Molly sat in the chair to the Queen's left. For the first time, Molly was able to see the Queen up close. Molly had looked at the Queen in paintings and at a distance during the royal performance. In her portraits, Queen Elizabeth was forever vital and forever young.

In reality, England's beloved monarch was as ornate and impressive as a decorated egg. The Queen's face was painted thick white. Her red, brushed curls were piled up and around her head, bedecked with teardrop pearls which matched her earrings. Her neck ruff stood high and proud about her neck, with the back swooping around like fairy wings behind her shoulders. Her black and gold-braided bodice had wide, puffed sleeves. These billowed out like the sails on the ships she had instructed Sir Walter Raleigh to steer against the Spanish Armada. The enormous mutton-shaped sleeves tapered tightly into her narrow wrists. Her wrinkly fingers were bedecked with rings with enormous gemstones.

What shocked Molly was the Queen's age. The people of England had been taught to think of Her Majesty, not as an aging human, but as a forever-young deity. Molly never thought it possible the Queen of England could get old. Her blackened teeth told another story.

A page brought in plates piled high with sweetmeats.

"We thought you might be partial to these," said Elizabeth. "They are simply delicious and we can't get enough of them. Along with honey, of course. But we mostly use honey for brushing our teeth. Do you?"

"I-I-I don't brush my teeth," Molly admitted, somewhat surprised that *brushing your teeth* was a thing to do. Why would anyone do that?

"You must. If you want to keep them in your head," admonished the Queen. "You must keep your wits and your teeth to survive in this life!" The Queen laughed at her own joke.

"I will, your Majesty," said Molly.

"Try this wet sucket. It's one of our favorites," said Queen Bess. A page passed a small pot of gooey fruit dessert to Molly, with a tiny silver spoon. The spoon had 'ER' engraved on the end.

Molly dipped her spoon into the sweet, red, jelly-type substance. Hesitantly, she raised the spoon to her mouth. What if she didn't like it? Would she have to pretend to the Queen she did? She took a tiny spoonful. Her mouth burst with sweet deliciousness. Molly thought, *This food is magic.*

The Queen observed the delight on Molly's face. Her Majesty opened her mouth wide in a satisfied laugh, revealing more of her blackened and misshapen teeth.

Molly gushed, "This is the best, best, best, best thing I have ever tasted in my life!"

"Ha ha!" she said. "Isn't it wonderful? We're so happy to have someone with whom to share this. Someone who will be as excited as we are! Now, try these!"

The page placed a shallow dish of candied fruit in front of the Queen and then another in front of Molly. The candied fruits were works of art. Each was cut into shapes Molly now recognized. There were red ones, shaped into roses with a white trim. These tasted like strawberries. There were yellow ones shaped into lions—these tasted of lemons. The rich, deep purple ones were shaped into unicorns. They oozed the flavor of plump, ripe blackberries. Before she knew it, Molly had devoured the entire plate.

The Queen laughed again, a full-throated, generous and loving laugh; not at all what Molly had expected.

"Those are our favorites!" said the Queen, showing Molly her own, almost empty plate.

"Your Majesty is most generous," said Molly. "I don't know what I have done to deserve such kindness."

"Your entertainment merits such attention," said the Queen. "In our life, we have learned that, while it is lovely to have nice things, it is even more pleasurable to share them with others." At this, she bit into a blackberry unicorn. Molly's face lit up. She clapped her hands with joy. The pages shuffled uncomfortably at Molly's obvious ignorance of courtly decorum.

"Which are your favorites?" asked the Queen, conspiratorially. To Molly, the Queen grew younger each time she spoke.

"Definitely the unicorns, your Majesty," said Molly, smiling.

"Ours too!" exclaimed the Queen, clapping her own hands with delight. With the smallest of gestures, she signaled her pages, three of whom bowed and left the room.

"We have something rather splendid we'd like to show you," said the Queen. "In the meantime, have you ever tried these?"

She slid a small, silver bowl filled with some sort of candied seeds. Molly bit into it and felt a rush of delight fill her brain.

"Aha!" exclaimed Queen Bess, clapping her hands again. Two pages returned, carrying an elaborate structure. Other pages helped them lower it onto the table. Then they cleared away the other bowls and plates.

"Don't take them too far!" joked Her Majesty.

"Majesty," said the pages quietly, who took everything she said seriously. They brought a small table close and placed the platters within reach of Her Majesty's grasp.

The pages slid the sculpture gently across the table until it was directly before the Queen and Molly. As Molly's eyes adjusted, she recognized it as a sculpture of the court performance of *Much Ado About Nothing*.

"It's… it's…" said Molly, speechless.

"Made entirely of sugar paste!" declared the Queen.

"That's remarkable, Your Majesty," said Molly, awed by the elaborate beauty of this creation.

"This is you!" said the Queen, picking up one of the tiny sugar-paste people. It was, indeed, Molly in her elaborate Hero costume.

"We could bite your head off right now, if we wished. For all the trouble you caused, my Lord Chamberlain."

"Majesty, I-.." suddenly Molly was worried.

"Don't be silly," said the Queen, "We are making a joke! We could have had your real head chopped off long ago had we found proper fault!"

Molly didn't know where to look. Could she run? No, they would catch her, before she had gotten through the door. The Queen burst out laughing.

"One is making another joke," she added, seeing the shock on Molly's face. Molly laughed, uncertainly. "One can have too much gallows humor for one's position. We forgive you for misjudging our merriment."

The Queen danced the sugar paste Walter Harcourt around in the air like a doll, repeating some of her lines. She picked up the sugar-paste Burbage and had him reply.

"We really did rather enjoy the play, Master Harcourt. Hence, we will leave you intact," said the Queen.

"Thank you, your Majesty," said Molly, smiling but still unsure.

"For now," added the Queen.

"Your Majesty is most gracious," said Molly, with a slight bow. She was starting to understand Her Majesty's humor.

Why must everyone she met who had power, play these odd games?

Seventy-Seven

"YOUR MAJESTY! How I wish the other actors could see this. It's stunning!" blurted Molly.

"My dear, that is one's plan!" replied the Queen, excited. "This is merely the prototype, created for our amusement. We had this fashioned for today's meeting. We had a vision, and voila! Between you and us, there will be future Royal performances. Then we will surprise the cast with a replica of the play! Tell us, will your brother join the acting troupe?"

Molly realized she was being asked a question.

"Uh…" she hadn't thought of that. Could Ben even act? Before she had a chance to answer, the Queen had changed the subject.

"Found him! Now *here* is someone from whom you might find pleasure in removing the head."

From the sugar theater, Her Majesty pulled out a carving of a young man with blonde hair. It was Harry Spleen.

"Bite his head off! We dare you," ordered the Queen.

"Is that safe?" asked Molly, uncertainly.

"We do it all the time. Look," said the Queen. She quickly grabbed another actor—it was Thomas Pope– snapped off his leg and ate it.

"Delicieux!" she declared, in French.

Molly burst into delighted peals of laughter, as did the Queen.

"Try it. It's very satisfying," she said.

Molly tentatively took the Harry Spleen sculpture. She tried to snap off the foot, but the leg broke up to the knee with a "snap!" Involuntarily, Molly let out a giggle.

"He'll be delicious, we promise," urged the Queen.

Hesitantly, Molly popped Harry Spleen's calf into her mouth. Her teeth crunched down onto the crisp sugar paste and the sweetness infused her mind.

"Does that not feel merveilleux?" asked the Queen, slipping into French once more.

Molly nodded a yes, her mouth filled with sugary deliciousness.

"Are you ready to bite off his head?" asked the Queen.

Molly swallowed the leg and brought the sugar head up to her mouth. Just as her teeth clamped down on the sculpture's neck, the Queen exclaimed, " Off with his head!" Molly crunched and laughed at the same time. She reached up her hand to catch tiny flakes of sugar, which broke off as she giggled.

"Do you desire to know a secret?" asked the Queen.

Molly nodded, her mouth full of Harry Spleen's head.

"When one has troublesome foreign dignitaries, we have the cooks make a model for us. We once left the annoying former French Ambassador in a full bow for fifteen minutes. That was fun. But biting off his entire sugar head was much more gratifying! It clears one's mind. We frequently do this with the Emperor of Spain. Ssh, don't tell."

The Queen bit off an actor's head. Molly thought it might have been Alvin. Oh, well. It was an honor, in an odd sort of way.

By this point, Molly had eaten almost all of Harry Spleen

and was feeling giddy. Her Majesty was right. It felt very lovely.

"And, just like that. You gobbled him up!" laughed the Queen.

Molly couldn't help herself. She giggled uncontrollably. She couldn't speak. The two of them laughed hard, doubled over, tears pouring down their cheeks. Who knew the Queen of England could be so much fun!

There was a loud commotion outside the door.

"I will enter, and you will not stop me!" said a voice.

Seventy-Eight

AN EXTREMELY HANDSOME young man burst into the room.

"Sir! Sir! Sir!" cried a page, hopelessly running after him, "Your Majesty, I -"

The very handsome man pushed past the page. He deeply bowed before the Queen.

"Your Majesty, pardon my interruption," he said in a velvety voice, "but I had to know...Oh."

His eyes rested upon Molly, who had the remainder of Harry Spleen's body sticking out of her mouth.

"But he's a child!" declared the handsome man, smiling. He promptly dropped to his knees, clasped the Queen's hand, and said, "I beg your Majesty's forgiveness. I had been led to believe you had a new favorite."

The Queen smiled and put her hand on the handsome man's head, as if he were her pet dog. Her demeanor changed to one of calm authority, total command, and complete composure.

"Was my Robert a little jealous? " she asked

"I was devoured by the green-eyed monster," answered Robert

The Queen reached into the theater sculpture and pulled out two actors.

"Benedict must trust his Beatrice," said the Queen

She handed Robert the sugary Beatrice.

Robert said, "Does Beatrice still love her Benedict? Un peu? Un petit peu?'

"As much as I will any man," she said, "And never as much as England."

The man humbly bowed head, "Your Majesty, I-."

"Leave us," ordered the Queen.

With his head still lowered, the man backed out of the room. Molly wondered how he could be so elegant. Even walking backwards with his head down, he was elegant; his flowing hair, his beard, his rapier dangling at his side.

After he left, the Queen sighed.

"Men!" she said. "We are surrounded by men all day long. Men who think they know better than us, merely because we are a woman."

"Your Majesty," was all Molly could think of to say.

The Queen, somewhat perturbed, paced the room, waving the sugar Burbage in the air. Without realizing, she took a bite and swallowed his head.

"We are the most successful monarch England has ever known. We have peace. We have prosperity. We brought England up from a nothing island to the greatest country in the world. We beat the Spanish Armada! And yet, and yet, these men continue to believe our success as monarch is in *spite* of us being a woman instead of *because* of it. They think we don't know what they say but we do! We have spies everywhere. We know exactly what is being discussed, where it is being discussed, and by whom! Did you know musicians and theatricals make perfect spies?"

Molly did not know how she was meant to answer. Was she asking Molly to be a spy?

"Which reminds us," said the monarch, standing behind

her glorious chair. "We like you. You are a spirit of another sort. We will afford you enough money to become a shareholder in the Lord Chamberlain's Men. You need a voice. And if anything were to… happen, you need security. To that end, we will afford upon you a royal stipend to be continued in perpetuity. How does that sound?" she asked.

"Your Majesty, I–I-I don't know what to say, I-" stammered Molly.

"You may begin with thank you," tittered the Queen.

"Thank you, Your Most Kind and Gracious Majesty!" said Molly, smiling in disbelief. "Your Majesty is most generous!"

"Well, if we can, why not? We have no children of our own, so-..We have taken the liberty to have drawn up a contract." The Queen glanced toward the door. As if he'd been standing there the entire time, which he most likely had been, her secretary approached with the paperwork and a gigantic quill. The secretary placed the document in front of Molly, dipped the quill into the ink and held it out to her. Molly signed "W.H."

"Ensure enactment forthwith. Inform my Lord Chamberlain," ordered the Queen.

"Your Majesty," said the secretary, making a deep bow. Carrying the contract as if it were gold, he backed out of the room.

The Queen silently studied Molly for what felt like a year, but was only a minute. Then she said, "Those like us, who swim against the tide, must throw out all the ropes we can. That way, those who follow after us have something to grab on to instead of drowning." The Queen looked away for a moment, a hand to her chest. Then, quickly, she said, "Master Harcourt, what a pleasure it was to meet you."

With that, Molly's meeting with the Queen was over. The page ushered her out. The experience had gone by so fast, Molly wondered if it had all been a dream.

As Molly was about to leave the palace, a page handed her a beautifully decorated wooden box.

"From her Majesty," he said.

Molly gently twisted off the lid. Resting atop a piece of stiff, waxed cloth, lay the sugar sculpture of herself as Hero. Molly's heart leaped with joy. She would treasure this gift forever. Just as she was closing the lid, she noticed a bumpiness beneath the waxed cloth. She carefully peeled it up to uncover a further surprise.

The bottom half of the box was filled with jellied purple unicorns.

Seventy-Nine

SAME SKY, *different life.*

Molly looked up through the circular hole in the open roof.

She stood alone in their brand new theater. A theater she helped to build. Molly breathed deeply. She took in the stage, with its two red pillars and three doors at the back.

Their new theater was called The Globe to celebrate the wide, new world in which they all now lived.

The Queen was as good as her, very honorable, word; Molly need never work again. On the other hand, audiences regularly flocked to see the famous young actor. The Lord Chamberlain's hearing and her meeting with the Queen had brought Walter Harcourt fame and notoriety. Molly loved it, and at the same time, hoped it would soon pass.

She smiled.

Same sky, different life.

"I love coming here when it's empty. The space is filled with possibility. It's the stuff dreams are made of," a familiar voice said.

Molly jumped.

"I'm sorry. I didn't mean to startle you," said Will.

"Can you feel the magic, too?" asked Molly.

"Oh, yes. Every time I come in here," said Will, his eyes sparkling.

They stood in silence. It was the first time they'd been alone since Molly's visit to the Queen.

"I haven't had a chance to ask you. How did it really go?" Will made a funny voice, "With she who was born great?"

"Oh! Well… It was a bit strange. Her Majesty is very gracious and entertaining, but she threatened to bite my head off," said Molly, still trying to find the words to describe her experience.

"Are you especially delicious?" joked Will.

"She bit Mr. Burbage's head off," Molly smiled,

"Should I be concerned?" exclaimed Will with mock concern.

"It was one of these," said Molly. She showed Shakespeare the sugar-paste figure of herself. Molly always carried it with her as a talisman. The locket rooted her in the past. The Hero sculpture symbolized future possibilities. The Queen had championed the alchemist, John Dee, for magical potions, but Molly thought her talisman much more powerful.

"That is remarkable," said Will, turning the figure around in his hands.

"It's supposed to be a surprise, so don't tell, but she had an entire sugar sculpture of *Much Ado About Nothing*," said Molly, speaking way too fast. "Everyone was there, this was me and you were there, but she avoided you, like you were gold or something, even Harry Spleen was there, but I ate him."

"You ate Harry Spleen?" laughed Will.

"Should I have done it?" asked Molly, suddenly doubtful. "She made me do it. She did."

"We must do as Her Majesty commands," said Will.

"Please give that back," said Molly, anxiously.

"Fearful I'll bite *your* head off?" joked Will.

"It means a lot to me," said Molly.

Will gently handed the sculpture back to Molly. She quickly wrapped and returned it to its reinforced leather holder. Ben had made it specially for her.

"He tasted ever so good," said Molly. "Harry, I mean."

Will burst out laughing.

I made Will laugh, thought Molly. *Things are definitely different.*

Will kicked some dust on the ground.

"I've been working on a new play," he said.

"No surprise there," teased Molly.

Will smiled.

"I've, uh. I've written it with you in mind," he said.

Molly lost her breath for a moment. "I don't know what to say. I'm honored."

Will brushed this off.

"It was only a matter of time," he said. "It's about a girl who loses everything in a shipwreck. She lands in an unfamiliar country - like you in London. She disguises herself as a boy and gets a job at Court. She rises through the ranks remarkably quickly."

Will held Molly's gaze. She felt her skin prickling. Was Will trying to say something?

"What happens to her?" asked Molly, trying to divert his attention.

"Things get complicated. A woman gives her a ring but insists he gave it to her. Her identical twin shows up, and they get confused for one another," Will said.

Molly hoped Will couldn't see her trembling.

"I'm very pleased with the opening line. Would you like to hear it?" asked Will.

"Very much," said Molly, quietly.

"If music be the food of love, play on," Will said.

Molly was overcome with the beauty of the words. She repeated them. "If music be the food of love, play on."

"What do you think?" asked Will, a little nervously.

"Oh. Mr. Shakespeare. It's beautiful," said Molly, breathless.

"Your little brother inspired that one. She's called Viola. Your character," he said. "Burbage says Viola is obviously written for you," he laughed.

"Is that an Italian name?" asked Molly, smiling shyly.

"Yes. Yes, it is. I once heard of a duke who said the English love everything Italian," teased Will.

"I don't know what to say," gushed Molly.

There was an awkward silence between them. Molly really didn't know what to say. It was all so much. Molly thought she saw Will struggle to find the right words, too. Instead, he reached for the latest London gossip.

"Did you hear the latest about Mary Frith?" asked Will.

"No," said Molly, feeling uncomfortable, again.

"Someone bet her 20 pounds she couldn't ride from Charing Cross to ShoreDitch dressed as a man without getting arrested," Will said.

"Did she win the bet?" asked Molly nervously.

"Not only did she win the bet, she rode on a show horse and blew a trumpet the entire way!" laughed Will. "She really doesn't care. I'll write a play about her someday. If another writer doesn't get there first. It's a silly law, don't you think?" asked Will.

"Which one? There are tons of silly laws," said Molly. She wanted this conversation to be over.

"The one making it illegal for girls to act," said Will.

"Oh! That one. Yes. But then again, if it were legal, I'd be out of a job," said Molly, a little too jovially.

"True," said Will. "One day, the law will change. Then, we'll see. Don't you think, Walter?"

"Absolutely," said Molly.

"Meantime," Will reached into his newly made leather satchel, designed by Ben, and pulled out a stack of curling paper. He plopped it onto the front of the stage. "There it is. It's the whole thing. Promise me you won't lose it."

"I promise," Molly whispered.

Will nodded, then headed to his desk, hidden behind the stage.

Molly trembled as she looked at the script. Was it possible that Mr. Shakespeare knew? That he knew and was fine about it? She started to jump for joy, when Will popped his head back through the door on stage. Molly immediately stopped jumping to look serious for the writer.

"I forgot to mention - The play is called *Twelfth Night* or, maybe, *What You Will*. I can't decide."

"You could keep both," suggested Molly.

"I could," he said. "I'm hoping it's a hit."

Molly nodded silently.

"Walter, were you jumping?" Will asked.

Molly nodded.

"Most excellent," Will said, then walked off stage.

Once she was sure Will had gone, Molly jumped up and down, punched the air and shouted, "YES! YES! YES!"

WILL SECRETLY WATCHED through a tiny gap in the back wall of the stage. He smiled.

"You'll do," he said.

Epilogue

MOLLY, Juliet, Ben and Aunty Anne made a pilgrimage to Bitford.

So much had happened since they sat on the riverbank watching their home burn.

The village was pretty much how they'd left it, with the exception of the trees. Mr. John Barnes had planted an orchard in and around the ruined houses. Aunty Anne identified cherry, peach, and apple trees, among others.

They stood in the wreckage of their old home, where Aunty Anne and their mother had argued, then fallen silent, "for the children." Aunty Anne placed the locket on a charred piece of wood, dropped her head, and cried.

Suddenly, Aunty Anne snatched the locket back up again.

"No!" she said. "While that would make a beautiful poetic gesture, this is the only depiction I have of the three of you as children. I am not prepared to leave that for Mr. John Barnes to find. Anyway, this locket brought you to me. I will cherish it forever." Aunty Anne reached into her leather pouch, designed by Ben. "Molly, I have this for you."

Aunty Anne pulled out an exact likeness of the locket.

"This is the original," she said, holding up the new locket.

"That is the copy," she referred to her own locket. Like identical twins, the lockets were exactly the same, even down to the tarnishing on the top by the latch.

Ben looked downcast.

"*Ben*, my dear, do you think I would have forgotten you?" She rubbed his cheek with her gloved hand and kissed him.

"Here," she said, reaching into her pouch. "I have one for you. *Yours* is the original. The others are copies." She smiled her cheeky smile as she handed him an exact likeness of the other two lockets. Ben popped it open. There was the tiny painting, exactly the same as the other two.

"What about me?" asked Juliet.

"*You?* Do you think I'd forget about you, my sweet little songbird?" laughed Aunty Anne. She reached into her purse and pulled out yet another locket.

"*Yours* is-" she began. The others chorused their interruption: "the original. The others are copies!"

Everyone laughed and tied the lockets around their necks. Who knew which was the original and which was the copy?

It didn't matter.

They were family, reunited forever.

Lady Shakespeare's Epilogue

(OR THE LAST WORD)

WELL, darlings, there you have it.

The *true* story of my rise to fame and good fortune.

If you ever hear anyone speak ill of Molly Shipton or, indeed, of Lady Shakespeare, you now have the facts and can put them straight.

I starred in every inaugural production written by William Shakespeare. So much so, the audience affectionately called me *Lady Shakespeare*. Mrs. Shakespeare laughed about it. "He always strives for grandeur," she quipped, " but reality keeps getting in the way."

Her Royal Majesty, Queen Elizabeth, was very gracious. Although, I did have to do a little work for her in exchange for my stipend.

As a spy.

But that is another story for another time.

Dearest of friends, adieu.

I have unclasped

To thee the book even of my secret soul.

WALK WISELY in the world and fare thee well.

Author's Note

This is a work of fiction. However, several of the characters and events are real. Richard Burbage was the preeminent actor of his age and he was the actor-manager of The Lord Chamberlain's Men. The Theatre was his theater built by his father. In a clandestine move against the landlord, the company took The Theatre down to build The Globe Theatre. William Shakespeare, Will Kempe and the other actors named in the story worked in his theatre company. Shakespeare wrote plays for Burbage and the company. Nathanial Giles was the Master of the Children of the Chapel Royal and had the power, by Royal Warrant, to take boys into his choir. He worked with Henry Evans at the Blackfriars Theatre, who could take young boys and force them to work in his acting company.

Acknowledgments

They say writing is a lonely profession. However, the characters felt so real to me and had *so much to say*, that I never felt alone.

I wrote this book shut in a two-bedroom apartment, in the middle of Manhattan, in the middle of a hotspot in the first pandemic in a century. The book began as a love letter to my children. I wanted to tell a story about another world, about resilience and following your dreams even when stuck indoors. I wanted them to know that there would be life after the shutdown.

This book would still be a series of scenes and ideas, were it not for the inimitable Mira Reisberg. Put simply, I would not have written this novel without Mira and her incredible, unending expertise. Her encouragement, enthusiasm and technical know-how gave me the precise tools I needed. Thank you, Mira.

"I would like to read this when it's finished," are some of the most motivating words I have ever experienced. They came from my publisher, Callie Metler of Clear Fork Publishing. Callie has been my enthusiastic champion from the moment she loved my pitch. Callie, also, took on the redoubtable task of being my editor. Thank you, Callie.

I met Dea Lenihan later on in the process but I feel as if I have known her for years. She transformed suggestions into artistic reality. What a talent! Dea is not only a wonderful illustrator, she always going above and beyond to create the best work possible.

Although I have performed Shakespeare my entire adult life, I still had to do an enormous amount of research for this novel. Thank you to the many professional historians whose hard work and writing I was able to draw upon (there is a bibliography on my website). In particular, I would like to thank the the BBC, the Folger Shakespeare Library, the Globe Theatre and the Shakespeare Birthplace Trust.

I will be forever be grateful for the generosity of Tudor enthusiasts, who were always ready with an immediate answer for my most obscure and specific questions. In particular, I would like to thank Heather Teysko for her Renaissance History Podcast and Brigitte Webster and her Tudor & 17th Century Experience Social Club members. I am so grateful to this energetic group of amazing folks, who are always so generous with their knowledge and support.

I am grateful to my wonderful young reader, Tahra Castro Alves Araujo. Thank you for your insightful feedback and for being gentle with my newborn book. You are brilliant.

Thank you to the Barnard Toddler Center. You are wonderful.

Thank you Chris, Amy & Gene for the quiet of your country house, where I was able to focus on edits. You are amazing.

Thank you to my friends and neighbors who kept reminding me of how excited they were for my book to come out. What is life without friends?

Thank you to my oldest child, Lila. I started writing this book when you were 8. Your eagerness to have me read a new chapter nightly, motivated me beyond words. Your enthusiasm, your sparkle, your perceptions and your excitement were the fuel to my creativity. You were, and are, my chief critic and greatest champion. You let me know when the story sagged and motivated me to keep it afloat. There would be no book without you, my real life Molly. I love you.

Sasha there would be no book without your help, especially your taking of regular, daily naps. Thank you for accommodating mummy's mental health activity during the NYC Covid shutdown. And thank you for making our lives richer with your daily, joyous observations. I love you.

Andrew, there are no words adequate enough to describe the continued, selfless support you gave me as I wrote this book. We all went through the shutdown but you took care of things so I could write. And then, you took time to be my at-home reviewer, cheerleader, editor and constant motivator. "Thank you" does not express the amount of gratitude I have for you. I love you.

About the Author

Sheri pretends to be other people for a living, or writes stories about them. Such sillybillyness has won her awards, prizes and publication. Sheri performed and taught Shakespeare for years, from the English Shakespeare Company and Cheek by Jowl to NYC's Student Shakespeare Festival and Theatre for a New Audience. SCWBI member & proud CBA graduate (PB, I & MG). This is Sheri's debut novel. Lady Shakespeare claims she wrote this novel but she did not. You have been warned

www.sherigraubert.com

Lightning Source UK Ltd.
Milton Keynes UK
UKHW040821191022
410730UK00004B/330